Praise for Alexis Fleming's
Handyman's Best Tool

"A Handyman's Best Tool is a winner in my book. Full of laughter, life and extremely hot sex, it kept me enthralled from beginning to end. I am happy to say that Alexis Fleming continues to be on my automatic read list and I am sure that other readers will feel the same way after reading A Handyman's Best Tool. I simply adored it!"

~ *Talia Ricci, Joyfully Reviewed*

"Alexis Fleming pens a fabulously charming tale with A HANDYMAN'S BEST TOOL. The characters are down to earth and could easily be somebody you actually know...but what I really love about this story is the dialogue. All the sexual innuendos and comebacks the characters use are laugh out loud funny...A HANDYMAN'S BEST TOOL has a wonderfully thought out storyline and is a sure-fire guarantee that you'll never look at a man in a tool belt without wondering about the tool that you can't see."

~ *Chrissy Dionne, Romance Junkies*

5 Red Tattoos! "I enjoyed this book and could have used a cold drink during the reading of it. It was a steamy story and had so much fun with double entendres through out the story line. In between all this there are things happening that bring Riley and Beth Ann closer together despite their ideas of just having fun with each other sexually. It's a story that I would not have missed reading...They are the perfect foils for each other, with snappy dialogue and steamy sexual appeal that makes this book a must read for the it had me smiling and wanting it to go on l The sex was incredible with the chemistry they had together. I hope there will be more from this author in the future."

~ *Judy King, Erotic Escapdes*

5 Red Hearts! "From the explosive first page until the very end, the reader will be mesmerized and held captive until the very last word. Ms Fleming has written about two very special people, very sensuous, sexy and hot, but very deep with their own fair share of baggage to lug around...Ms Fleming has done a wonderful job of getting into the emotions of these two characters and the reader can feel each one...The love scenes are extremely hot, very passionate and deeply romantic. This reviewer will gladly read this one again."

~ *Valerie, Love Romances*

A **5 Pink Hats Off Salute** to Alexis Fleming for a wonderfully written story with endearing characters, great humor and sizzling hot sex...I was hooked from the first line...I laughed out loud and knew I was going to enjoy this book. This story is a fun read and will have you checking out Ms. Fleming's other stories. A Handyman's Best Tool will make it to your keeper shelf. Enjoy!"

~ *MA, The Pink Posse*

4 Cups! "This is an excellent story. The characters are lively and the dialogue very witty and loaded with humor. Both Beth Ann and Riley have understandable commitment issues, but fall in love anyway. Their love story is very well written and full of extremely hot love scenes. The secondary characters are equally vivid, making the reader feel part of the story. I especially like the cooking scene with the two neighbors. It was very funny. I could not put this one down once I started, and will definitely look for more by Ms Fleming."

~ Maura, Reviewer for Coffee Time Romance

A Handyman's Best Tool

By Alexis Fleming

A Samhain Publishing, Ltd. publication

Samhain Publishing, Ltd.
PO Box 2206
Stow OH 44224

A Handyman's Best Tool
Copyright © 2006 by Alexis Fleming
Cover by Scott Carpenter
Print ISBN: 1-59998-127-0
Digital ISBN: 1-59998-017-7
www.samhainpublishing.com

First Samhain Publishing, Ltd. electronic publication: March 2006
First Samhain Publishing, Ltd. print publication: June 2006

A Handyman's Best Tool

By Alexis Fleming

Dedication

To Crissy and Samhain:
My thanks for taking a chance on me. The ride is fantastic.
To Angie:
My thanks for being such a great editor, not to mention a dab hand with the whip.
To Carla, Publicist Extraordinaire:
My thanks for taking me on and putting up with all the bimbo questions.
You ladies rock!

Chapter One

"Are you the man who's going to plug my hole?"

Riley Osborne's eyes boggled. His mouth dropped open and he stared at the little pixie in front of him. Surprise kept him frozen on the spot for a moment. He shook his head and tried to gather his scattered wits. Freakin' hell, he couldn't believe a woman had just said that to him. *I know I have a dirty mind, but I don't even think she's aware how that sounded.*

He couldn't help himself. His zany sense of humor demanded he answer in kind. The weighted toolbox connected with his thigh as he propped one hip against the door jam. "What would you like me to plug it with?" Despite his best efforts, his smile broke free.

She frowned and blinked her eyes as if she needed time to assimilate his question. Big, baby blue eyes, with the thickest, darkest lashes he'd ever seen. She couldn't be more than five feet...five-one at the most. Dark red hair, at the moment dripping wet, hung in corkscrew twists that fell forward over her shoulders.

He wondered what color it'd be when it was dry. If he knew women—and he did—he'd hazard a guess that the red was real, not a bottle job. He could be wrong, but she had the fair skin that went with red hair and a sprinkling of little freckles across her nose. Cute.

"Um, what do you suggest we use?" she said with a frown.

She raised her hand and tried to push the wet curls back from her face. He would have to be blind not to notice the way her tee shirt pulled across her breasts. It didn't help that the top was soaked. Damp fabric and the obvious fact that she didn't have a bra on. Hell of a combination. *Wonder if she knows white material is almost see-through when it's wet?*

Riley straightened up and stepped over the threshold. The little pixie backed up a pace to allow him entrance. His grin was pure devilment. He had to say it. There was no getting away from it. He just couldn't ignore that perfect opening sentence.

"Hmm, let's see. There are certain things designed especially for filling holes. Tailor-made, you might say. Depends on what your specific needs are. Soft and malleable works fine for some. Then there's hard and rigid, but with surprising strength. A little heat behind it and it will amaze you what can happen."

Beth-Ann Harris allowed his words to sink deep. A slow curl of fire ignited low in her belly. Her face burned with a flush of heat. Surely he hadn't said...?

She looked into his chocolate-brown eyes and saw the twinkle. *And* the oh-so-sexy smile on his face. Hot damn, he was coming on to her.

With a frown, she cast her mind back over what she'd said when she'd flung open the door. As she picked up on the sexual connotation implicit in that simple little question, her eyes widened. Lord, she was at it again. Terminal foot-in-mouth disease. All she ever did was open her mouth long enough to change feet.

Her immediate reaction was to take him to task. Instead, she hesitated. It had been a bitch of a day. Heck, the last forty-eight hours had been a nightmare.

First that jerk, Brad, dumped her for not being adventurous in bed. For crying out loud, they hadn't even got as far as going to bed. Not that he'd really dumped her. He'd told her she needed to go away and rethink what she wanted out of a relationship with a man. It was at that point she'd walked out, his comment that he'd be in touch ringing in her ears.

If he'd been a bit more particular about personal hygiene, she might have been willing to discuss the idea of going down on him. As it was, the whole thing was a total turn-off.

She wasn't a prude by any means. As far as she was concerned, as long as both partners were comfortable, anything was fair game between the sheets. But, come on, there had to be at least a strong physical attraction there, and with that bozo, she'd only just been getting to know him. What she'd seen to date hadn't impressed her in the least.

Okay, he hadn't been important to her. Her emotions weren't involved and it had only been their second date. Heaven knows why she'd let him talk her into going back to his apartment. The squalor in his home had given her a pretty good idea that she wasn't far off the mark in her assessment of the guy. She could tell a lot from the way a man lived.

Damn, this had become a habit. A girl could get bent out of shape after being ditched three times in a row because she wouldn't play kinky games.

For some reason she always attracted the wrong type of guy. She didn't want a lifelong relationship, but a bit of steamy one-on-one wouldn't go amiss. She needed a red-hot fuckfest to raise her sexual self-esteem because it had sure taken a beating in the last six months.

Put your money where your mouth is, Beth-Ann. She had the perfect specimen right in front of her and he wanted to play.

She backed up into the flat, hands on hips to emphasize her tiny waist. "And which one would you recommend?" She lowered her voice to a husky drawl, dragging in a deep breath to push her breasts high.

His gaze slid down the front of her tee shirt. She knew her breasts weren't big, but they were enough to catch his attention. And the soggy fabric sure helped matters somewhat. She should have been embarrassed, but she wasn't. If anything, she was titillated and eager to see how far he'd go.

"Hot and hard will do it for me every time," he drawled. The toolbox dropped from his hand and hit the tiled floor with a heavy clunk. He leaned back against the door and hooked his thumbs through the belt loops of his tight blue jeans.

Boy, talk about confidence. This guy had it in spades. She conducted her own examination. He was so darn tall, she had a mental picture of having to stand on a chair to kiss him goodnight. Or perch two steps up on the nearest staircase with him on the other side of the railing. Hard to get hot and heavy when a metal bar comes between a girl and the object of her lust.

She raised her eyebrows. "So you reckon heat does the best job, do you?"

"Sure does, ma'am." He straightened up and moved away from the door, his hands spread wide. "I'm a builder. Would I lie to you?"

Something about his tone of voice and even the fact he'd called her *ma'am* struck a chord deep in her mind. She tried to pin it down, but it was too elusive. One thing was for certain, she had a strange sensation she knew this man. How weird. There's no way she'd forget someone like this. So why did she have such a strong sense of recognition?

She shook the thought away and concentrated on her sexy visitor. Backing up even further toward the far side of the living room, she lowered her brows in what she hoped was a come-hither look. "Okay, Mr. Hot and Hard, prove it. Fill my hole up."

Riley almost choked as he fought to contain the crack of laughter bubbling up inside him. She was outrageous, and one hell of a lot of fun. Today had been a totally shitty day and he didn't have the time to deal with the insurance side of R & J Constructions. That was his father's field of operation. Only problem was, John, his dear old dad, was at home in bed with a cold. Mind you, if *dear old dad* ran into little pixies like this one, he wouldn't mind taking on the work.

When the woman reached out, grabbed hold of his arm and pulled him closer, he grinned in anticipation. She gave a sudden jerk and pranced away from him, her finger pointed at the ceiling. Without thought, he looked up. And in an instant, regretted his action.

Cold water trickled down onto his face from the foot-wide, gaping hole in the ceiling. Underneath was a soggy bunch of towels to sop up any further downfall. Off to one side were two full buckets of water.

The little witch. She'd caught him good and proper. That would teach him to mess with the customers, even if she was officially his dad's client and not his.

Stepping back, he shook the rain from his hair and wiped a hand over his face. He started to laugh. Oh, she was good. She'd really had him going. "Your hole, I presume?"

She simply raised her eyebrows and grinned at him.

"Let me get my toolbox and ladder and I'll see what damage has been done."

"Want me to help you carry your...tool?"

Lord, this was going to be a hell of a job. He struggled to hold his laughter as he retrieved the ladder. He had no doubt this time she knew exactly what she'd said.

The ladder erected under the hole, he turned to face her, his hand held out in the time-honored fashion of greeting. "We never did get around to introductions," he said as he slid his palm against hers. He frowned at the arc of static electricity that seemed to flow from her hand to his. Weird. He shrugged and smiled at her again, the same killer smile he used on any woman he wanted to impress enough to get into bed.

"I'm Riley, the R bit of R & J Constructions. The J belongs to my father, John. Your insurance company contacted us first thing this morning to come fix your—" he couldn't say it "—roof. Normally my father does all the insurance work, but he's off sick, so I'm it today."

He tipped his head back and stared up at the hole a moment before flicking a lazy grin back at the pixie, all without letting go of her hand. "I take it you *are* Beth-Ann Harris?" He gave in to her slight tug and released her hand. "Why don't you tell me what happened here?"

Beth-Ann took a step back from Riley and dragged in a quick breath, pulling the damp tee shirt away from her chest. Enough fooling around for now. It was time to get down to business. "I noticed a slight bulge in the ceiling last night when we had all that heavy rain. So the first thing I did was climb up and have a feel."

Feel. Now there was a good word, with myriad uses. She ran her gaze over Riley's body, stopping at his hips where the tight cut of his jeans showed off his...attributes. She had to clear her throat before she could go on.

"It was sort of squishy and cold to the touch so I didn't need to be too smart to know I had water in the roof." She shook her head, amazed at how hard it was to keep her mind on the matter at hand. Her gaze kept sliding back to the bulge clearly outlined by his jeans.

She beckoned to him to follow her out the back door of the low-set house and around to the side. Once there, she backed him up against the hedge that marked the boundary of the property and pointed to the roof.

He stood so close the brush of his arm raised goose bumps on her flesh. A little shiver slithered along her spine and it had nothing to do with the fine drizzle that damped down everything in sight, her tee shirt included. Somehow, his very nearness made her more aware of her body. The hardened tips of her nipples abraded by her soggy shirt. The throbbing ache that had started deep in her womb and now centered on her clit. She rubbed her thighs together to try to relieve the tension as heat streaked through her blood. It was all she could do to continue the conversation.

"This morning I got a ladder and climbed up onto the roof to have a look." She pointed over her shoulder to indicate the ladder where it lay on the grass behind them. "I can't see any cracked tiles. The only thing I can figure is that the rain has come in under that bracket thingy that holds the pole for the main power supply to the house."

"You know you shouldn't be climbing ladders when there's no one else around, don't you? It's too easy to fall when everything is wet and slick." He paused a moment and angled a glance at her. "You are alone, aren't you? No significant other who could have done the job for you?"

She grinned at his roundabout way of asking her if she were heart-whole and fancy-free. She inclined her head at him. "I'm free."

"I'm gla—"

He cut off the word as if he'd only just remembered this was a professional visit. After what had gone on inside, it was way too late for that. Beth-Ann had an insane desire to burst into giggles and she *never* giggled.

"When I rang the insurance company's emergency service, the man told me to shove a screwdriver up into the roof to release the water so the whole ceiling wouldn't fall down." She grimaced.

"I take it you didn't get to it in time?"

"Yeah, right. The man could have told me to hold a bucket underneath when I did it." She grinned. "Okay, okay, I should have been smart enough to work that one out for myself. Anyway, I'd just pushed the screwdriver into the squishy bubble when the whole chunk fell out on top of me. Good thing I'm small and can move quickly. That, in a nutshell, is how I came to be soaked. I haven't played in the rain since I was a kid, even if the rain *was* on the inside, not the outside."

"The insurance company told me to go ahead and arrange to fix the problem so I'd best get on with it before any more water gets in."

Turning, he grabbed the ladder from where it lay beside the hedge and propped it up against the guttering. He disappeared back inside for a moment, only to return with a silicon sealant gun and an old toweling cloth in his hands.

Beth-Ann watched as he scaled the ladder with the ease of long practice. Incredible view from this position. His denim jeans molded the nicest set of buns she'd seen in a long while. Some women went for good looks or bulging muscles, but she was rather partial to a well-shaped ass. This guy seemed to have the lot.

Nothing wrong with his muscles. His tight black tee shirt showed bulges in all the right places, but not overdone. One thing she did find a turn-off were those muscle-bound jerks who thought they were God's gift to women. The one time she'd been stupid enough to go out with one of them, he'd paid her no attention whatsoever. He'd been more interested in flexing his muscles in every reflective surface he could find.

Riley bent over to check out the bracket that secured the metal pole to the roof. Beth-Ann started to salivate. *Oh my giddy grandmother, he is hot.*

He turned his head and winked at her before he focused again on the job at hand. That one little eye twitch had the effect of causing a major rise in body temperature. She grinned. He was fun, and right about now she could do with some fun in her life. If she was involved with a man like this... Her libido kicked in and a raft of raunchy pictures sprang to life in her mind.

She wondered how he'd respond if she took him up on his blatant flirting and put the move on him. Might be interesting to find out. She imagined he'd be quite fantastic in bed. Adventurous? Oh, yeah, she'd stake a bet on it.

"Here's your problem."

Riley's voice dragged her thoughts away from the erotic scenario that had formed in her head. "Um, sorry?"

"You've got cracks in the bracket holding the base plate onto the roof," he called down. "That's how the water got in."

He used the old towel to blot up any moisture, laid a silicon trail around the whole thing and smoothed it into place with his fingers. Within minutes, he was back down on ground level.

"That should hold it. At least it will prevent any more water from seeping in." He took her arm and turned her toward the back of the house. "Let's get in out of this drizzle and have a look up in the ceiling."

Beth-Ann shivered at the touch of his hand on her upper arm. Despite the haze of light rain, heat arced from his palm and created a warm patch that quickly spread.

Sex, kid, that's all it is.

She chuckled. Sex she could handle. She risked a quick sideways glance to find his gaze fixed on her, so she tipped him a wink and smiled in response to his grin as they paused at the back door.

His grin suddenly morphed into a grimace. "We're going to track water through your house." He shook his head and turned to look at her.

Beth-Ann almost drooled. She loved his eyes. Chocolate-brown, puppy-dog eyes, with that sad expression that will make you give your favorite canine anything his little doggy heart desires. A slow smile curled his mouth and the twinkles sprang to life in those expressive eyes.

A multitude of hormones went on immediate alert and started a mad rampage throughout Beth-Ann's body. Heat burst low in her belly with an explosive flash, hard enough that the breath caught in her throat. Those eyes alone would get him anything he wanted.

"Don't happen to have a towel handy, do you? I could blot up some of this water before I dirty up your house."

"Ah, yeah, no problem." She took herself to task and scooted inside and down the hallway to the linen closet. Three thick towels clutched in her hands, she made her way back to him. It wouldn't have mattered if he'd come right in. She'd just tracked so much water into the house they'd have to be careful they didn't slip on the wet tiles. Her floors needed a wash, but this was ridiculous.

Riley removed his shoes and socks and as he straightened up, she handed him two of the towels, the third draped around her own shoulders. "Sure you don't want to take your tee shirt off as well? It's pretty soaked."

"Nah, it'll dry. And it's not like it's cold. The rain might have caused a bit of havoc at your place, but we sure needed it. It might help cool things down somewhat."

Rats. And here she was thinking she was going to get him at least stripped down to his jeans.

"Okay, let's see what damage has been done inside," he said.

He stepped past her and moved to where he'd set the ladder up under the hole. Only a few lonely little drops plopped through now, the residue of what had collected up in the roof cavity.

"I'll have to break away more of this damaged part so I can see what's what up here. Don't get underneath. It's pretty spongy. The whole area could drop."

"Be my guest," she replied, her eyes trained on the ripple of muscles as he worked. At the same time, she dug back into her memories. Something about the way he talked and moved jangled that chord in her mind again. Darn it, she was sure she'd met him, or at least seen him, somewhere before. She shook her head and water droplets ran down her neck, making her squirm.

She watched as he flipped open his toolbox and extracted a well-worn builder's tool belt. He cinched the leather strap about his hips and adjusted the belt so the hammer hung down his side. Each little compartment and loop was filled. A flashlight poked out on the opposite side to the hammer, various screwdrivers, measuring tapes and like paraphernalia completed the assorted collection without which no good builder would be seen.

He grinned at her as he gave the buckle a final pat. "Yeah, I know, it doesn't lend itself to the picture of sartorial elegance, but it's the handyman's best tool."

When he wiggled his hips so the screwdriver didn't hang down right over his cock, Beth-Ann's lips twitched. She had to struggle hard not to give in to the desire to make a play on his use of the word "tool" and what every handyman needed. The sensual look in his eyes told her he was well aware of where her mind had headed.

Darn, he was good.

He tossed his head back and moved toward the ladder. The simple action sparked off that sense of recognition again. She'd only been in Sydney for six months. Someone like this she would have remembered. Perhaps it was further back in her past.

A big, fat blob of water trickled down her face and reminded her she was dripping moisture all over the tiles. She glanced down at the puddle forming at her feet. Time to get out of these wet clothes.

"You okay if I slip off to have a shower and get changed?"

"Go for it," he said without turning his head. "I'll be a while yet."

Beth-Ann took herself off to the bathroom, her mind still fixated on where she may have run into her sexy handyman before.

❊ ❊ ❊

Riley pulled a bit more of the damaged plasterboard away and let it fall to the floor. The hole was big enough now he could at least fit his head and shoulders through. More by feel than anything else, he pulled the flashlight and a long-handled screwdriver from his tool belt and clicked on the light.

It was time for work. Shame of it was, thoughts of Beth-Ann intruded and made it difficult for him to keep his mind on the job.

The sound of water running in the shower at the other end of the house filtered down the hallway. His mind filled with images of his little pixie, naked and slathered with soap. It wasn't difficult. Her wet clothes had given him a fairly good idea of what her body was like, at least the upper half. His jeans pulled tight across his crotch as all the blood that should have been driving his brain rushed to his cock. *Hmm, wonder what she'd do if I joined her?*

Down, boy. She may have flirted with him, or at least responded to his overtures, but she hadn't handed out the right signals. Yet. She was funny and sexy, even soggy wet. He wouldn't mind being in a situation where he could spend some time with her. Provided she knew the score, that is.

His father called him a playboy and maybe he was. He liked women. In fact, he loved them. The women he took out always had a good time and never went away unsatisfied, but he wasn't about to get serious with any female. Lay it on the line, give 'em a good time and walk away if they looked like they wanted more. That was his credo, and so far, it had worked for him.

His father had a hankering for grandkids, but it wasn't going to happen. Riley made damn certain he always used protection. And if he didn't have any condoms on him, there were other ways to scratch an itch, his or the lady of the hour's. He was as willing to play as the next man. He just didn't want to get caught.

Memories of his childhood surfaced. He'd grown up in a small country town where everyone knew each other's business. The townsfolk had been well aware that his mother had played around with anything in trousers. *And* she hadn't been discreet about it. She'd walked out with the proverbial traveling salesman when he was sixteen. Within weeks of that happening, his father moved them to Sydney and set out to rebuild his life.

If seeing his father go through the pain and humiliation of that hadn't soured him on the idea of the so-called holy state of matrimony, the debacle he'd been involved in with his fiancée and his old college buddy, Seth, would have done it.

It was enough to put a guy off making a commitment to any one woman. You never knew when they were going to kick you in the teeth. He may not trust them, but he could certainly enjoy them. If that made him a sleaze, so be it. No sir, no way was marriage for him.

The sound of the shower being turned off reminded him he had work to do. Enough with the deep thoughts. He poked his head through the opening in the ceiling to check out the damage. With the tip of the screwdriver, he probed at the silver foil insulation and created an escape hole for the water trapped between the insulation and the outer roof. He ducked, but still managed to get wet, although it wasn't as bad as he'd thought it would be.

When the water had drained away, he pushed his head and shoulders through the damaged ceiling, reached up and peeled the foil back to allow it to dry. With a prod of his screwdriver, he tested the main support beams. Good thing they were hardwood. Not much damage there.

A slight sound alerted him that Beth-Ann had entered the room. He had a burning desire to check out how she was dressed, but he resisted. Damn, he'd miss that soggy top. She could feature in any wet tee shirt competition going and she'd always come out the winner as far as he was concerned. She wasn't over-abundant in the boob department, but as the old saying went, any more than a handful was a waste. Now a mouthful—

The ringing of the telephone cut off the thought before it had fully formed. Good thing, too, or he really would be in trouble. His jeans were tight enough without having to accommodate a raging hard-on.

"Hello."

He ceased his tapping on the timber support beams as Beth-Ann answered the phone. Probably should give her a bit of quiet. He thought about slipping outside to allow her some privacy, but her next words held him rigid.

"Brad, I can't talk to you now. I'm way too busy. I've got a man here with his head up my hole."

Riley slammed his hand over his mouth and stepped down two rungs on the ladder. Leaning against the cold aluminum, he tried to stifle his chuckles. He couldn't believe she'd said that. Bloody hell, her turn of phrase was priceless.

"Get your mind out of the gutter, Brad. What I get up to is none of your business."

Good manners dictated he not listen, but Riley couldn't help himself. He risked a glance, the grin still on his face. She looked so cute standing there in a very short, bright blue dress. Her hair was a fluffy nest of towel-dried curls that framed her face and brushed her shoulders. In her free hand, she held a hairbrush she was trying to drag through her disheveled locks.

Cute wasn't the word for it. Even the little frown that creased her forehead was sexy. He took a closer look at her face. A flush of red colored her cheeks and she stabbed the brush into the air in front of her for emphasis as she talked. One angry lady.

"Oh, shut up, Brad. There's nothing wrong with me. If you didn't use half a bottle of aftershave to hide the fact you have an aversion to soap and water, we might have gotten on a little better. By the way, you'd better buy a new toothbrush. I think your old one has lost all its bristles."

She paused and dragged in a deep breath. "Hang on a minute, maybe you don't use one at all. Duh, color me stupid. Why didn't I think of that last night when your breath just about blew me out the front door of your flat? I could have offered to buy you one and teach you what it's for."

Ooh, nasty. Riley smothered another chuckle. He couldn't have turned away now if he'd wanted to. He had to know how it worked out. What a brush-off.

"I'll have you know I have as many erotic fantasies as the next person. So maybe I don't play them out, but I sure don't need you to take me on a guided tour. I'll learn on my own, thank you very much"

Riley raised his eyebrows. He wondered what it would cost him to find out what those fantasies were.

"No, Brad, there's no point calling me again in another day or so. I'm simply not interested."

Beth-Ann slammed the receiver back on the cradle. She hoped like hell it hurt his eardrums. The cheek of the guy. And he wasn't even good-looking. Why on earth had she allowed herself to be talked into going out with him the first time, let alone the second? She just had to learn to say no.

"One thing's for certain, you don't need anyone to teach you how to get rid of a guy. Tell a man he's got bad breath and it'll do it every time."

It was only then Beth-Ann remembered she wasn't alone. Riley stood halfway up the ladder watching her. She shook her head, exhaled with a noisy rasp, and tried to cool down. "Not that jerk. He's so thick-skinned I'll probably have to be really personal to get it through his head that I don't want him to ring me again."

Riley let out a rumble of laughter. "That wasn't personal?" He stepped down from the ladder and strutted over until he was right in front of her.

She sucked in another deep breath and this time caught the scent of warm, wet male. A definite libido kicker. He moved closer still, until his heat reached out to her and she had to strain to look up at him. A grin as sexy as sin curved his lips and that twinkle was back in his eyes.

"Sounds like the...jerk didn't think you could cut it in bed."

She grimaced. "He reckons I need lessons on how to be more adventurous in the bedroom. For crying out loud, we didn't even get that far."

"So do you?"

Beth-Ann dragged her mind back from the accusations Brad had thrown at her. "Do I what?"

"Need lessons in how to make some of those fantasies come true? Someone to teach you all the naughty and nice things about sex. You game, ma'am?" He leaned forward and ran the tip of his tongue around the curve of her ear.

She shouldn't do this, she really shouldn't, but she was tired of being dumped by losers. Truth be told, they hadn't even turned her on. This one sure did. Why shouldn't she have some fun?

A light bulb suddenly went on in her head. The *ma'am* had finally done it. Memories flooded back. So she was right. *Riley Osborne*. She did know him. Oh, this could be so much fun. She propped her hands on her hips and leaned close enough for her breasts to brush his chest.

"You offering?" She almost burst into laughter when she saw him swallow hard.

"I'm offering," he said in a husky voice.

A shiver of shock at her daring sliced through her. Then a surge of good old-fashioned lust swept in to take its place. Her heartbeat accelerated and the level of her breathing upped a notch. *What the hell. I'll prove I'm game for anything, if only to myself.* And this was *Riley.*

"No strings attached?" she inquired.

"No strings attached. Just a lot of fun. I'm not into the happy-ever-after bit."

"And I get to keep control? When I say it's finished, no discussion will be entered into, right?"

He inclined his head in acquiescence. She stared at him for a few moments. Did she dare?

"Is that offer for real or are you just a tease?"

"I'm offering."

"Then I'm accepting."

Oh, yeah, she was finally going to get a chance to make Riley Osborne sit up and take notice, even if she had to screw the ass off him to do so.

Chapter Two

Beth-Ann couldn't believe she'd committed herself to a no-holds-barred affair with the object of her teenage fantasies. She'd lusted after Riley all through her high-school years and he didn't even remember her.

Part of her was slightly miffed that he didn't, but it was no big surprise. Way back then, she'd been as wide as she was tall. Her hair had been a nondescript, washed-out red—thank God for dye jobs to enhance the color—and she'd sported a mouthful of metal and a face covered in pimples. Even in the folds of fat on her face, those little beggars had managed to erupt and turn into the most unsightly zits ever imaginable.

Not to mention the freckles, the bane of every redhead's life. Okay, so she only had a sprinkling across her nose, but that was enough. She'd spent years trying to bleach them out with lemon juice. Now she just relied on a good foundation when she went out.

The pimples had disappeared as hormones settled. The braces had been shed and with a lot of exercise and dieting, and a whole load of self-control, the weight had fallen off. Now she didn't even look like the same girl and it was blatantly obvious Riley had no memory of the truly nasty comment he'd once made to her.

Payback. It was time to make him eat his words.

Riley, you are going to want me so bad, you'll salivate just at the though of getting hot and heavy with me.

"So where do we go from here?" She knew her smile was mischievous, but what the heck? This was fun. "Want to check out the bedroom?" She took a slow step backward, flicking a glance over her shoulder in the general direction of her newly decorated boudoir.

Riley reached out and curled his fingers around her arm to stop her, before giving a gentle tap on the end of her nose with the tip of his index finger. His lips tilted upward in the same sexy smile he'd been famous for when he was sixteen.

"Let's take this one step at a time. I like to build the tension a little before I jump into bed. I want to give you a good time, make certain you have some fun. Take you out and show you off. You're one hel—er, heck of a lady, Beth-Ann. I may not be into the marriage and forever-after scenario, but I don't believe in keeping it in the dark either. We'll just be a regular couple on a date and see where it goes."

As she opened her mouth to speak, he raised his hand again. "Oh, we'll get to the fun in the bedroom, but not yet. Besides, I don't have any condoms with me. I didn't expect to meet a sexy little minx when I took on this insurance job. And talking of insurance jobs..."

"You're right. I guess we'd better take care of business first before we play." Beth-Ann walked across the room to lounge against the wall opposite the damaged section of the ceiling. "So what happens now?"

She knew her position outlined the curve of her hips and pushed her breasts forward. That was the idea. When Riley's gaze immediately zeroed in on the outline of her nipples, she wanted to laugh outright. "The roof, Riley," she said, eyebrows raised.

"Um, right. The roof."

He paused and dragged in a deep breath. Then he shoved his hands into the pockets of his jeans, which only served to pull the fabric tight across his lower body.

This time Beth-Ann couldn't help the grin that crept across her face. She dropped him a cheeky wink as she ran her gaze over the bulge in the front of his pants. Oh, yeah, he was interested all right.

"The roof," Riley repeated. He couldn't believe how arrogant he'd sounded when he'd given her that spiel about making certain she had fun. He hadn't meant to come off that way, but he had a policy. Make certain the lady enjoyed herself as much as he did *and* received her fair share of pleasure.

He struggled to collect his thoughts. Shit, the little witch had him hot as hell. A wave of heat washed up over his face as she continued to keep her attention fixed on the front of his jeans. The longer she did it, the harder his cock grew. Too much more and he wouldn't be able to crawl, let alone walk out the door.

"I can't do anything until it's dry up there," he said. "We'll give it a few days, then come back and get started. The insulation will have to be replaced and we'll check out all the main support beams for any further damage."

"And what about my hole?"

Riley gulped and tried to keep his mind on business. "We'll probably have to cut out that section of the ceiling and replace it. Depends how it shapes up when it dries. After that, it gets plastered to cover the joints and the whole ceiling—living room, dining, kitchen and hallway—gets repainted."

Beth-Ann straightened up and moved closer to him. "You mean I get the whole lot done?"

"Yep. Because it's a flow-on effect with the open-plan style. Not all whites match so we'll do the entire area for you."

"Hey, terrific. I haven't gotten around to painting the ceilings yet. You'll save me a job. Will you do the work yourself?"

He slid his hands around her waist and moved her so she stood in front of him. "Normally I'm the architect and I design the projects and just oversee them. But in this case, I think I'd handle the job personally." No way was he going to let any of his men get their hands on this assignment.

"I'll send a painter over tomorrow to do a quote for the insurance company. Don't show up in that wet tee shirt, will you?" He grinned. "You'll cause the poor guy to have a heart attack."

He put her aside and started to clean up his tools, placing them back into the toolbox. "You got a broom handy so I can get rid of all this broken plasterboard?"

Beth-Ann grabbed the broom and dustpan and brush from the hall closet and handed them over, watching the play of muscles as he swept up the mess. She passed him a rubbish bag before going back to the delightful task of checking out his ass. She could just imagine going down on her knees and running the tip of her tongue over that butt. And when she'd finished, she'd spin him about and start on his cock. Take him deep, until she could feel his balls on her chin.

"So would you like to go out tonight or would you rather do something tomorrow?"

His voice dragged her back from the X-rated thoughts filling her brain. "Why wait? Let's strike while the mood is upon us. You might change your mind by tomorrow."

He looked up from his position on the floor. "Uh-uh, no way. Tonight it is. I'm a great believer in spontaneity."

"I don't want to be too late though. I need to get up early so I can make a start on the preparations for painting the spare bedroom. I've taken two weeks off my job to renovate. The plan is to get as much finished as I can before I have to go back to work."

"So what do you do for a living?"

He flicked another quick glance at her as he tied off the bulging rubbish bag. Beth-Ann grinned. From his position on the floor, and given the way she was standing with hands on hips, she figured there was a good possibility he'd be able to see the edge of her panties as the abbreviated excuse for a dress hiked up.

"I'm a legal secretary for a firm in the city called Bradford & Tyler. You know it?"

"Sure do." He stood up and handed the broom and dustpan back to her. "That big construction job at the end of the same block is one of ours. Inner city apartments."

She raised her eyebrows. She walked by that job every day on her way to and from work. *And* she'd received her fair share of wolf whistles from the workmen. She'd even passed the time of day with quite a few of them. One of the older guys, Charlie, seemed to have adopted her, making a point of greeting her each day, handing out paternal advice along with a coffee-to-go. Even if she happened to be a few minutes late, Charlie was still waiting to see how her previous day had gone. But with all that time standing around the front gate of the site, she'd never seen Riley.

Hmm, interesting. With Riley so close...

"Where do you want to go tonight? Anything you fancy?"

Oh, yeah, you. "How about we go dancing? You must know all the right nightspots."

She'd spent all her early years dreaming about being held in his teenage arms. Too many times he'd even invaded her adult fantasies, although she'd had to guess what the grown-up Riley would look like. The reality was even better than she'd imagined. Wow, a chance to satisfy her schoolgirl crush. This was the perfect opportunity.

A fizz of excitement whipped through her veins. Her libido reared up, filling her mind with all manner of naughty thoughts. Somehow, the fact that he didn't know who she was laced the whole scenario with erotic overtones.

Riley unbuckled his tool belt and tossed it into his box. Tucking the ladder under his arm, he reached for the handle of his toolbox. "I'm not much for ballroom dancing, even if I knew where to go, but how about a nightclub? They even have slow dancing on occasion. The type where you can get up close and personal with your date. That suit you?"

"Sounds great. I haven't hit the nightclub scene since I arrived. Should be fun."

She preceded him to the entrance and flung the door wide. He slipped past her and propped the ladder up against the front of the house, dropping the toolbox at his feet.

"Okay, nightclubbing it is. I'll pick you up at eight. And don't forget, no wet tee shirt look when my painter comes to call tomorrow. That pleasure is mine." He leaned down and captured her mouth.

Heat hit Beth-Ann at the touch of his lips on hers. She opened to him, welcoming the thrust of his tongue and reciprocating in kind. Her heartbeat sped up, like a freight train that rushed through all the stations, fire trailing in its wake as it headed for the juncture of her thighs. One little kiss and her pussy was already dripping wet.

She wanted to grab him, throw him to the ground and climb all over him. She wanted to fuck the daylights out of him until he cried for mercy. Hell, no hands and he could achieve this effect? *Wow.*

He broke off the kiss and moved away to pick up his tools. "See you tonight," he whispered in a husky voice as he turned toward his truck.

Beth-Ann hugged her arms about her body. *Hot damn.*

✻ ✻ ✻

When the cab drew to a halt outside Beth-Ann's little house, Riley jumped from the backseat and strode up the footpath to the front door. His date waited for him in a circle of brilliant illumination cast by the porch light.

His eyebrows lifted. Holy shit, he'd hit the jackpot. This was one sexy lady. She might be small, but she packed a hell of a punch. His gaze slid from the top of her cluster of deep auburn curls, down her body, to the fuck-me black heels on her itty-bitty feet.

She had on a slinky black top with tiny spaghetti straps. One pull and they'd break they were so thin. The top clung to her breasts, outlining the peaks. He wanted to lean down and place his mouth over the telltale marks. Erotic thoughts about the taste and texture of her nipples filled his head. His cock started to throb as his body tightened in anticipation.

Where this woman was concerned, his mind was stuck in a groove. Hang it, a pit—deep enough to swallow him whole if he wasn't careful. And judging by the way her nipples hardened and pushed against the fabric of her top, he had a good idea where *her* thoughts were headed, too. A perfect match for his.

The top ended just below the waist of the shortest skirt he'd seen in a long while. Sexy red, it was tight enough to show off the curve of her hips and, as she stepped toward him, the slits in the sides parted to give him a flash of naked thigh. The high heels added an extra few inches, but he'd still have to bend to kiss her.

He did so, dropping a swift caress on her red lips. "Baby, you are hot."

"Why, thank you, kind sir." She gave a breathy chuckle. "Shall we go? That cab must be costing you a fortune."

"To hell with the expense. You're worth it." He stepped close and rested the palm of his hand in the small of her back to guide her to the vehicle.

Fucking hell, there's no back to this. The thought hit him round about the same time as the heat of her naked skin seeped into his hand. He risked a quick glance. The tiny straps in the front snaked over her shoulders and hooked through the sides of the top level with her breasts, then tied in a bow in the center of her back.

One little tug and the whole thing would come away. He dragged his gaze free before he fell over his own feet. Just the same, the image of that fragile bow remained in the forefront of his mind.

"Keep salivating like that and you'll drool down the front of your shirt. Time enough for that later."

He didn't know what to say for a moment. Then he chuckled as he opened the back door of the car for her. "Am I that transparent?"

"I've never known a man to be able to resist a bow," she said with a grin. "But I have to warn you, it's tied double. You'll have to work for your dessert."

"Where to, buddy?"

The question jerked his attention away from Beth-Ann and her bow, and onto the driver. "If you can take us to the Fantasia Nightclub in the city, that'll be fine."

The cab driver started the engine and negotiated the suburban streets until he hit the freeway. For a Friday night, traffic wasn't too bad and Beth-Anne's house wasn't far from the city. Riley settled back to enjoy the view in the backseat, rather than what flashed past outside.

"What are you doing all the way over there?" He reached out to grasp Beth-Ann's hand and urged her to slide across the seat toward him.

Just then, the cab took a sharp turn off the freeway onto the city access ramp. Beth-Ann slid sideways and Riley, with snap-fast reflexes, wrapped his arm around her shoulders and hauled her nearer. When she was snuggled so close he could feel the heat of her against his side, he grinned down at her.

"That's a C.O.D. corner," he said.

"C.O.D?" She shook her head. "You've got me there."

"*Come Over, Darling.*" Riley grinned and wiggled his eyebrows as she chuckled over his play on the abbreviation for the postal "Cash on Delivery".

"Riley, that is so—"

"Yeah, yeah, I know. So juvenile. The kids have used that one for years, but it did make you laugh. Have to keep my end up, don't ya know?"

"Oh, I don't think you'll have any problems in that department."

Boy, she was quick. He wanted to answer that one. He really did, but maybe he should hold fire until later. After all, the night was young. Instead, he pulled her even closer and tucked her head against his shoulder.

"You still haven't told me which of your fantasies you want fulfilled first," he said as he twined his fingers with hers.

"Hmm, I have to think about this." There was silence for a moment before she said, "There's a certain piquancy about the idea of being in a situation where discovery is possible. Ups the tension somewhat." She chuckled. "Or how about getting hot and heavy in the backseat of a city cab?"

"Not in my cab, lady."

Beth-Ann slapped a hand over her mouth at the total horror in the driver's voice. Laughter bubbled up, the sound muffled from behind her palm. Riley took one look at her and joined in. The poor cab driver must think they were demented—or sex maniacs.

"Anyway, you don't have time, unless you're Quick Draw McGraw, mate. We're here."

The driver's pithy comment caused another round of chuckles as Beth-Ann allowed Riley to help her from the vehicle. While he paid the driver, she took a moment to study the front of the nightclub. She'd expected a slightly sleazy look, but it was very understated.

Situated in the center of the block of businesses and shops, the only thing that marked it as a nightclub was the name picked out in blue neon, and the muscle-bound bouncer at the dark-painted front door. That, and the pulsing music that filtered out and danced on the night air.

"Ready?" Riley slipped his arm about her waist and urged her over to the entrance.

"If you're ready, so am I," Beth-Ann said, a cheeky grin sliding across her face.

"Honey, I'm game for anything." He raised his free hand in a salute to the bouncer. "Hi, Danny, busy night?"

"Hey, Riley, the boss said you'd be here tonight. Haven't seen you in a while."

"Haven't had anyone cute enough to show off," he retaliated.

Beth-Ann let the chauvinistic comment pass. She was having way too much fun and the night had only just started. Riley was one hunk of a man. The odd sexist remark she could ignore, provided he didn't take it too far.

When they stepped inside, she took a moment to look around. She'd never been to a nightclub before—they weren't the norm in her tiny country town of Wattle—but it fitted the image she'd built up in her mind.

Bright lights flashed on and off in the dim interior. She felt an instant of disorientation before she adjusted. The music was loud. The heavy thump reverberated throughout the room and would probably result in a headache before the night was done, but what the heck? It was an experience to add to her repertoire of new adventures since her move to the city.

It was early so the club wasn't too packed, but she imagined it would be a crush later on. The dance floor was small and patrons hovered on the fringes, drinks in hand, as they enjoyed the atmosphere. The D.J. spun another song and everyone started to gyrate to the catchy rhythm. Beth-Ann found herself tapping her foot in time.

A smoke machine puffed out vapor that collected at floor level, thickest around the dancers' feet, and slowly wafted upward. Tendrils curled about the mobile bodies and gave the whole image a surreal effect.

She felt Riley's presence beside her moments before he slid his arm around her waist. She snuggled closer to him and cast him a grin. "So what now?"

Before he could answer, a bear of a man bounded up to them and slapped Riley on the back. He had to be at least six-foot-six; he made Beth-Ann feel like a dwarf. Muscles bulged below the edge of the short sleeves of his shirt, his chest was immense, and it didn't take a degree in rocket science to work out he was into weight lifting and bodybuilding.

"Riley, old chum. Great to see you."

"How are you, Max?" Riley shook his hand and turned to Beth-Ann. "This is my good friend and the owner of the club, Max Myers."

Riley hugged her to him, as if intent on getting a little male message across. Like the fact that Beth-Ann was his and definitely hands off. "Max, this is Beth-Ann."

"Great to meet you, little lady." His gaze ran quickly over her petite figure before he focused again on Riley. "I've kept the back booth for you. It will give you some privacy. I'll send a waiter over to get your drink orders. That'll save you having to brave the crowd around the bar. Don't want to waste time hanging round in line, right?"

"Thanks, mate," Riley replied before he pointed Beth-Ann in the direction of the rear of the club. He paused a moment and said over his shoulder, "You could send over some of those cylume sticks, if you have any spare."

"Anything for you, old boy," Max called out.

Max disappeared through the dancers as if swallowed by a giant mouth. Beth-Ann shook her head at her fertile imagination, but the analogy fit. One minute he was there, and then he was gone. For such a big man, he was surprisingly light on his feet.

Riley led her to a partially hidden booth, roped off and with a large *Reserved* sign parked in the middle of the table. She frowned as she sat down. What on earth was a cylume?

Before she could ask, Riley slipped in beside her, so close his thigh brushed against the length of her bare leg. Shivers feathered down her spine in anticipation of things to come.

Oh, yeah, this was going to be fun. It was time to play Riley a bit to see if he remembered her. If nothing else, she was going to make him sit up and take notice, even if it meant reading every raunchy magazine she could get her hands on to learn what turned a guy on.

She leaned close enough that her breast brushed his arm. "I'm not much of a drinker. An occasional cocktail, but mostly I stick to soft drinks. With my small frame, I can't handle alcohol." She gave him a slow smile from under lowered brows. "Of course, this could be a cocktail night."

The tip of her tongue bathed her bottom lip. "You do know what alcohol does to a girl, don't you?"

Before he could answer, a waiter appeared at his elbow.

"Table service tonight, Riley. Boss's orders. What can I get you?" He leaned down and placed a handful of three-inch plastic tubes in the center of the table.

Beth-Ann frowned as she stared at them.

Riley nudged her with his elbow. "What would you like?"

"Huh? Oh, I'll have an orange juice." She reached out and picked up one of the tubes.

"Ever seen those?"

"I take it this is one of those cylume thingies you asked for."

"Check out the people on the dance floor. See the glowing sticks they're holding or have in their hair or tucked into their clothes?"

She nodded.

"That's a cylume or glow stick. If you bend it slightly it cracks inside and two chemicals mix to form a substance that glows. They're all the rage in the nightclubs. The military uses them."

Beth-Ann did as he said and grinned when the little tube started to glow. "Cool." She pointed the glowing tube at him. "So when do I get to hear your life story?"

Riley waved her question away. "Nah, too boring. Born in a small town—I hate small towns where everyone knows each other's business—moved away from said town after mother left when I was sixteen..."

She'd heard all the rumors about his mother when she was growing up. About how she went after anyone in pants and how everyone in town knew about it. Poor Mister Osborne. She remembered him as a kindly man who always had a gentle word for the introverted chunky teenager she was then.

"...went into business with Dad after I got my degree, and the rest is history. That's me in a nutshell." He trailed the tip of his finger down her arm. "I'd much rather talk about you."

"Uh-uh, too boring," she echoed his words. "Come dance with me instead." She dropped the glow stick on the table—the only illumination in their dark little corner—and stood up. Backing away from the table to allow the waiter to set down their drinks, she held her hand out.

With a grin, Riley slid his hand around hers and led her onto the floor. A new wave of dancers had taken to the small space set aside for dancing, making the area look crowded. Which was fine by Beth-Ann. It meant she had to stand close enough to Riley that they almost touched. Now to see if she could get a rise out of him—in more ways than one.

She may have been the resident fat kid all through school, and she'd never attended a school dance, but she'd practiced for hours in front of her mirror behind a locked bedroom door. Now to see what affect it had on Riley.

Riley raised his eyebrows as Beth-Ann lost herself in the music. Her body gyrated and bumped in perfect synchronization with the tempo. He grinned. His pixie liked to dance. As the song changed to a heady Latino beat and Beth-Ann moved closer and thrust her hips toward him, his grin disappeared.

First the thrust. Next she glided in even closer and ground her body against his. He took up the rhythm and reciprocated, his hips rotating in time with hers. They could have been having sex their movements were so well timed. Then she slid around behind him and repeated the action and he was hell bent on keeping up with her.

He snaked an arm behind him and hauled her back round in front, his hands clamped on her hips. Thank God it was dark in the nightclub. That way no one knew he had a raging hard-on that would be evident to anyone with the slightest bit of brainpower. His old John Henry pulsed in time with the beat and he couldn't remember any other woman who'd ever turned him on so hard, so fast.

Hell, she was screwing up his brain. He almost burst into laughter at the thought of calling his cock by the old John Henry tag. He hadn't done that since he was in high school. All thoughts of laughter fled as Beth-Ann ground her hips against his front and leaned back, trusting him to take her weight. Her hands skimmed up her body to tangle in her red curls, before sliding down again to outline the curve of her breasts.

With a sinuous stretch, she straightened up and a sexy smile tilted her lips as she winked at him. His cock throbbed, his hips jerked forward and the air gusted from his lungs. *Holy crap, she's got me hotter than a bug on a barbeque.*

Beth-Ann smirked as she caught the bemused look on Riley's face. His eyes glazed over, his chest heaved as he dragged air deep into his lungs, and she had a feeling it had nothing to do with the strenuous rhythm of the dance. She angled her hips and pushed her pubic area harder against him. Darn shame she was so much shorter than he was. The fit wasn't quite spot on.

The hard, hot ridge of his erection pressed against her belly, made her curl her hands up around his neck and press her breasts to his chest, so close she couldn't have fitted a blade between them had she tried. Rock-hard muscles nudged at her nipples, sensitizing the peaks until she felt she would go crazy with wanting. No, more than that. Sheer need.

Heat pooled between her thighs as Riley held her hips tight against him, rotated his pelvis and thrust. Her legs trembled and the breath gusted from her throat. The skin on her arms pebbled. She shivered, but it had nothing to do with being cold. This was lust, pure and simple. *Pure?* She chuckled, the sound bitten off when he thrust again.

Hot damn, she was about to combust. Heat licked through her veins, making her heart race with excitement. She stared up at him to see a knowing smile flit across his face before he wiped all expression away and raised his eyebrows.

Dammit, she was supposed to be putting *him* on the spot, not the other way around. She was the one who said she wanted to be in charge of this affair, to have control over what they did or didn't do. It was time to put her money where her mouth was.

She broke away and danced behind him. Before he could turn around, she plastered herself to his back and slid her arms around his waist. Then, the beat of the music a metronome to time her movements, she walked her fingers across his chest, between the buttons of his shirt, to stroke at his warm skin. At the same time, her hips moved in an advance and retreat strategy designed to entice him into a sexual frenzy. Well, that was the general idea anyway.

When he least expected it, she dragged her hands down and knocked against the belt of his trousers before moving lower. Her palms glided over his hipbones, fingers angled inward so they just brushed against the bulge in his trousers. The husky groan that rippled from his throat was reward enough.

He reached down to grasp her questing fingers, but she eluded his touch, broke away and twirled around in front of him. Their gazes connected and she kept him pinned there on the spot as she thrust her hips to first one side and then the other. At the same time, she kept up a constant caress of his chest, only dancing away when he tried to reach for her.

Tease me, will he? Hah, let him get a taste of this.

She continued to taunt, to raise the tension between them until the set of music ended. When the D.J. finally announced a break, she was glad. Her breathing was fragmented. Her chest heaved so much, it was a wonder her breasts didn't escape the abbreviated top.

Okay, they weren't that big, but they sure kept Riley's gaze busy. She grinned as she reached for his hand and tugged him toward their booth. Like a tame puppy dog, he trailed after her without a word. Maybe he was having trouble breathing, too.

Lord, she could drink a river dry right about now. She ran her tongue along her lips. As they reached their table, she turned and rested her hands against Riley's chest as she tried to catch her breath.

"Ohhh," she said in a husky voice as she dragged in the scent of his aftershave, "I really, really need a quick fuck after that."

Chapter Three

Riley's thought processes ground to an abrupt halt. He tried to swallow, but his throat felt like it was sealed shut. He gave it another shot, downed the lump lodged in the back of his mouth and dragged in a shaky breath.

Quick fuck?

Did she say quick...? He shook his head. Damn, only twenty-nine and old age was already catching up with him. Didn't they say hearing was the first of the senses to go? He must have heard her wrong.

He might have misunderstood, but his old John Henry figured he had it right. His lower body throbbed, his erection straining against his trousers for release. *Fucking hell, this woman sure knows how to push my buttons.*

All that wild dancing had left Beth-Ann's skin dewed with perspiration. The slinky top clung to her chest and left nothing to the imagination. She might have small breasts, but she had the most prominent nipples he'd ever seen. So okay, he hadn't seen them yet, but wet tee shirts and clingy black tops didn't exactly hide them from view. A guy with a good imagination wouldn't have any problem visualizing the real thing.

At the moment, the tips were hard little nuggets that pushed against the damp fabric of her top. He could even see the ridged outline of her areoles. Oh, boy, overload here.

On a tide of sexual hunger, he let his hand follow where his thoughts had led him. In a moment of total clarity, he acknowledged the tremor in his fingers as he reached out and used the tip of his pinky to trace that telltale outline.

She sucked in a sharp breath, but didn't turn away or smack him one in the face, which is what he deserved for attempting this in plain view.

It wasn't really open to any passing voyeurs. This part of the club was mostly in shadow, although the odd flicker of spinning red light flashed across Beth-Ann's face and created a bizarre pattern. He had a sudden desire to see her naked body clothed in the same spirals of color.

Instead of moving away from him, she leaned in closer, until her chest brushed his and he had no choice but to flatten his hand over her breast. Her engorged nipple nudged at his palm. He'd been correct in his assessment about her breasts. Just the right size to fill his hand—and his mouth—if he ever got that far.

Beth-Ann fought to catch her breath. *Oh my giddy grandma, Riley Osborne has his hand on my boob.* Her teenage fantasy had come to life. All those times she'd pretended it was Riley's touch after she'd learned what masturbation was about, and it didn't even come close to the real thing.

She moved her body experimentally so her nipple grazed his palm. When he groaned, low and husky, her ego took a giant leap. She grinned. "I'm talking about the cocktail," she managed to drawl. "You know, a Quick Fuck, mostly referred to as a QF. One part each of Kahlúa, Bailey's Irish Cream, Midori and Amaretto. Layer into a shot glass, finishing with the Bailey's."

With a lopsided grin, she stepped away from him and slid into the booth. "I did say I like a cocktail on occasion. I think this warrants a splash of alcohol."

The desire to burst into laughter at the stunned expression on his face was immense. She squashed it. *I've got you, Riley Osborne, high-school football stud.* Wouldn't do to tip her hand too early.

"Ahh, you wait right there and I'll go and get you your Quick Fu..." His voice trailed off and he backed away from the table, almost losing his balance as he swung around and raced for the bar.

Now she did laugh. It bubbled up as she craned her head and watched him elbow everyone else out of the way so he could get to the front of the line. If he wasn't careful, he'd end up in a brawl for barging in, and if that happened, the bouncer would toss him out on his ass.

In less time than she would have believed possible, he was back at the booth with her drink in one hand and a fresh mug of beer for himself in the other. He placed the glasses down on the table before he slid in beside her.

There was no pretense this time. He moved right up close and deliberately allowed his thigh to brush against her leg. One arm snaked around her waist and his fingers caressed the underside of her breast. Heat slammed into her and her nipples started to ache.

"You're a witch, you know that?" He lowered his head and nuzzled the side of her neck. "You did that on purpose, so I *would* squirm."

"Hey, I just wanted a drink." She angled her head to allow him an unrestricted path. "If the shock value worked, so much the better."

A shiver trickled down her spine as he nipped at the column of her throat before bathing the love bites with open-mouthed kisses. Her breathing sped up, along with the beat of her heart. Thank heavens their booth was almost in total darkness. If she was going to make out in a nightclub, she'd prefer there were no onlookers.

Although, come to think of it, maybe that was part of the turn-on. She sucked in a shaky breath as Riley moved his hand up and covered her breast. When his fingers tweaked at the nipple, heat shot downward to center between her thighs. She wriggled around on the leather seat and rubbed her legs together as the tension escalated.

"Are you hot, Beth-Ann?"

His warm breath whispered across the side of her face as he trailed the tip of his tongue around the curve of her ear. The breath caught in her throat and her heart thumped so loud it was a wonder he couldn't hear it. She was so hot she thought she'd disintegrate at any moment. The reality of being with Riley was so much more than she'd expected.

"You want me to put out the fire?" he whispered.

When he placed his hand on her bare leg, she jumped before she gave in to the delicious feelings that swept through her as he moved higher on her thigh. He turned her slightly more toward him, lowered his head and took her lips in a heated kiss.

Thank you, Lord. She'd wanted this for so long. She opened her mouth when he nibbled on her bottom lip. Dampness gathered between her legs as he brought his tongue into play. She met him halfway, joining him in the thrust and parry. Her hips wanted to take up the rhythm, but she restrained herself.

Despite her attempts at self-control, she lost it when Riley moved his fingers up under her skirt and brushed at her swollen pussy through the silk of her panties. She moaned, the sound absorbed by the rapacious hunger of his mouth. Her breathing was harsh by the time he broke off the kiss and pulled back to look at her.

"Open your legs a bit," he whispered.

"Riley, we can't—" She couldn't even finish the sentence.

"Can you honestly say this isn't a turn-on? To do this in public where the risk of getting caught is high?" He moved his fingers the slightest amount, eliciting a gasp from her.

"Bet I can make you come in public." He flicked his fingers again and a cheeky grin broke out on his face.

Beth-Ann was grateful for his humor. It helped to lighten the tension that arced between them. She needed a moment to regroup. Her grin matched his as she shook her head. "Can't be done," she crowed. "I have too much control to allow it to go that far."

He waggled his eyebrows. "Wanna bet?"

A gurgle of laughter escaped, abruptly cut off when he slid his hand down between her thighs. Throughout their banter, she'd relaxed the muscles in her upper legs and he'd taken immediate advantage.

Her thin panties were no barrier to his scalding touch as he ran the tip of his finger along her cleft. Without her brain giving the order, she widened her legs even more, allowing him greater access.

"You're already wet," he whispered as he leaned forward to shield her from anyone who might come too near. "I can feel the dampness through your panties. Right here." He fingered the crotch of her underwear, pushing the fabric against the heat of her pussy.

Beth-Ann's hips bucked. *Wet?* What an understatement. Her panties were so wet they were darn near soaked. Without conscious volition, she slid further down on the bench seat, her head drooping forward to rest on his chest.

As she dragged in a shaky breath and opened her mouth to speak, the scent of her desire mingled with the spicy tang of his aftershave. She snapped her mouth closed again. There wasn't a thing she could say. Her libido had taken over.

"Take them off."

She frowned as she tried to process his words. "Wha—"

"Your panties. Take them off."

"Here? I can't... Someone will see me." She lifted her head and stared at him, at the wicked glitter in his chocolate-brown eyes. The hangdog look, filled with longing, caught at her heart and drove rational thought from her mind.

"How?" She rolled her eyes at the husky croak that came out. Here she was with Riley Osborne willing to pleasure her and she couldn't even put a cohesive sentence together.

He slid his hand around behind her and hooked his fingers over the elastic. "Lift your ass," he said in a low voice, his gaze never wavering from hers.

When Beth-Ann complied, he slipped her underwear down beneath her. A gasp escaped as his knuckles brushed at the cheeks of her bottom. She'd never thought of that region as being erotic, but hot damn.

"Lay back a fraction."

Well, heck, she'd come this far. May as well go the rest of the way. She still maintained her control was rigid enough to avoid the final fulfillment, but she wasn't averse to a little playing around. Manual stimulation had a lot going for it. Besides, she was interested to see how far *he'd* go.

Her heart skipped a beat as he moved his hand across the slight swell of her stomach and inserted it under the front of her panties. His fingers tangled in her pubic curls and he gave a slight tug.

"You ready?"

Oh, yeah. It was impossible to verbalize her response, but she nodded so vigorously it was sheer dumb luck she didn't knock him out.

Quick as a wink, he slid her panties down her legs until they pooled at her feet. With the added advantage of his long reach, he bent beneath the table, snagged them up and stuffed them in his pocket. Beth-Ann blinked like a moronic bimbo, astounded that he had achieved it with so little fuss. No one appeared to have taken any notice at all.

She tried to even out her breathing, but he didn't give her the chance to come down. His hand settled over her mound and slid forward to cup her between the legs. With a groan, she collapsed back against the seat and let him have his way, because right at that moment, it was what she wanted, too.

"I was right," he whispered against her mouth.

He parted her labia and ran the tip of his finger along the length of her. Beth-Ann whimpered and tilted her hips. *Don't stop, please, don't stop.*

"You are so hot and wet, so ready for me," Riley said as he delved deeper, then dragged her creamy moisture up over her clit. "You want me in there, don't you?"

"God, yes, don't tease, Riley."

With a smile, he leaned down and nibbled at the outer edge of her mouth. "Teasing is good. It builds the tension."

"Much more tension and I'm going to shatter," she managed in a shaky voice.

"Oh, I'm going to make you shatter, darlin'. That's the whole point of the exercise."

Beth-Ann made a move to shake her head in denial, but all she could do was gasp as Riley covered her mound of springy curls and pressed his fingers down. When he slid one finger inside, she moaned and spread her legs even more.

"You feel that?" he murmured against her lips. "See how wet you are. I can smell your desire. You like me doing this, don't you?"

Without any direct command from her brain, her hips moved in time with the thrust of his finger. Her muscles clenched as she tried to drag him deeper. Lord, it wasn't enough. And it was too much. Fire gathered at his touch. Her heart raced, threatening to jump right out of her chest. Her eyelids drooped as her mind turned to soggy mush and her body took over.

"No, look at me, Beth-Ann. I want to know you're thinking only of me."

She couldn't believe how hard it was to focus. Where was her much-valued control now? She struggled to gain the upper hand. After all, she was supposed to be putting *him* on the spot. Her gaze fastened on his glittering brown eyes, she leaned forward and ran the tip of her tongue around his mouth before bathing his full bottom lip with wet strokes.

He groaned and when she pulled back and looked at him, she could have sworn his eyes had glazed over. She grinned, then released a gasp as he withdrew his finger and replaced it with two. Her hips bucked in response to the tightness, the stretch of her body. A shudder raced through her as he set up a steady pace. Thrust and withdraw, only to plunge deep again.

"Go for it, darlin'. No one can see you, and even if they could, think of the spice possible discovery adds to the scenario."

Beth-Ann forgot about anyone or anything else around her. Her body took up the rhythm, her hips angled to take him deep. It still wasn't enough. She wanted more. Control forgotten, she clamped her hand on his wrist, pushing down so the friction was where she wanted it most.

Her breath gusted out in short pants, interspersed with soft moans she couldn't have prevented if she'd tried, and she was way beyond the point of trying. All she could do was feel, and trust Riley to be there for her when she fell.

Riley couldn't believe how responsive she was. He wasn't really into public displays of sexual excess, but damned if this wasn't the greatest turn-on he'd ever experienced. Beth-Ann held tight to his wrist and ground her hips against his hand in concert with the thrust of his fingers. Her thighs clamped around his hand as if she feared he'd pull away.

No chance in hell. It was a major effort to keep control of his body as she rode his hand. His cock was rock-hard, almost to the point of pain. He needed to sink himself into her heat, bury himself to the hilt and pound away at that delectable body. Small, but dynamite.

He wanted to slither down under the table and replace his hand with his mouth. Drink of all that fiery slickness, tease her clit until she screamed out his name, and to hell with the consequences.

Beth-Ann's eyes closed as the movement of her hips became more frenzied. Her long fingernails dug into the back of his hand. Her moans increased in volume and if he kept this up, everyone would definitely know what was going on in this darkened corner of the nightclub.

"Let go, Beth-Ann, I'll catch you," he whispered as he dragged her head forward and slanted his mouth over hers. His tongue swept inside and tangled with hers, thrust in time with his fingers. The muscles in her thighs tightened and her hips pressed forward, ground against his hand in desperate appeal. He thrust his fingers deeper, harder, faster—and Beth-Ann came apart in his hands.

At the moment of ultimate surrender, he caught her breathy moans in his mouth and swallowed them. Took the sounds of her climax deep inside where they lodged in his heart.

Removing his hand from under her skirt, he dragged her close, her head pushed against his shoulder. His breathing was as hoarse and raspy as hers. Teeth clenched, he struggled to control the unrelieved sexual tension that hummed throughout his body. His trousers were so damn tight in the front he was in danger of doing himself an injury. And as for standing up... Forget it. He couldn't move if his life depended on it.

Beth-Ann dragged in a shuddering breath. *Oh, my.* She couldn't believe she... Heck, she couldn't even finish the thought. Her brain felt as if it had turned to sludge, rational thought impossible.

She kept her head buried in Riley's chest for a few more minutes as she tried to regulate her breathing. Her thighs quivered as she pressed them together on a lingering spasm and sought to ignore the throb between her legs.

So now she knew why all the girls in high school had raved about Riley Osborne. Hot damn, he was good. If that was the appetizer, she couldn't wait for the main course. Given half a chance, she'd go for the whole darn banquet.

With a final, shaky sigh, she pulled back and glanced up at Riley, grateful for the darkness as a wave of heat washed up over her face.

"You okay?" she managed to whisper. She ran the tip of her tongue along her dry lips and wiped one hand across her forehead, surprised to feel the sheen of sweat.

Riley let out a crack of laughter. "Hell, I should be the one asking that."

"Oh, yeah, I'm fine, but what about you?" She allowed her gaze to slide down his body. Turned sideways as he was, it wasn't difficult to discern the bulge in the front of his trousers. She raised her eyebrows. "You didn't—"

"Plenty of time for me later," he interrupted with a grin.

He reached out to grab the beer from the table. When he raised the glass and took a greedy gulp, Beth-Ann was surprised to see the tremor in his hand. Sooo...he was just as affected as she was. Interesting. She propped her arms on the edge of the table and laid her head down, her face turned toward him. "I can't believe you did that. Made me—"

"Made you come? Or made you come in public?" He leaned forward and dropped a light kiss on her flushed cheek. "So does it up the excitement any, to know you're doing that where you could be caught?"

Beth-Ann turned her face into her arms. So much for her self-control. All those years she'd worked to reinforce her belief in her self-restraint and Riley had shot it to pieces with a few moments of sexual gratification. If he hadn't kissed her at the exact same instant she'd climaxed, she would have howled to the moon it had been so intense.

For a minute, she struggled with the idea that her willpower was so fragile where Riley was concerned. She shrugged it aside. She'd gone into this with her eyes wide open, for one reason and one reason only. To make Riley sit up and take notice of her. Tonight's little episode had certainly engaged his attention. His breathing was ragged and if she moved her head a little, she could tell by the bulge in his trousers that he still had a hard-on. Oh, yeah, he was as turned on as she was.

"Your turn's coming, Riley Osborne," she murmured as he bent over her again.

"Promises, promises," he whispered right back.

She dropped her hand and trailed the tip of one finger over his engorged cock. "Not a promise, a fact. When you least expect it, I'm going to turn you into a raving sex maniac."

He dragged in a harsh breath and released it on a growl. "Hell, with you, darlin', I'm already a sex maniac." He grasped her hand and moved it away from his crotch.

"Hi ya, Riley, got a problem with the little lady? Quick Fucks have a lot to answer for, you know?"

At the same time as Riley twisted to glare over his shoulder, Beth-Ann lifted her head and looked into the knowing eyes of Max, the owner of the nightclub. Lord, how mortifying. She didn't need to ask what he was thinking. She could see it in the raised eyebrows and the smirk on his face.

She glanced at Riley, caught the half smile on his face and the twinkle in his eyes. Suddenly she saw the funny side of it. *Oh, my God, I asked for a quick fuck and that's exactly what I got, even if it was a finger fuck.*

The chuckles started deep inside her, rising up to bubble out in a steady stream of contagious hilarity. Riley's mouth twitched and it wasn't long before he joined her. Beth-Ann collapsed against his chest and held on while the laughter rocked her. They both looked at Max and laughed even harder at his confused shrug as he turned and walked away.

Beth-Ann wiped at her eyes and prayed her mascara hadn't run. A play on words she could handle. Looking like a pathetic panda bear with black-smudged eyes she couldn't. "I can't believe we did this," she said.

"Actually, it's a first for me, too," Riley said, a grin curving his lips. "What say we get out of here? We can go on to another club or I can take you home if you've had enough."

"If that's a sample, I'll never have enough," she teased. "But, yes, time to go home. I need a good night's sleep so I'll be fresh for all that painting tomorrow."

"Who said anything about sleep?" He raised his eyebrows in query.

"You staying?" Beth-Ann couldn't believe she was being so bold.

"You asking?"

She nodded in reply.

"Then, yeah, I'd like to stay. We've only just started, darlin'. One thing, though…"

"Hmm?" Beth-Ann sat up and straightened her top, conscious all the while that she had no panties on. It gave her a delicious sense of wickedness.

"Do you mind if we swing by the building site downtown? I want to check in with Mel, the security guard. We've had some strange things going on over the last week or so."

Beth-Ann propped her chin on her hand and frowned at him. "What type of things?"

"Supplies have disappeared, equipment busted, that sort of thing. Mainly nuisance value, but I'd still like to find out who's responsible. That's why I employed a security firm to keep watch on the place."

He stood up, smoothed his hair back and pulled at the front of his trousers. "Okay, let's get out of here," he said as he held out a hand to her. A dismayed look suddenly flashed across his face and he dropped hurriedly back onto the seat. "Holy crap, I've still got your panties."

As he dug into his trouser pocket to retrieve her underwear, Beth-Ann leaned forward and placed her hand over his. "Don't bad boys collect panties as trophies?"

She didn't wait for him to answer. Instead, she stood up and smoothed the skimpy skirt down over her hips. "Keep them. I've decided I quite like being bad. Very liberating to know I have no underwear on." She edged past him in the confined space of the booth. "Of course, I also know that *you* know I have no panties on, and that's the greatest reward I can think of."

With a twitch of her hips, she set off across the nightclub, followed by a husky growl. When she flicked a look over her shoulder, Riley was right behind her. She didn't need to be too smart to work out his body had responded to the knowledge of her lack of underwear. The tight fit of his trousers did that.

She drew to a halt just outside the nightclub. He fitted in behind her, hands on her shoulders, his erection nudging her bottom. One thing had become blatantly clear. He may have made her climax in public, stripped her of her self-restraint along with her underwear, but right now she was back in control and she intended to stay that way.

With a sinuous movement, she rubbed against him, gratified to hear his groan. "Control, my lad," she whispered. "We have all night for that."

Chapter Four

Beth-Ann slid into the backseat of the cab, conscious all the while of her brief skirt and the fact that she had no panties on. A grin caught her unawares. Who would have thought it? Fat old Beth-Ann, the object of everyone's jokes at school, and here she was, running around without any underwear, totally bare-assed. And talking about butts...

She squirmed around, lifted up and attempted to pull her skirt down before she clipped on the seat belt. Then she twisted some more as she tried to get comfortable.

"Are you all right?" Riley moved closer and reached for the center seatbelt.

"I've got a problem. My skirt's caught and my bottom is sticking to the plastic cover on the seat. Besides, it's cold."

Riley chuckled. "Can't have that. I like my women hot."

Oh, yeah? You haven't seen hot yet, Riley Osborne.

Unclipping her seat belt, he reached behind her. "Lift up and I'll smooth your skirt down. Although it's so short, I'm not certain there's enough to tuck under your thighs."

She used the back of the driver's seat to lever herself up a few inches. Riley swept his hand under her backside and dragged her skirt down. A delicious shiver slid down her spine at his touch. As he trailed his finger along the split in the side of her skirt, the breath caught in her throat.

"That better?"

"Riley, you're playing with fire. You're supposed to help me, not make it harder for me to sit still."

"Hmm, talking about harder, how do you think it makes me feel to know you have no panties on?" He feathered a soft kiss up near her ear.

"And you're still not doing it in the back of my cab, buddy. This ain't no knocking shop. Now, where do you want to go? I haven't got all night."

Beth-Ann took one look at Riley and burst out laughing. Oh my God, what were the odds of getting the same cab driver they'd had before? The look on Riley's face was priceless. He might like to play with women, but she had a feeling he'd never had to deal with this type of situation before.

"Um, the R & J construction site on Castlereagh Street in the city, just off Martin Place. I need to stop there for a few minutes and then back to the house where you picked us up."

The driver twisted his head to stare at Riley, his expression filled with suspicion. "That building site is shut up at night, mate."

"I know, I'm the owner. Just need to check in with the security guard." He settled back in the seat, his shoulder brushing against Beth-Ann's.

An occasional flicker of neon lighting from the shops and business premises they passed lit up the inside of the cab for an instant before they were again plunged into semi-darkness. Not a lot of illumination, but enough that Beth-Ann could see the two spots of color high on Riley's cheekbones.

She leaned in close enough that she could whisper in his ear. "First time I knew men blushed." Then she ran the tip of her tongue around the furled edge.

Riley turned his head and captured her lips in a quick caress. "You are a minx, madam. You've turned me into a testosterone-filled school kid. The thought of you without your panties is driving me crazy. If we weren't in the back of this cab..."

"It's nice to know I'm turning you on," she said, pressing closer still.

He nuzzled at her neck. The brush of his new whisker growth made the fine hairs stand up on her arms and sent a shiver down her spine as if an ice-cold finger had trailed over each separate vertebra. His lips were warm on her skin, igniting an answering fire deep in her belly that drove downward to center between her thighs. Sitting still was almost a physical impossibility.

She wanted to turn into his arms and go for broke. Hell, she wanted to climb all over him, savor every bit of him, start at his lips and work down. Talk about dreams coming true, even if they were left over from her school days.

"Just make certain you don't turn anyone else on," Riley said. "I may not be into happy ever after, but I'm certainly into exclusivity while I'm seeing a woman."

She grinned. "That sounds a tad chauvinistic there, Riley Osborne. I hope that cuts both ways."

"Here you are, buddy. Don't take too long. I'm due to go off for a meal break."

Riley pulled away as the driver interrupted and drew the cab to a halt outside the security booth of the building site. "I won't be long," he murmured, unclipping his seat belt and sliding out of the cab.

He stuck his head through the open window of the vehicle. "Just keep the meter running, *buddy*. The size of your fare will make it worth your while to be a bit late for dinner."

Beth-Ann pulled her legs up and curled sideways on the seat. The driver stared at her through the rearview mirror. She wasn't certain how much he could see, but she wrenched down her skirt to cover her naked butt just to be on the safe side.

Forgetting the driver for the minute, she turned her attention to Riley.

A grin surfaced as she watched the shape of his ass as he approached the building. Man, she was a sucker for a tight set of buns. An older man stepped forward to meet him, hand extended in welcome, and the two disappeared inside the security booth.

Five minutes stretched into ten before Riley returned to the cab. He opened the back door and leaned over, but didn't enter the vehicle. Beth-Ann raised her eyebrows and waited. Something must be wrong.

"I'm going to be a bit longer than I expected," he said. "Mel's got a problem. Seems kids are on the loose throughout the building site. God knows how they got in."

"You want me to wait in the security booth?" Beth-Ann moved across the bench seat toward him.

Riley frowned and ran his hand through his hair. "I have no idea how long I'll be. Look, why don't you take the cab back to your place? If it's not too late after I finish up here, I'll join you."

He stood up, reached into his back pocket for his wallet and peeled off a couple of large denomination notes. Poking his head through the front window of the car, he handed over the cash to the driver. "I'd appreciate it if you'd take the lady home." He nodded at the money in the driver's hand. "That should cover it. Keep the change."

"Right you are, buddy," the driver replied.

When Riley turned back to her, Beth-Ann had separated out the key to the rear door of her house, leaving the front entrance one on the key-ring She held it up to him. "Doesn't matter what time it is. Just let yourself in the back door. I'll leave the side gate unlocked for you."

"You're sure?" Riley clasped his hand about the key, her fingers trapped in his grasp.

Beth-Ann snaked one arm around his neck and pulled him down to her. Before he could say a word, she fastened her lips on his and swept her tongue inside, tasting his heat before withdrawing.

"I'll be waiting," she said in a husky whisper. "I still have a lot of fantasies to explore. For one thing, I've never gone down on a man. How'd you like to be the first?"

She laughed outright at the shocked but intrigued look on his face as she slammed the door of the cab and waved him goodbye.

✵ ✵ ✵

Riley pulled the utility truck he'd borrowed from the building site into the driveway of Beth-Ann's low-set house and cut the engine. For a moment, he sat and rubbed at his eyes. Then, rotating his shoulders, he slid from the cab of the vehicle and closed the door with a quiet click. Raising his hand, he squinted at the luminous dial of his watch.

Shit, three in the morning. Way later than he'd planned. Beth-Ann would be well and truly asleep by now. Perhaps he should get back in the truck and...

He let the thought trail off. She did say it didn't matter how late it was and he had a hankering to crawl into bed beside her warm, delectable body.

Checking out the building site had taken longer than he'd expected. He and Mel would get down to one end of the site before having to tear back to the other in response to a crash or the sound of someone talking. Whoever it was—maybe it was more than one given they'd heard conversation—had been playing them for fools.

He didn't agree with Mel that it was kids out for a lark. Something told him it had more sinister overtones than that. Not only had the vandal poured fresh concrete over all the tools, and smashed and mangled the equipment, but someone had sawed almost all the way through one of the main support beams of what was going to be the foyer of the inner-city apartment block. Which meant he'd have to check all supports and beams before any further work could take place. Thank God he'd spotted it, and if the idiot hadn't left the handsaw on the concrete slab beside the beam, he wouldn't have thought twice about it.

His contract specified he had to finish the project by a certain time. If he didn't, the penalty clauses in the document would blow his budget sky-high. He'd allowed for weather variations, but he hadn't counted on sabotage, and that's what this felt like. He was probably being paranoid, but something about this whole thing didn't sit right with him.

There'd been a lot of rivalry for this job, but he couldn't believe his competitors would go to these lengths to prevent him bringing the project in on time. Well, worrying about it in the wee smalls of the morning wasn't going to help matters any. He'd have a session with his father tomorrow—um, later today—and see what he could come up with.

He levered himself away from the truck and paced around to the side of the house. It took less than a moment to reach over the top of the gate, undo the latch and push the gate open. As he started down the side path, the dog in the next yard set up a frenzied barking. Riley jumped in shock, cursing under his breath. He tried to shush it, but it only made the animal bark louder and launch itself at the timber fence separating the two properties.

With a silent prayer that the animal wasn't big enough to clear the fence, he continued down the path, cringing as the barking rose in pitch, the sound an assault to the ears in the night air. Christ, the neighbors would think he was a burglar at this rate. Just what he needed, damn it. If they rang the cops, how the hell would he explain he was about to sneak in to crawl into bed beside the hottest woman he'd met in a long time?

The dog settled down as Riley rounded the house and approached the back door. The key turned in the lock with a slight click and he let himself in. The living area was in darkness but for the soft glow that emanated from a table lamp Beth-Ann had left on, a small courtesy for which he was grateful. He didn't fancy trying to negotiate an unfamiliar house in the pitch black.

He paused long enough to shed his clothes and fling them over the arm of the couch. Anticipation dried his mouth, made his heart beat faster. When he'd stripped to his boxers, he tiptoed down the hallway, surprised the loud performance of the dog next door hadn't woken Beth-Ann.

The first bedroom on his right was empty so he moved on to the next one. The master bedroom, lit by a small, wall-mounted nightlight that cast a halo of brilliance onto the king-sized bed taking up most of the room. The sight that met his eyes almost floored him.

Oxygen wheezed from his chest in a harsh whistle. His mouth dropped open. He snapped it closed and dragged fresh air into his lungs, struggling to clear the fog from his brain.

Holy crap, what a sight to walk in on.

Testosterone raged through his body and awoke the most basic of functions—the need to indulge in carnal knowledge. And that wasn't all it woke. His cock hardened and throbbed with expectancy, his boxers tented over his erection. Thank God he didn't still have his trousers on. He'd be in serious pain with *this* hard-on.

Beth-Ann lay before him, a feast for not only the eyes, but also the senses. She might be small, but she sure knew how to use what she did have to best effect.

The bed linen was deep scarlet and against it, her naked body looked like an alabaster statue. She'd curled up on her side, her face turned toward him, one hand cradled under her cheek. Her other arm lay in the curve of her waist.

Pink-tipped nipples peaked at him, her breasts the perfect size. He wasn't into overly endowed women. There were more important things than a big set of boobs. Maybe in his teenage years, he might have lusted after size, but these days he went for quality over quantity. Hell, one never knew in these times what was real and what surgery had enhanced.

His gaze tracked downwards, skimming over her bare skin. Her hips were tiny, but exquisitely shaped, her bare legs enough to start him salivating. His cock throbbed in response to the visual feast.

She lay with one knee drawn up to hide the juncture between her thighs. He felt like a voyeur as he stood staring at her. He was one sick puppy. Sick for Beth-Ann, that is. Something about her made his insides turn to jelly, morphed him into a quivering mass of need. Of hunger. But also a desire to please her in whatever way possible, not just the sexual.

With a shake of his head, he tried to analyze his reaction, but his brain wouldn't cooperate. A memory moved on the edge of his mind, then slithered out of reach, driven by the thunderous beat of his heart. He pushed away from the doorframe and approached the bed.

Beth-Ann took that moment to roll over. A lump lodged in his throat as she moved onto her back. Now *there* was a picture. The breath gusted from his throat at the sheer eroticism. Then he nearly choked himself as he struggled to contain the chuckle that threatened to break through. He moved nearer the edge of the bed to check that he hadn't imagined it.

Nope. A tiny, neatly tied bow. She had combed her pubic hair upward and caught the topmost curls together with a narrow strip of bright crimson. And yeah, she was a true redhead, a slightly softer shade, but real nonetheless. He shook his head at the idiotic thoughts cluttering his brain.

Fucking hell, what a present.

His immediate response was to dive onto the bed beside her and fuck the daylights out of her. He reined in his impatience. "Finesse, old boy, finesse," he whispered.

"You ever coming to bed?"

Beth-Ann grinned as Riley jumped and swung his gaze back to her face. She'd heard the vehicle pull into her driveway, but a sudden bout of embarrassment, and a lifetime of insecurities as the fat kid on the block, had kept her where she was.

Now she was glad. She may not have been able to see everything with her eyelids cracked open only the smallest amount, but she'd seen enough. The front of his boxers was about eye level as he bent over the end of the bed. Hard to mistake where *his* mind was.

"I thought you were asleep," he said. "I was just debating whether to wake you or not."

A gurgle of laughter burst from her. "Riley, that's a big fib. Come on now, `fess up, you were copping an eyeful." She pushed herself upright until she rested on her knees.

"Do you blame me? What red-blooded male would be able to ignore you if he walked into a room and found you stretched out on the bed dressed in nothing but a bow?" He grinned and reached down to flick at the red ribbon caught in her pubic curls.

Beth-Ann thought she would burst into flames. He hadn't even touched her and she was as hot as... She couldn't even think of a comparison. She just knew she was in danger of burning up and if she wanted to take control of this situation, she'd better do so right now.

"Shuck your shorts, mister," she purred, hands braced on her hips. "I'm way past the hungry stage. Now I'm ravenous."

He darn near wiped the smile from her face when he obeyed her order. Instant compliance was not what she'd expected.

Her eyes opened wide as she focused on his crotch where his erection stood at attention. No need to ask him how he felt, it was blatantly obvious. She couldn't believe how much of a struggle it was to find her voice.

"Remember what I told you in the cab?" *Real sexy. A croak like a frog.*

"Oh, I remember. Did you mean it?" he asked in a husky growl.

In answer to his question, she crept to the edge of the bed, slipped her legs over the side and sat down. Her gaze never wavered from his engorged cock. Before he could speak, she reached out, circled his hips and dragged him into the vee of her thighs.

"Don't I get my present first?"

"Later," she whispered as she laid her cheek against his lower belly.

The feel of his cock against her face was like a wash of satin that trickled over her skin. She shivered and ran the tip of her tongue along the length of him. His hips jerked in reaction and she moved back to look up at him, a grin on her face.

"Want me to stop?" She held her breath, praying he would answer in the negative. This was one feast she planned to savor.

"Hell, no. You can—"

The words strangled in his throat as she lowered her mouth and swirled her tongue around the smooth head before trailing down the thick length of him again.

So hard, yet so soft. His skin was heated as if he'd stood too close to a fire. A bead of pre-cum glistened on the very top and she lapped it away before she took him deep into her mouth.

A shudder ripped through him and his hips set up a rhythm that matched the glide of her lips. He buried his hands in her hair to keep her in place, not that she was going anywhere. She was having way too much fun. Then the fun turned to a hot, wet bombardment of hormones as she realized it wasn't just Riley getting a charge from her going down on him. Her own libido was way up there with his.

She brought her teeth into play, scraping gently down the side of his cock. He groaned, his hips bucking. The sound of his hoarse breathing filled the room. Her body temperature increased right along with his. Her pussy throbbed and she squirmed on the bed, rubbing herself against the sheets, trying to easy the tension.

Rational thought slipped away as she cupped the weight of his balls with one hand and gave herself up to the feel and taste of him as he glided wet and slippery in and out of her mouth.

When he released a strangled growl and tried to pull her away, she drew him deep, sucking at his swollen cock with enough strength to keep him there. The movement of his hips sped up as he pumped himself into her mouth, a cry torn from him as his body tightened for an instant and then convulsed.

He drooped forward over her, his weight supported by his braced hands on either side of her body. Beth-Ann released him, lay back on her elbows and stared at him. Her breathing was as ragged as his. She ran the tip of her tongue along her bottom lip, tasted him again and felt her control slip. She wanted him in the most elemental way, her hunger so fierce she felt she could swallow him whole.

A chuckle caught her by surprise. Reality check here. She just had. And now she needed her own desires fed. Her teenage dream—to *have* Riley Osborne.

Riley lifted his head at the sound of the sexy chuckle and stared at the woman on the bed in front of him. Sweet Jesus, he couldn't believe she'd made him come like that. He was no innocent where this sort of thing was concerned. For fuck's sake, he'd been engaged once, if only for a short while. He wasn't a Casanova, but he'd had his fair share of women, and always before he'd been able to control his libido to the point where he could make certain the woman was along for the ride as well.

He shook his head and leaned down to take her lips in a quick kiss, but the moment he touched her, the flames flared higher again. He thought he was spent, but she was well on the way to teaching him that he had a lot more to offer.

She opened to him, driving her tongue forward to tangle with his. And as she stroked and sucked, his cock came alive again, hardening with need. He had a moment to process the thought that it wasn't possible so soon, so fast, before she ran her hand down his body and cupped his balls, giving a gentle squeeze.

"You'll kill me, Beth-Ann," he growled as he knelt down between her legs.

"What a way to go," she murmured in a soft whisper.

"Can I have my present now?" He didn't wait for her to answer. He lowered his head and outlined the triangle of red curls with the tip of his tongue. Her hips rose to meet him and a tiny moan escaped her parted lips. He grinned. "Your turn now."

"Yes, please."

She rotated her hips and he couldn't wait any longer. He grasped the end of the bow with his teeth and pulled. The whole thing came away so easily it was a wonder it had survived her movements when she'd gone down on him. He lowered his head again.

"Wait."

Her whispered command dragged him to a halt. With raised eyebrows, he waited.

"On the bedside table." She tilted her head and tried to look backward.

He followed her line of sight and saw the handful of foil-wrapped packages. It took a bit of contorting, but he was able to reach across her and snag one of the little packets. He handed it to her. "You hold it. We won't need it yet."

"What are—"

He didn't give her time to finish the question, let alone the thought. Instead, he trailed his mouth up the inside of her thigh until he reached her moist heat. Her hips bucked in reaction as he placed an open-mouth kiss right over her pussy. And when he parted her with his tongue and thrust into her, she let out a keening cry.

She was hot and wet. He couldn't get enough. She tasted like all his dreams come true. Her hips undulated in conjunction with the movement of his mouth as she met every thrust of his tongue. When his teeth grazed the little nub hidden within the silken folds, she screamed out and jerked so hard he had to tighten his hold on her hips to keep her there.

"Enough," she whimpered.

"Not nearly enough." And he lost himself again in the delectable feast, flicking at her clit with the tip of his tongue.

Beth-Ann struggled to find her breath, but it was difficult, if not impossible. Every time Riley plunged his tongue into her pussy, he drove the air from her lungs. God, she wouldn't survive this. It felt as if her heart had slammed into her rib cage with enough force it was a wonder it didn't jump right out of her chest.

In an effort to raise her upper body, she used her elbows to prop herself up. One hand slid down to tangle in Riley's hair.

She didn't know whether she wanted to pull him away or drag him closer. The sight of his dark head buried between her thighs was such an erotic image she almost came apart in his hands.

Heat coiled deep inside, centered in that place where his mouth worked its magic. Tiny spasms gathered force and threatened to rip through her body. She wanted Riley with her when she climaxed, inside her where he could share the experience. She wanted to scale the heights wrapped in his arms.

"Riley," she managed, "I need you inside me. Now." She tugged on his hair, not certain she'd last.

When he lifted his head, she continued to tug, grateful he obeyed her frantic command and climbed up beside her. He slipped his hand under her back and shifted her higher on the bed. Beth-Ann's fingers shook as she passed him the condom. Her mouth dried up and her body trembled with need as she watched him roll the rubber over his swollen cock.

She snaked her hands around his neck and pulled him over her, perfectly aware that his compliance had nothing to do with her strength and everything to do with *his* sexual hunger. A groan feathered from her lips as she took his weight. It was as if he'd covered her in a blanket of fire. Her hips angled to take him deep as he thrust forward and buried himself inside her, his thickness stretching her, filling her, driving the tension higher.

"You are so hot, so tight," he whispered just moments before he took her mouth in a soul-shattering kiss, the movement of his tongue an imitation of the rhythm he established.

Finesse disappeared out the door as the primal act of having sex took on new meaning for Beth-Ann. She couldn't take him deep enough. Each time he pulled back, she whimpered at the loss, then moaned as he thrust home again. When he drew her nipple into his mouth and suckled hard, she arched her upper body off the bed.

Fire streaked from her breast, down her body to join with the swirling tension that pooled low in the pit of her belly. The only sounds in the room were the harsh rasp of their breathing and the slap of perspiration-drench flesh as they hurtled toward the finish line.

The spasms broke free and started to ripple through her. For a moment, she hung suspended on an uncharted precipice, until a final thrust from Riley sent her over the edge. She screamed as the climax hit her and heard the echo of his yell as he joined her.

There was one moment of clarity, one instant of sanity, before a tidal wave of molten feelings swept her away. A realization that hit her, hard and fast. The lust she'd felt for Riley Osborne since she'd been a gawky teenager was so much more. She wanted to be this close to him for the rest of her life. She wanted to lay down with him and wake up again the next morning with him curled up by her side.

She wasn't the type to indulge in torrid affairs with men she'd only just met, but the startling discovery she'd just made was as good a reason as any to explain why she'd committed herself to *this* liaison. Because a small part of Riley was better than nothing—a memory to last a lifetime.

The thought scared the living daylights out of her, but she didn't have time to dwell on it. The sexual maelstrom inside her caught her up and tossed her about as she clung to Riley and floated in that obscure world where only lovers can go. All rational thought ceased and she drank in the sensations through every pore in her body. And when the world finally righted itself and she could think clearly, Riley still held her clasped tight in his arms.

"*Wow.*"

Riley lifted his head and grinned at her, his breathing labored. "Wow is right." He dragged in a shaky breath. "Darlin', that was amazing. You are—"

"Okay?" She bit her lip and waited for his reply. A reply she suddenly realized was important.

"Okay?" He grinned. "That doesn't even describe it. The tension was so great I thought I'd burst."

"You did," she said, tongue-in-cheek.

Riley started to chuckle, the sound filling the room with warmth. Beth-Ann grinned. Better he laugh with her than push her aside now he had what he'd been after.

"That's one of the things I like about you, darlin'. Your ability to use humor to lighten a situation. You're an incredible lady."

He lifted her up and pulled back the sheet beneath her, laying her head on one of the pillows. "You want me to leave?"

"Do you want to?"

"Uh-uh." He shook his head. "I'd like to curl up beside you and go to sleep with you in my arms. And still find you there when I wake in the morning."

"I'd like that," she replied. *Oh, Beth-Ann, what have you gotten yourself into?*

He rolled off the bed and bent to pull the sheet over her. "You curl up and I'll go turn the living-room light off. I won't be long."

As he disappeared out of the bedroom, Beth-Ann turned onto her side and hugged her hands to her chest. Her heart still raced, but now it had nothing to do with an approaching orgasm. This was a cold rush of fear as she realized where her internal revelation had led her.

She'd gone into this with her eyes wide open. To make Riley eat his words and to convince herself she was attractive to the object of her teenage crush. She'd wanted a casual relationship. Just good fun and even better sex.

Right?

Maybe not. Because she didn't just lust after Riley Osborne. She could very well be slightly in love with him, or at least the teenage version she remembered.

Damn, she couldn't be in love with him. To love a person meant giving over control of your life. Her mother had loved her father to distraction, had wanted to do everything for him, and in doing so, had turned herself into a doormat. He'd had control of every aspect of her life. What she wore. Where she went. He'd believed a woman was there simply to keep the man happy.

Take the way her mother had focused on food. She'd equated it with love. Her self-confidence had been so shaky, if her father had rejected something she'd cooked, her mother had felt unloved. Her father was of the old school; a woman's job was to cook and clean house. And when her mother had cooked all those fancy meals, he believed she had fulfilled her role in his life.

No wonder the whole family had ended up fat. Both parents had died of heart attacks because of their unhealthy diet. Beth-Ann had developed the same tactics in pleasing her mother and she'd ended up a big tub of lard.

No way would she ever hand that type of control to anyone, let alone a man who had the power to twist her insides into knots. Could she continue to see Riley, to enjoy his company and the fantastic sex, without losing her sense of self-worth?

Damn right she could. She hadn't spent years carving out a new life to give up control now. She'd take pleasure in the experience and then walk away. She did not love Riley Osborne. She lusted after him, but that was a whole different ballgame.

At that moment, Riley came back into the room and climbed into bed beside her. As he gathered her close, she silently repeated her new mantra.

I do not love Riley Osborne.

Chapter Five

Riley rolled over onto his back and stretched one arm up above his head. The slither of cool satin against his skin dragged him closer to full consciousness, although he still didn't open his eyes.

Hmm, not his bed. That much was certain. He didn't sleep on slippery satin sheets.

His mind engaged and his body remembered. *Beth-Ann.*

He moved his hand and patted at the sheet beside him. No warm body. That did make him open his eyes. The room was in semi-darkness, the drapes pulled shut across the large window at one end. He lifted his arm and squinted at his watch, made his eyes focus on the luminescent dial.

What he saw jerked him upright, the sheet falling down to his waist. Crap, it was nearly lunchtime. He'd slept half the day away. No wonder Beth-Ann was no longer beside him.

With a yawn, he slid to the side of the bed and sat up. He braced his hands on the edge of the mattress and dropped his head forward to stretch the kinks out of his neck. Another yawn caught him unawares. Was it any wonder he still felt tired? It must have been well after five before they'd settled down to sleep.

Fists propped on his hips, he stood and arched his back. Amazing, he could work all day on the building site and not have the same type of muscle ache he had now. A grin surfaced. What a way to get a workout.

Beth-Ann had collected his clothes from off the couch in the living room and folded them neatly on the end of the bed. He should get dressed and go find her, but first he needed a shower.

Off to one side of the room was a door that gave access to a small bathroom. Surely she wouldn't mind if he borrowed it for a minute? He saw she'd anticipated his needs. A couple of towels were folded on the vanity with a new disposable razor and toothbrush on top of them. A lady after his own heart.

While the water came up to the right temperature in the shower, he made short work of the business of shaving. Then it was under the warm water and a hasty application of Beth-Ann's rose-scented soap. Within minutes, he'd showered, dried off and shrugged into his clothes.

A big cheesy grin reflected back at him as he bent in front of the vanity mirror to comb his wet hair. He couldn't believe how eager he was to find Beth-Ann. And it wasn't because he wanted a second go around—okay, so he did, but not right now. No, this was more to do with a desire to spend time in her company.

She made him laugh and he still hadn't worked out if she said the outrageous things she did out of pure innocence or a need to be humorous. He suspected the former. She spoke before she thought about what she wanted to say. Or maybe he had a dirty mind and gave everything she said a sexual connotation.

He shrugged. The simple fact of the matter was he liked being with her. That was unusual for him. He liked women and he loved making love, and for him, it was always more than a biological urge. More than the mechanical act of slotting A into B.

He gave his whole attention to the woman of the moment, but once he was out of bed, or wherever else they chose to get down and dirty, he liked to get off on his own. He wasn't into playing happy house the next day, and he almost never slept the whole night through in a woman's bed.

With Beth-Ann, it was different and he didn't know why.

A thread of memory teased him again, hovering on the fringes of his mind before it slid away. He couldn't work it out. Sometimes, when he thought about it, he almost had the sense he'd met her before.

Nah, not possible. This woman he would have remembered, if only for her sassy mouth. He shook his head and threw the comb back onto the vanity. Enough with the deep analysis. That wasn't his style. He lived for the moment and that was exactly what he planned to do right now.

He went in search of Beth-Ann. The pungent odor of fresh oil-based paint filled the hallway. He grinned. Beth-Ann had said she'd be painting today. Looks like she'd made a start while he was sound asleep.

Maybe after he'd raided her pantry and had something to eat—funny how ravenous he was—he'd give her a hand. After all, it had been part of his trade before he'd become an architect. He could still turn his hand to it when the need arose. Besides, it was a good excuse to spend the rest of the day with her.

The house was small and it didn't take him long to work out it was empty. The back door stood wide open and he stepped out to soak in the full sunshine of a balmy summer day. Still no sign of his little pixie.

A sound floated to him from the side of the house, the opposite side to where the dog had scared the crap out of him last night. Barefoot, he ducked around the edge of the building. A paved path cut through a jungle of semi-tropical plants, curved around the base of several large bushes and disappeared from sight.

Before he could move more than a few steps along the path, Beth-Ann's voice filtered through the thick foliage. Damn, she had good hearing. He'd figured he'd surprise her.

"If you lift up a bit, I might be able to fit it in."

Riley stopped in his tracks, his eyebrows raised. What the... Okay, so she hadn't heard him, but who...

"It's not going to fit."

A man's voice, slightly muffled, but he still had no trouble making it out. He took a cautious step closer to the bushes.

"Hmm, it's a lot bigger than I thought," Beth-Ann said. "Maybe if I try and squeeze it a bit like this..."

Her voice trailed off. Riley shook his head. He wasn't a man to jump to conclusions, but who the hell was behind that bush with Beth-Ann? She was *his* pixie.

"No, too wide. No way is it going to fit," the man said.

"Maybe if I lift it up higher, it might go in, but if it's too much, say so. I don't want to be responsible for you having a heart attack."

"Men are made for this, girlie," the voice answered, followed by a husky chuckle and a grunt.

That was it. He'd had enough. He'd told her he was exclusive when he was with a woman, even if he wasn't into the gold rings and white veil. Riley struggled to breathe. The fire in his gut burst into a full-fledged bushfire. Damn her, if he vowed to concentrate only on her, she should give him the same courtesy.

He moved up to the bush, dragged in a deep breath and tried to regulate his pulse rate before he confronted her. Shit, he'd never been jealous in his life so why the hell should it suddenly happen now? Something about Beth-Ann got to him, slid under the careful guard he kept about his emotions, and no bloody way was he going to put up with her messing with another man. He'd tell her what he thought of her and then get the fuck out of here. He didn't need this.

"Well, darn, it really isn't going to fit. I guess it will have to be a hand job then."

Okay, that did it. He couldn't believe she'd said that. It was time enough to put a stop to this. He blinked his eyes to try to clear the red haze from his vision. Waste of time. Nothing, but nothing, would cool the rage in his blood and the hurt in his heart.

He rounded the bush at a rush, his hands curled into fists, ready to thump the bastard into a pulp. What he saw dragged him to an abrupt halt.

Beth-Ann, dressed in shorts and an overlarge tee shirt, her small hands clad in gardening gloves, lifted a pile of dried leaves and garden cuttings from a wheelbarrow and shoved them into a trashcan. Her fiery hair curled about her shoulders, tendrils brushing her face, emphasizing the cream streak of paint on one cheekbone. Beside her stood a man well into his fifties, a grin on his face as he held the trashcan at an angle to make it easier for her.

Jason Rouch, the painter he'd arranged to come and do the quote for the painting of Beth-Ann's ceiling. A solid family man, not the least interested in scoring with the ladies.

His little pixie lifted her head and grinned at him.

"Good morning, sleepy head. Shame you didn't make it out here a few minutes earlier. You could have helped us lift the wheelbarrow up and tilt it so I could just push the rubbish into the bin."

She straightened and dumped the next handful into the receptacle. "Turned out it was too wide to fit so I have to do it by hand. I like the gardening bit, but I'm not too taken with having to get rid of the debris."

Riley felt like an idiot. The knowing grin on old Jason's face didn't help matters much either. A wave of heat washed up over his cheeks. He shuffled his bare feet like a kid in trouble before he caught himself and tried to control the flush he had no doubt colored his face.

Maybe Jason would think it was because the boss had been caught sleeping with one of the clients—strictly speaking she was his father's client, but it amounted to the same thing—and not because he'd been about to make the biggest fool of himself ever. He could take the teasing from the guys on site as long as he preserved his dignity.

"Morning, boss." Jason flicked a glance at his watch. "Or should I say good afternoon? Big night last night?"

"Something like that." Riley struggled for a professional tone despite his embarrassment. "Had to spend a few hours at the building site. Mel had a bit of trouble."

Jason released his hold on the trashcan and moved over beside Riley. "What sort of trouble?"

"In the beginning I thought it was kids, teenagers out for a lark and a bit of mischief. Now I'm not so sure." He frowned and ran his hand through his hair. "The cement mixers are wrecked, the power tools smashed, paint splashed over the fresh timberwork. It's going to take some time to clean it up."

"Don't think it's kids, boss. Too pointed." Jason shook his head.

Riley was nobody's fool. If one of his workers had picked up on something he'd missed, he'd be an idiot not to listen to them. "How do you mean, too pointed?"

"You think about it. Kids these days would get in there and spray some graffiti about, maybe kick in a few of the wallboards. You'd find the odd soft-drink can, or even empty beer bottles, and food wrappers. These teenagers all live on junk food."

Beth-Ann stripped the gardening gloves from her hands and sidled up to Riley. With a shrug, he casually reached out, pulled her close and dropped his arm over her shoulder. It was too late to try to hide his interest in her now Jason knew he'd slept here last night. "So not kids," he said in response to Jason's comments.

"And if it were kids looking for a place to shoot up," Beth-Ann chimed in, "you'd find some evidence of it. They're not real careful about cleaning up their mess most of the time."

"True," Jason said. "Given the fact every piece of machinery that has been trashed or disabled is vital to keep the project on course, I'd say it was personal. Anyone you've annoyed lately?"

Riley scratched his head as he tried to remember. "A few employees fired for non-performance, but no one who'd go this far to get even."

"What about competitors," Beth-Ann said.

"Can't see it. The other bidders for the job were well-known companies. It's too unprofessional. They'd lose their licenses if they were caught."

He paused for a moment, debating whether he'd share his latest discovery, then decided to go ahead. Jason had been with his father ever since the company started. He was loyal to a fault. "After what Mel and I found last night, we're going to have to beef up security. It's gone beyond simple pranks now."

"How so?" Jason stared at his boss with a frown on his face.

"One of the main support beams on the bottom floor was sawed almost all the way through. We'll have to check the lot before we can continue."

"You callin' the police?"

Riley shook his head. "No, not for the moment. I'll take a shift with Mel tonight and see what happens."

"Let me know if you need an extra pair of hands," Jason said. "And since you're here, I'll give you this now." He tore the top copy off his quote pad and handed it to Riley. Turning, he flicked a snappy salute at Beth-Ann. "I'm outta here, missy. Wife wants to go shopping. If you need any help with those lawn grubs, just let me know."

"Thank you, Jason," Beth-Ann called as he left the garden.

Jason was a great guy and Riley enjoyed his company, but right now he was glad he'd gone. A flash of jealousy still hovered inside his mind. Beth-Ann seemed to get on well with everyone she met, his painter included. He couldn't believe he was feeling like this. Hell, he was the original love-'em-and-leave-'em guy from way back. Maybe it was time to step back and evaluate this whole thing. But first...

He slid his hands under Beth-Ann's arms and lifted her clear off the ground. "You are such a tiny thing, I'll have to start carrying a box around with me. Otherwise, I'll never be able to do this unless we're lying down."

With a determined effort, he buried the little voice inside his head that tried to point out that, only moments ago, he'd decided to back away from this relationship. Beth-Ann opened her mouth to speak, but he didn't give her a chance. Instead, he sealed her lips with a hard kiss. It felt like ages since he'd tasted her.

She threw herself into the morning greeting, opening her mouth and thrusting her tongue deep. Her arms wrapped tight about his neck and he could feel the swell of her breasts against his chest. His libido reacted to her nearness. The blood rushed from his head, moving south, until his cock snapped awake with a painful throb. At this rate, he'd have to go around with a permanent hard-on.

"Are you kissing Beth-Ann?"

The childish treble broke through the sexual fog clouding his brain. He released Beth-Ann's mouth and lifted his head to look for the owner of the voice. A little girl, dressed in shorts and shirt, no more than eight or nine, stared at him with suspicion from the edge of the bushes. A boy, probably about ten or so, joined her, a small fluffy dog by his side.

"Nah," the lad said, "he just wants to get his rocks off."

Beth-Ann gasped and stared at the kid. "Peter Phillips, I can't believe you said that."

She wiggled for Riley to put her down, but before he could do so, the little bundle of white fluff launched itself at him and fastened his teeth onto a wedge of trouser fabric. Riley shook his foot, trying to dislodge the mutt. At the same time, he allowed Beth-Ann to slide down his body until she stood before him.

"What'd I do? Get him off of me."

His pint-sized pixie made a poor job of stifling her laughter. "It's a she and her name is Susie. She thought you were hurting me." She turned to the boy. "Peter, call your pet off. Riley is a friend."

Peter whistled and the white fur-bag raced back to his side, although she continued to growl as the boy clipped a lead onto the animal's collar. Riley bent to check out the hem of his trousers. No damage done. As he straightened up, he caught the look on Beth-Ann's face and laughed.

"Okay, so I don't do well with dogs, male or female." He grinned at her and waggled his eyebrows. "But I've been told I'm not so bad with the human variety of females."

"Yeah, and you're truly modest, aren't you?" She turned to face the children and wiped all sign of humor from her face. "Peter, if I ever hear you say anything like that again, I'm going to wash your mouth out with good old soap and water. Is that clear?"

Peter hung his head for a moment before tilting his face back up, a cheeky grin plastered across his mouth. "Can I still stay? Can I? Can I?"

Riley watched the twitch on Beth-Ann's lips as she tried to stop her answering grin. Before she could respond to the boy, a young woman came around the side of the house and drew to a halt behind the children.

So much for making out with his pixie. Every time he thought about it, someone turned up. Beth-Ann had the type of nature that attracted people to her, almost as if she had a talent for picking up all the lame ducks in the area.

Hang on, that wasn't correct. It was just thwarted sexual tension talking. He hadn't known her long enough to make that type of judgment. She was a warm, loving woman and he had a feeling that's what people saw in her. That and the fact she actually listened to them.

"Riley, this is Cindy, Peter and Julianna's mother."

Riley waved a greeting and tried to concentrate on the new arrival instead of the soft planes of Beth-Ann's face.

"You sure you don't mind babysitting?" Cindy said.

Oh-ooh. There go my plans for the day. Riley tried not to allow his disappointment to show. He'd had something more adventurous in mind and it didn't include contributing to the education of minors. Not that he didn't like kids—he did—just not right now when he couldn't think of anything but the feel of Beth-Ann's sexy body close to his.

"No, I'll enjoy it," Beth-Ann said. "The kids are going to help me strip the wallpaper off the small bedroom. Right, guys?"

She grinned when the children jumped up and down with barely restrained energy. Riley found himself fascinated with the curve of her lips. What the hell? It could be fun to hang out here today with Beth-Ann and the children.

"Now, shoo, out of here, Cindy, and I'll see you later this afternoon." She took the children by the hand and followed the young woman round the side of the house. After Cindy had gone, she waltzed the kids inside. "Okay, I've set up the buckets of warm water and the sponges. You two head up to the bedroom and I'll be there in a moment."

She called out to them as they disappeared up the hallway. "And don't touch anything before I get there. Otherwise, there'll be no biscuits for either of you for afternoon tea."

"And you..." She turned toward Riley, slipped one arm about his waist and reached up with the other to tug at his hair.

Riley responded to her urging. When she fused her mouth with his, he suddenly felt like he'd received a kick in the gut. The ravenous thrust of her tongue and the erotic glide of her lips drove the air from his lungs. His heartbeat accelerated and his cock filled with blood. Unable to help himself, he pulled her closer and ground his erection against her.

When she'd tasted her fill, she drew back and grinned up at him. He wheezed as he drew fresh oxygen into his starved chest.

"Good morning, Riley," she murmured. "And who said we need a box? Hmm?" She spun away from him and into the kitchen. "You hungry?"

"Um, you could say that," he managed to get out.

Beth-Ann shook her finger at him. "Uh-uh, careful. We have little ears present. You'll just have to wait to satisfy *those* appetites until later."

He stepped up behind her and fitted his body to hers. Despite the height difference, he could feel her pressed against the length of him. Heat hit, burned through his skin and sensitized his flesh. Unable to help himself, he slid his hands under the bottom of her tee shirt and caressed her bare tummy.

She gasped. "Ahh, Riley, the kids—"

"Are up the other end of the house," he finished for her. He walked his fingers upwards until his palms cupped her breasts. No bra. Just the way he liked it...er, them.

Tiny they might be, but they fitted his hands to perfection. Beth-Ann gasped again and arched her upper body as he kneaded the soft flesh. When he took her nipples between the thumb and forefinger of each hand and tweaked the pebble-hard points, her breathing fractured, the sound lodging deep down inside him.

She drove her ass backwards, rubbed against the swelling erection that filled the front of his trousers. Just as he was about to bend his knees to align himself with the juncture of her thighs, he heard a slight noise at the entrance to the kitchen. He jerked back, pulled his hands from under her tee shirt and tried to look innocent.

"Beth-Annnnn, Peter won't gimme a sponge."

Riley stepped aside, his gaze fixed on Beth-Ann. A sweep of color rode high on her face. She swallowed convulsively and kept her back to Julianna, no doubt to hide the telltale peaks of her breasts where they pressed against the worn fabric of her top.

He grinned at the shaky quality of her voice as she tossed over her shoulder, "Tell Peter to leave the sponges alone. I'll be there in a minute."

When the little girl left the room, Beth-Ann turned toward him, hands planted on her hips. "You are wicked," she said with a grin.

"And you are so damn responsive." He bent down and placed his mouth over the budded point of her breast and suckled, gratified with the sharp gasp that escaped her. When he pulled his mouth away, the dusky rose color of her nipple showed through the damp white fabric.

Beth-Ann folded her arms across her chest. "As I said, definitely wicked. Now, to change the subject, do you want something to eat?" She held up her hand and grinned. "And I do mean food."

Riley felt an absurd need to wrap his arms about her and hold her close. He frowned. It wasn't just a sexual need. This went much deeper and it scared the shit out of him. He needed some time alone to think this through so he grabbed on the first excuse he could find.

"Given what happened last night at the building site, I probably need to touch base with my father."

She played with the fingers of his left hand. "So you need to go?"

"Yeah, I think I should." A childish squeal filtered down the hallway from the spare bedroom. He grinned. "And you'd better get in there with the kids before Peter drowns his little sister."

He moved over to the table where he'd left the keys for the truck last night.

"Will I see you tonight?"

"I promised Mel I'd keep watch with him at the site." He stopped, then couldn't help himself. "Ah, I'm going over to the old man's for lunch tomorrow. How about I pick you up and take you with me?"

"Um, n-no, I don't think so. I'll be worn out after mucking around with this wallpaper all afternoon, and tomorrow I want to get the undercoat on the walls." She turned away, grabbed the dishcloth and scrubbed madly at the already clean bench.

Riley frowned. He tilted his head to catch a glimpse of her face. She looked nervous. In fact, she looked downright terrified. Now why the hell should that be?

A shaft of disappointment arrowed through him at the thought of not seeing her tomorrow. Shit, what the hell was wrong with him? First he exhibited all the classic signs of jealousy. Now he was pining because he couldn't see her? Holy fuck, he was in too deep.

He dragged in a sharp breath, and hands on hips and head thrown back, exhaled noisily. For the moment, he was off center, at a loss for words. His gaze flicked around the kitchen as he struggled to make sense of the emotions that raged in his chest.

Suddenly, he spotted it. A photograph in a silver frame on the top of the refrigerator. If he hadn't been so tall it would have escaped his notice. Beth-Ann still had her back to him so he shuffled closer.

Bloody hell, this explained the odd feeling that floated on the edges of his mind, then darted away before he could grasp hold of it. Little Beth-Ann Harris and her parents.

Not so little back then. What a way to go into high school. The kids had been downright mean to her. He cringed as he remembered his parting shot to her just before he'd left Wattle. It was a time in his life he didn't like to think about, but that was no excuse for his nastiness.

Why hadn't she said something? He frowned. Was it possible she didn't recognize him? After all, he'd only been sixteen then. Or maybe she didn't want to focus on that period of her life. He'd respect her wishes and wait for her to tell him.

She'd done a great job at reinventing herself. If he hadn't seen that photo, he wouldn't have known. She'd sure made him eat his words. He couldn't get enough of her now. And therein lay the problem. If a fit of pure green jealousy wasn't enough to tell him it was time to step away and re-evaluate the affair, this certainly was.

"I'll get out of your hair, but I'll ring you tomorrow afternoon to let you know what time we'll be here Monday morning to start on that hole in your ceiling." He moved close enough to drop a quick kiss on the top of her head. "I'll ring," he reiterated as he disappeared out the back door.

Beth-Ann sighed and threw the dishcloth in the sink. Her insides still trembled at the thought of a confrontation with Riley's dad. She really wanted to spend tomorrow with Riley, but it wasn't possible.

His father might not recognize the new Beth-Ann, but if he happened to ask her where she came from, she wouldn't be able to lie to him. After that, it was a short jump to putting together her surname of Harris and the red hair and he'd have her pegged. She didn't want Riley to know who she was. At least, not yet.

Maybe it was a good thing they had the weekend apart. Something niggled in the back of her mind. She'd received mixed signals from Riley. He wasn't exactly blowing hot and cold, but there was something not right.

Not that she was much better. One minute she wanted to throw him down on the floor and fuck him silly. The next she wanted to run a million miles from him in order to protect herself.

Her reaction when she'd risen this morning was to kick his ass out of her house before she became even more involved with him. But she found she couldn't do it. She really wanted this time with him. It was just a hangover from her teenage years. She needed to prove to him that she was desirable. It couldn't be anything else. She was *not* in love with Riley Osborne.

She fancied him—a lot—but that's all it was. She was a strong woman. Keeping a rein on her emotions should be a snap. As far as she was concerned, loving meant a loss of control and she had no intention of going down that path. Marriage and a committed relationship were not in her life plans.

However, the sex was a different thing altogether. Now *that* she could enjoy. This was all about fun and adventure. Oh, yeah, and maybe teaching Mr. Riley Osborne a little lesson. She stretched and smiled at the achy places on her body. Muscles she didn't even know she had. Last night had been wild, at least for her. She grew still as a thought hit her.

Maybe Riley hadn't enjoyed himself as much as she had. Was it possible that's where the mixed signals had come from? Would he even bother to ring her again?

She glanced down at the dining table and chuckled. The key to the back door she'd lent him last night, and which had rested beside Riley's truck keys, was gone.

Oh, yeah, Riley was coming back.

Chapter Six

Beth-Ann frowned as she hung up the phone. "What am I supposed to glean from that conversation?"

"Problem?"

She jumped and spun about to face the back door. "*Cindy.* You scared the bejesus out of me. I didn't hear you there."

Cindy moved further into the dining room. "You were so caught up in your phone call you wouldn't have heard a bomb go off." She pulled out a chair and sat down, her elbows propped on the table.

"Where are the kids?"

"It's their father's Sunday with them. He'll drop them back later tonight. I thought I'd grab a bit of girl time without the children." She pulled another chair up and balanced her feet on the edge. "Ahh, bliss. Now tell Aunty Cindy all about it. What's the problem?"

Before she answered, Beth-Ann filled the electric jug with water and set it to boil. Fetching down two mugs, she spooned instant coffee into them. After adding a dash of sugar to Cindy's, she leaned back against the bench and waited for the jug to complete its assigned task.

"That was Riley." She stared at the silent phone.

"The stud you were with yesterday when I dropped the kids off?"

"He *is* a bit of a stud, isn't he?" She grinned, unable to help herself.

"Girl, he's hot." Cindy fanned her face with her hand and rolled her eyes in an expressive gesture. "If you don't want him, pass him over to me. I could do with one of those to fill my bed. So what's wrong with him?"

Mugs in hand, Beth-Ann joined Cindy at the table. She took a sip of the hot coffee before setting it down on the table. "That was the most unsatisfactory conversation." She indicated the telephone. "I don't know what to make of it."

"How do you mean? After seeing the two of you yesterday, I know you're involved. You had enough electricity sparking between you to light up the town. So what's gone wrong? Come on, girlfriend, give. I'm the expert on twisted relationships."

Beth-Ann sighed. "That's the problem. I don't know what's gone wrong."

"Who is he? I haven't seen him around before. Believe me, I'd remember if I had."

"He's the guy who came to do the insurance quote on my leak in the ceiling."

"Oh-hoo, getting hot and heavy with the hired help, eh? Never known you to get into the one-night stand thingy. I know you don't want a committed relationship, but you're not promiscuous."

"There's more to it than you realize. I know Riley, but he doesn't know I know who he is." Beth-Ann took a leaf from Cindy's book and propped her feet up on the spare chair. She allowed her taut muscles to relax although her insides still felt as if someone had tangled them into a knotted mess.

Cindy shook her head. "Run that by me again," she said. "Sorry, but it doesn't make sense."

"Yeah, I know." She grinned at the perplexed look on the other woman's face. "It doesn't make sense to me either."

Cindy was not only her neighbor, but also the first friend she'd made when she'd moved to Sydney. Over the past six months, they'd grown quite close. Just the same, Beth-Ann wasn't certain how much to tell her. She felt a big enough fool as it was. Ah, rats, she may as well go for broke. There was no one else she could talk to about her problems.

"Remember I told you how fat I was when I was a kid?"

Cindy nodded, her eyes wide with anticipation.

"Riley was one of the people responsible for giving me the backbone to develop some self-control. Of course, I couldn't put it into practice until I was on my own after Mom and Dad died, but he certainly helped. He just doesn't know it."

"Sorry, but I'm still lost."

Beth-Ann grinned. "Let's see if I can simplify it for you." She dropped her feet to the floor and turned toward the table. "Riley Osborne and I grew up in the same small town. In fact, my father worked for his. He just doesn't remember me. I doubt he ever gave me a thought after he left, and if he had, it would have been as the chunky kid who followed him around like a bad smell."

A gurgle of laughter caught her by surprise. "Heavens, when I look back now I can see how pathetic I was. I had such a thing for him. My first and only teenage crush."

"From where I'm sitting, it looks like that crush lasted a long time. You practically glowed when he was beside you yesterday." Cindy chuckled. "The kids told me about your hot kiss in the garden. Peter said he was trying to eat you."

"Your Peter has picked up some rather raunchy sayings from school," Beth-Ann responded.

"Don't I know it. Anyway, back to your stud."

"He was the high-school jock and I thought I was in love with him. Until the day he caught me spying on him down by the football field while he stripped off his jersey."

She closed her eyes and the scene unfolded as if it had happened yesterday. Her overweight body crammed into the grey school uniform, dull red hair tied in straggly pigtails. Protruding teeth restrained by braces. Riley and several of the team had just finished training for the day and were changing their football uniforms before going home.

"Hey, don't leave me hanging here," Cindy said, cutting across the memories.

"Sorry. The upshot of it is Riley Osborne said something really nasty to me that day and at thirteen, it shattered not only my heart, but also any budding confidence I might have had."

"What did he say?" Cindy moved closer to the table, her chin balanced on her cupped hands.

"I'll never forget his words. He told me he was sick of my hanging around and when I said I liked him, he said—and I quote—'*Are you crazy? Why would any man want a fat slob like you? All those rolls of fat would swallow me whole. I could never be turned on by you.*' End quote."

Cindy sat up straighter in the chair, a flash of anger on her face. "You let him near you after that? Girl, you must be mad."

"He was sixteen and going through a tough time." She grinned at the fierce look on Cindy's face. "His mother had just left him and his dad, walked off with some guy. I think any female would have copped an earful right about then."

She held up her hand as Cindy opened her mouth to speak. "In actual fact, it's because of his comments I decided I needed to do something about my weight. Took me years, but I finally got there."

"And now you want to rub his nose in it?"

Beth-Ann chose not to answer that for the moment. "I didn't recognize him at first and we got into this banter about me needing my hole filled up."

She paused as Cindy went off into peals of laughter. When she'd calmed down somewhat, Beth-Ann continued. "You know me and my foot-in-mouth disease. I gave him the perfect opening and he took it and ran with it. I played along because it was fun. That idiot I'd gone out with the night before had given me a hard time because I wasn't adventurous enough and I wanted to prove him wrong. When Riley came on to me, I was flattered. And all that before I realized who he was."

"How do you feel about him now?"

"I still fancy him like crazy and I guess I need for him to want me, if only to wipe out the sting of that earlier memory. And before you ask, he definitely wants me."

"So you going to make him suffer?" Cindy inquired.

"Maybe... A little bit, I guess." Beth-Ann stared out through the open back door at the sunlit garden beyond. "A part of me would like to get him all hot and bothered so I can throw his words back in his face and walk away. I know it's juvenile, but if I don't get him out of my system, I think his comments will haunt me forever."

"Go for it." Cindy shrugged and spread her hands wide in silent question. "Where's the problem?"

"Two things. Friday night Riley was all over me like a rash. Then today I get that call telling me what time they'll be here tomorrow to fix the roof. He was so, oh, I don't know, businesslike, I guess. Not like he was yesterday. Maybe I've read the signals wrong."

Cindy stood and took the empty coffee mugs into the kitchen before returning to lean against the bench separating the kitchen from the dining room.

"Hey, that *is* business for him," she said. "Why don't you wait and see what he's like tomorrow? You said two things. What's the second?"

Beth-Ann ran her hands through her curls, not at all concerned she'd turned her hairdo into a bird's nest of tangles. Right now, she had more important things to worry about. Like the fact that maybe—only maybe—she actually felt more for Riley Osborne than she should.

She'd tried to convince herself otherwise, but it just wouldn't fly. Why else could he tie her in knots so easily? She looked up to find Cindy staring at her with narrowed gaze. "How can you tell if you're in love with a guy?" she questioned, trying for nonchalance.

"Does it make your heart beat fast when you think of him? Do you want to spend all your time with him? Does he make your insides melt, and I'm not talking sex here?" She seated herself back at the table. "Heck, girl, only you can decide if you love the guy. Are you sure this isn't a crush left over from when you were thirteen?"

"I don't know," Beth-Ann whispered, to herself as much as her friend. "I've dreamed about Riley for years. I've measured every guy I've ever gone out with against him, against the way he used to make me feel as a kid. Now that I've spent some time with him—okay, so it hasn't been long—but he makes me laugh. He turns me on, but he makes me feel cherished, too. And I'm scared."

Cindy frowned. "What's to be scared about?"

"I don't want to love him because people in love give control of their life to their partner. My mother did that. As far as Dad was concerned, a woman's place was in the kitchen and that's where she stayed. She did everything for him. She probably would have thrown herself on the fire if he'd asked. He even chose her clothes. No way am I going to get married and let someone else take over my life."

"Whoa, girl. It's a big leap from being in love to getting married. Love doesn't have to be, or shouldn't be, controlling.

And maybe your mother liked doing for your dad. Ever thought of that? Why don't you just go with the flow and see where this leads? You'll know soon enough if you love the guy. When you get to the stage where you can't stand to spend one minute away from him, you'll have the answer. There's one other thing, too."

"What's that?" She glanced at Cindy in enquiry.

"I suspect you're already in love with the man. It sure sounds like it from the way you talk about him and the look on your face every time you mention his name."

Beth-Ann pushed away from the table and paced across to the back door. "I can't be," she whispered as the fear of commitment gathered force inside her. "I won't turn myself into a doormat for any man."

Cindy walked over and gave her a quick hug. "Honey, love doesn't have to be like that."

"From what you've told me, your marriage was exactly like that." Beth-Ann regretted the words the moment they left her mouth. She bit her lip and grimaced. She hadn't meant to mention Cindy's break-up with her husband. "I'm sorry, I shouldn't have said that."

"Why not? It's true, although to be quite honest, I brought most of it on myself. I was this meek and mild little miss when I got married and I encouraged him to treat me like a slave. I made myself a victim, just like your mother did." She grinned. "I've grown a fairly solid backbone over the past twelve months and could even give good old Barry a run for his money now."

"You wouldn't!" Beth-Ann stared at her friend.

"Who knows?" Cindy shrugged and raised her eyebrows. "One thing about Barry, he sure knew how to pleasure a girl. Anyway, we're talking about you, not me. You can't allow your childhood hang-ups to overshadow the rest of your days. If you do, you could miss out on the greatest adventure of your life."

Beth-Ann couldn't help herself. She burst out laughing, shaky though it was. "That's what this was meant to be. An adventure."

"So go for it and don't worry so much. It's time you had some fun in your life."

"The only good thing is Riley wants no more strings than I do." Her attempt at a smile was weak. "But you're right. Maybe I'll just enjoy it while it lasts. If neither of us gets too serious it should be all right."

"Way to go, girlfriend," Cindy crowed. "Nothing like a hot and heavy affair to boost a girl's ego."

⚒ ⚒ ⚒

Love or lust? Beth-Ann still wasn't certain, but she had a feeling it was time to find out, because if she didn't, she would always wonder. She had a strong premonition Riley would feature in all her fantasies for the rest of her life and she wasn't about to give a guy that type of control.

She flicked a glance at her watch. Almost nine. He'd be here any moment to start work on her ceiling. With a twist to catch the rear view, she posed in front of the mirror.

Her lips twitched. Let's see how he reacted to this. Did she dare? Then she grinned outright. Her navy shorts were the briefest she could find. They hugged the top of her hips and ended just below her butt. In fact, brief wasn't the right word. The rounded curves of her ass peeked beneath the hem of the shorts. If she bent over too far even more would show.

With it, she'd teamed a bright yellow halter-top that cupped her breasts and tied around her neck. Forget the bra. Wasn't possible with this get-up. She slipped her feet into low sandals and stood back to get a better view.

Bare from the bottom of the top to the upper edge of the navy hipster shorts, her body looked longer than normal. All that skin on show made her feel taller. Not that her lack of height seemed to worry Riley. He managed to overcome any hurdles when it came to kissing her. She twirled in front of the mirror one more time.

"Eat your heart out, Riley Osborne."

A shiver raced through her and her heart started to flutter. She sprawled on the end of the bed and stared at her reflection in the mirror. A wave of pure terror burst over her. A cold sweat broke out on her forehead and she gasped as the breath caught in her throat. A cloud of butterflies took up residence in her stomach. Shit, forget the butterflies. This felt like a whole herd of elephants on a rampage.

She clasped hands that trembled to her mid-section. It hit her like a ton weight. She didn't just lust after Riley. It really did go much deeper. That instant of realization moments before she'd climaxed the other night came back to haunt her.

Oh my God, she was in love with Riley Osborne.

Cindy had been right all along. She didn't just want him in her bed, she wanted him to share his life with her. The mere thought of seeing him this morning was enough to put her into an emotional tailspin. She didn't ever want that sensation to go away.

Oh, no, how could she have done this to herself? She loved Riley, had probably done so for years. All it had taken was a few hours in his company to revive the teenage angst she'd felt and turn it into this white-hot torrent of emotion.

Before she could worry herself to death about how she'd handle the situation, the doorbell rang. Riley was here. Her heartbeat immediately accelerated and her palms grew sweaty again. She wiped them on the back of her shorts as she raced down the hallway toward the front of the house.

As she opened the door, a smile trembled on her lips. When she saw the stranger standing there, her jaw dropped, the smile disappearing.

"You Beth-Ann Harris? Riley Osborne from R & J Constructions sent me over to fix the hole in your roof. I'm Larry Bates and this," he indicated the young lad behind him, "is Chris. He's the apprentice."

"Where's Riley?" A surge of disappointment swept through her. "I thought he'd be here."

"The boss said to tell you he'd call later. Did a stint with the security guard last night and needed to get some sleep, but he'll be back at the building site before lunch."

Beth-Ann waved the man and his helper inside and pointed the way to the living room. She felt self-conscious in her brief top and shorts. Larry couldn't keep his eyes off her boobs and poor Chris looked like he was about to swallow his tongue.

"I'll...um, I'll leave you to it," she said. "I'll be in the small room at the end of the hallway if you want me."

Larry nodded and turned to issue instructions to the apprentice. Beth-Ann beat a hasty retreat to the master bedroom, where she stripped off the halter-top and shorts and donned an old tee shirt and a pair of cut-off jeans. Then she slipped into the spare room, closing the door behind her.

Well, shoot, all that soul-searching and she wouldn't even get to see Riley. At that moment, a thought hit her. She opened the door and stuck her head out. "Hey, Larry?"

"What can I do you for, Ms. Harris?" he shouted back.

"Ah, it's Beth-Ann, not Ms. Harris, and I'm expecting a friend. Can you send her down here when she comes?"

"Will do."

Beth-Ann closed the door again and looked at the mess around her. With the wallpaper now stripped off, she wanted to get the first coat of paint on the walls and Cindy had offered to help. She'd meant to do it yesterday, but hadn't been able to motivate herself.

Rats, she didn't feel like painting today either, but it had to be done. She was due back at work in a week and hadn't achieved anywhere near what she'd wanted.

"Get on with it, you dummy," she whispered. The command had no effect. All she could do was stand there with her back pressed to the closed door and think about Riley and the predicament in which she found herself.

"Hi, Beth-Ann, coming in."

The words filtered through the timber door, but before she could move, Cindy pushed on it and Beth-Ann stumbled with the force of the movement.

"I thought you'd locked yourself in for a moment." Cindy stepped into the room. She took one look at her friend and frowned. "Are you okay?"

Beth-Ann untangled her feet from the drop cloth and bent to straighten it out again. Without looking at Cindy, she pried the lid off the can of paint and poured some into the paint tray, before hammering the lid back on the paint pot.

"Come on, girl, give. What's wrong?"

She handed Cindy a paintbrush. "Question. How can I have a raging affair with Riley if I've just discovered I love him?"

"Hmm, thought as much. The signs are all there." Cindy dipped the brush into the paint and started to cut in along the cornice of the wall nearest the door.

Roller loaded and ready to go, Beth-Ann waited until Cindy was far enough along before she started to layer the paint onto the bare walls. "I don't know what to do," she said. "When he didn't come this morning, the disappointment felt like it would cripple me. Darn, that scares the heck out of me. It's like I've already given up control of some part of my life."

Cindy turned and waved a dripping paintbrush at her. "It doesn't have to be like that. Here's my take on the situation. Loving the man should make the affair all the more satisfying."

"But what about—"

"Hang on, haven't finished yet." She poked the end of the paintbrush in her mouth and clamped her teeth about it while she pulled her hair up into a ponytail.

"This doesn't have to lead to marriage," she continued when she'd removed the brush. "I know how you feel about that. But why can't you just enjoy your time with him? It can be as exclusive as you like, but if you don't move him into your home, you still have control of the whole thing. See what I mean?"

"So he can stay over—"

"Just not every night," Cindy interrupted. "Otherwise, it gets to be a habit. Then you could find yourself sliding toward co-habitation and marriage."

She moved on to the next wall. Beth-Ann followed close behind. "There is one thing, though," Cindy said.

"What's that?" Beth-Ann grabbed the rag hanging out the back pocket of her shorts and wiped a drop of fresh paint off her face.

"How are you going to handle it if Riley breaks it off? You said he already seems to have pulled away. You could get seriously hurt here."

"Nah, now I'm aware of my feelings, I can make certain I control them. I'm not the queen of self-control for nothing." She laid the roller down on the side of the paint tray. "And as far as how Riley feels..." She grinned as a plan burst to life in her mind. Oh, how Machiavellian, but it was a sure way to find out how things stood with her football jock.

"Um, Cindy?"

"Methinks the girl has a plan." Cindy gave a trill of laughter. "So what do you want me to do?"

"Can you baby-sit for me?"

"Huh?" Cindy shook her head. "What or who do you want me to baby-sit? In case you didn't realize, you ain't got no kids, honey."

A mischievous chuckle bubbled up out of Beth-Ann. Her mind worked overtime. Larry said Riley would be back at the site by lunchtime. Sooo, she just might go visit him. Offer him a picnic lunch—and maybe herself? If she could pull this off, she'd know for sure whether Riley wanted to continue their association.

"Seeing as how you don't have to go to work today," she said to Cindy, "how about you look after the painters for me? I think I'll catch the train into the city and pay a call on my stud."

Cindy grinned. "Girl, what are you up to? You have the most evil look on your face."

Beth-Ann raised her eyebrows and pulled her face into a haughty look. "Evil? Me? No way. I'm going to have a shower, find the sexiest bra and dress I have and go visit Riley."

She started to leave the room, then spun around at the doorway and waited, hands propped on hips. Her friend didn't let her down.

"Okaaay. Bra." Cindy ticked it off on her fingers. "Dress, sexy of course." She held up the next finger. "You forgot panties."

"Who said I have to wear them?"

Chapter Seven

"Glad you could come down at such short notice, Seth," Riley said as he removed his hard hat and ushered his old friend into the site office. "I'd hoped to keep the police out of it, but it's way too serious now."

"No problem." Seth dropped down into a chair. "You're lucky I was on duty when you rang. Detectives do get time off on occasion." He propped one booted foot up on his knee and leaned forward. "So what can you tell me?"

Riley settled back down on his side of the desk and slid a sheet of paper across the surface, careful to touch only the corner. He remained quiet as Seth read the note, silently praying he'd know how to stop the strange happenings at the site.

He and Seth Gallagher had gone through college together and had remained firm buddies since. Except for that disastrous time just after Riley had turned twenty-two when he'd decided to go against everything he'd believed and had committed to one woman. Though, normally when the two of them got together, it was to sink a few pints of beer or shoot hoops. This was the first time Riley had called on Seth in his official capacity as police detective.

"Take me from the top," Seth said. "When did all this start?"

Riley released a deep sigh and ran a hand through his hair. "A few weeks ago now. In the beginning, I thought it was a group of kids out for a lark. Just things knocked over, items shifted and thrown around, that type of things. Although I must admit, we didn't see any of the normal signs of street kids on the rampage."

"No food remains, empty cans or bottles?"

Riley shook his head.

"And, forgetting this note for the moment, what makes you think something's changed?" Seth said.

"The acts of vandalism have become more pointed. Wet cement poured over vital pieces of equipment, tools smashed or missing. The worst was when I realized whoever it was had sawed through a half dozen of the main support beams on the bottom floor. We thought it was only one until we did a check. Then there was a fire last night. Granted, it was only in the rubbish bin, but had it got away, it would have been a different matter."

Seth frowned. "So now it's become dangerous. If the building had gone up without you finding those beams, there could have been dire repercussions. Weaken the main structure and the whole lot could tumble down when least expected. That worries me more than the fire at the moment."

Riley stood and paced about the office as the anger at this senseless vandalism built up and refused to allow him to sit still. "We've increased security. In fact, I'm doing a stint almost every night myself, but we haven't managed to catch anyone. I've walked the perimeter fence, but can't for the life of me work out where they're getting in." He turned to face Seth. "Or maybe it's singular. One person with a grudge."

"Competitors?" Seth raised his eyebrows and waited.

"No, I've done some checking and I don't think it's any of the companies that put in for the job." He turned and pointed to the letter in front of Seth. "And that note makes it personal."

He moved to the desk and leaned over Seth's shoulder so he could read the threatening words. "It sure sounds like it's aimed at me. *'Osborne, you've wrecked my life. You took everything away from me. Now I'm going to do the same to you. I'll see you suffer the same type of agony I'm going through.'* I've been through my personnel files and I can't work out who it is. The two guys I've sacked this last month have new jobs on other sites. I can't see it being either of them."

Seth pushed himself to his feet, picked the letter up by one corner and slid it into a plastic evidence bag he removed from his pocket. "And this was shoved under the door of the office when you came in this morning?"

"Yep, which means he was on the site again last night and we had no idea. He's good, whoever he is."

"You don't recognize the writing?"

He shook his head.

"All right, I'll take this back to the station. Meanwhile, I want you to go back a bit further. Say, six months. Make me a list of anyone you've had to sack or lay off, or had trouble with. The officers on night shift can do regular patrols around here and we'll see what we can pick up. I'll get back to you on this."

Riley escorted him to the door of the office. A sense of relief filled him now he'd given in and called the experts.

Seth turned at the door. "Haven't seen you about much over the last few weeks. You missed the good news."

"Been a bit busy. What's the latest?"

"I've gone and done it. You'll get an invitation soon. I asked Maggie to marry me."

"You? The confirmed bachelor?" Riley started to chuckle. "Never thought I'd see the day."

"Remember what your father said?" He thumped Riley on the shoulder. "There's one special woman out there for each of us and I just happened to find mine." He opened the door. "What about you? Anyone interesting on the scene?"

"You know my dear old dad. He might have been through one disastrous relationship himself, but he still believes in the gold ring. A soul mate for everyone." He grimaced. "Look how that turned out for him. A woman who'd go after anything in trousers."

"A lot of time has passed since your mother walked out on you and your dad," Seth said. "Thought you would have gotten over that by now."

"Sure I have, doesn't mean I'm going to put myself in the same position as my father though. Tried it once and not going there ever again."

A frown settled on Seth's face. "I know you don't like to talk about it—hell, we never, ever mention it now—but that episode with Denise was seven years ago. That's long enough to get over the hurt."

"Hey, there's no hurting left, but that doesn't mean I trust women. Look at Denise. The sweetest girl on the face of the earth. Loved me to distraction, so she said. The moment she gets the proposal, she does a total turn-about, morphs into a raving nymphomaniac and fucks anyone who'll have her."

Seth shook his head. "Nah, she was always like that. You were just too close to the situation to see it. At least you found out before the '*I do*'."

Although he kept it partitioned in the back of his mind, Riley would never forget that time in his life. Finding his fiancée naked in his best mate's room had almost finished his friendship with Seth. He'd wanted to kill him.

It had taken Seth introducing him to some of the guys she'd been screwing before he'd believe Seth was an innocent victim in the whole thing. Hell, she'd left behind a trail of fucked-over schmucks as long as his arm. Thank God he'd found out when he did.

"So if you're over it, why do you still hate women?" Seth raised his eyebrows in question.

"Hey, I don't hate 'em. I love women. I'm just not about to get caught."

Seth grinned. "That doesn't answer my question. Is there anyone special at the moment?"

Riley gave up. He knew Seth would continue to dig at him so he may as well spill the beans. "There is someone." A smile crept across his face. "And she sure knows how to push my buttons."

"Mate, that's sex," Seth responded. "How does she make you feel? That's the important question."

With that, he lifted a hand in salute and vacated the office. Riley closed the door and moved back to settle behind his desk, the smile still on his face.

Good question. How *did* Beth-Ann make him feel? One thing for certain, she could shoot his body temperature sky high with a simple look. She made him laugh, the more so as her sassy comments seemed totally off the cuff. But there was more to it than that.

She'd awoken a protective instinct in him he hadn't even been aware he possessed. Thoughts of Beth-Ann filled his mind. Even when he was up to his eyebrows in work, her image intruded. He worried about how she was getting on. Damn fool woman was just as likely to climb up on the roof and decide to replace the tiles or something.

For the first time he questioned his previous dealings with women. Was he being fair with his no-strings-attached policy? Beth-Ann had agreed to it, but he didn't want to hurt her in any way. He needed to keep it light-hearted enough that both of them could walk away without regret. A kernel of pain flared to life somewhere inside of him at the thought that he might never see her again.

The most worrying thing of all was the surge of jealousy he felt whenever he though of her with another man. That had never happened to him before, except with his ex-fiancée, and then he'd had good reason. Oh, boy, he was in trouble. It was time to shore up his defenses before he saw her again. Enjoy her he would, but he was not about to get caught in the marriage trap.

⚒ ⚒ ⚒

Beth-Ann's shiny black heels clacked on the concrete pavement as she left Wynyard Street Station. A cane basket of picnic foods clunked against her leg as she cut across George Street and into Martin Plaza. It was the quickest way to reach the building site. A smile teased at her lips at the thought that no one knew about her state of semi-undress. It made her feel decidedly wicked.

Cindy thought she'd been fooling, couldn't believe she would go through with it. This was one sure way to make Riley sit up and take notice. If he ignored her invitation, she'd know where she stood.

She grabbed at the full skirt of her bold black and red summer frock as the breeze that tunneled down through Martin Plaza shopping center teased at the soft fabric. It was Riley she wanted to shock, not all the innocent shoppers and workers out for a bite of lunch.

The building site loomed in front of her as she rounded the corner. Without a falter in her stride, she approached the security booth. A man, the same one she'd seen the other night, stepped out to greet her.

"Something I can do for you, Miss?"

Beth-Ann lowered the basket to the ground at her feet, crossed her arms under her breasts and exerted upward pressure so her cleavage was visible above the scooped neck of her dress. Even the lace trim of her half-cup bra showed. She felt mean for trying this on Mel, but after all, a man was a man, and she needed all the ammunition she could get.

"It's Mel, isn't it?" She tried not to smile as his gaze slid down her chest. "I saw you briefly on Friday night."

"Ahh, you're the young lady who was here with Riley. I caught a glimpse of you in the cab." He grinned and moved closer.

Boys will be boys. "I need to see Riley. I know it's a closed site, but is there any chance I can visit with him for a little while?"

She raised one hand to twist a red corkscrew curl around her finger and plastered a needy little-girl expression on her face. "I promise I won't be a nuisance. Please, pretty please? You're such a nice man, sure you can't do this for me?" She reached over and dragged the tip of her fingers across the top of his hand where it rested on the doorframe of the booth.

A spasm of guilt hit her at her manipulation of Mel. She should be disgusted with herself. He was in all probability an upstanding family man and she shouldn't be doing this. She justified it with the thought that maybe she'd stroked his male ego a bit and given him a cheap thrill. Anything was fair game if it got her in to see Riley. She had a desperate need to know if Riley was still interested, one that wasn't going to go away until she satisfied it.

"Okay, little lady, you can stop with the flirting now." Mel grinned at her. "I've got daughters your age. If it ain't been tried on me, it ain't been invented yet."

Beth-Ann chuckled. "Sorry, but it really is important I see Riley."

Mel turned and reached into the little booth, a red safety helmet in his hand when he faced her again. "It's a hard hat area so you'll have to wear this."

She took the hard hat and clamped it on her head. Who cared if it messed up her carefully arranged curls and clashed with the auburn color? That was the least of her worries. She gave it an extra tap on top and waited for Mel to direct her.

"I'll just let Riley know you're here."

He grabbed a hand-held radio, but before he could switch it on, Beth-Ann intervened. "No, I'd like to surprise him." She reached down and grasped the handle of the cane basket. "I've brought him a picnic lunch as a treat."

He laughed, the sound rolling up from his barrel of a chest. "Okay, little lady. Never let it be said I stood in the way of true love." He walked her over to the front entrance of the site and pointed across to the far side. "See those demountable buildings over there? One of them is the site office. You'll find the boss there, probably up to his eyebrows in figures."

He waved her on. "Now don't you go and fall over in those spiky heels. Strictly speaking, you should have work boots on, but I didn't think they'd go with that spiffy dress."

"Thank you, Mel." She reached up and planted a quick kiss on his weathered cheek. "I owe you one." She started across the site.

"You can bring me one of those picnic baskets when I'm on night duty, only add a flask of coffee instead of that wine bottle I can see sticking out under the tea towel," Mel yelled after her.

"You're on," Beth-Ann called back over her shoulder.

As she picked her way across the cluttered building compound, the workmen on lunch turned to stare at her. A few wolf whistles floated on the air, doing her ego a world of good.

"Yo, Beth-Ann, haven't seen you around for a few days. I missed our morning chats when you were on your way to work."

She turned toward the voice. "Yo yourself, Charlie. Wanna point out which building is the site office? I need to see the boss."

"I didn't realize you knew Riley," Charlie said as he pointed out the correct building.

"I do now." *Oh, yeah, did she know Riley!*

"You be careful there," Charlie warned, a frown pleating his brow. "I've been with this company since the beginning and I've seen him go through a lot of women. If you're looking for marriage, forget it. Not Riley's thing." He shook his head. "Someone should teach that boy a lesson or two in how to treat women."

For a moment, Beth-Ann entertained the idea that maybe Charlie was involved in the sabotage. Had he elected himself to be the teacher? She turned the idea over in her mind for a moment and then dismissed it. Nah, Charlie was too nice a man and from the discussions they'd had on her way to work, he pretty much thought of Riley as a son.

Before she could say anything else, a gust of wind swept through the yard, caught at her skirt and lifted one side of it to flash the length of her thigh. She grabbed for it and held it against her leg. She had to struggle to control the surge of fright that rolled over her. It was Riley she wanted to tempt, not every workman on site.

As she reached the site office, she had a sudden distressing thought, one she hadn't entertained until this moment. What if Riley's father was here? Worse still, right behind this very door?

Did she want Riley to know who she was? Uh-uh, no way. She had a feeling he wasn't going to be happy that she hadn't come clean with him. Heck, he might even toss her out on her ass, not want any more to do with her. She wasn't finished with Riley Osborne yet.

Still after your revenge for his unkind remarks when he was nothing but a kid?

The question caught her by surprise, making her pause mid-stride, mere inches from the bottom step. And in that instant, she came to a blinding realization. She didn't want retaliation. Revenge was the last thing on her mind.

No, what she wanted was very simple. Time with Riley, the one person who'd been able to make her pulse speed up, her libido go into overdrive, and her heart turn cartwheels since she was thirteen years old. Lord, she was in deeper than she'd thought. If she had any sense, she'd turn her back and run like crazy.

She couldn't, because then she'd never know if Riley was still interested. She'd be reduced to hovering by the phone, praying he'd ring, and that path wasn't for her. Being in control had been her mantra since she was a teenager.

So practice what you preach, Beth-Ann Harris. Walk into that office and see if Riley still wants you, and if his father is there, brazen it out.

As quiet as she could, she stepped up and opened the door, wincing as it creaked in protest. The sound was enough to make Riley lift his head from the mess of papers and blueprints on the desk in front of him.

A quick glance around the small room showed her Riley was the only occupant. A sigh of relief emerged as she slipped inside the office, pulled the door closed behind her and locked it.

"Hi, Riley, thought you might like to join me for lunch." She held up the picnic basket, plucked the hard hat from her head and sashayed over to the desk.

Riley felt a thud in his chest as his little pixie walked toward him. If he'd been given to flights of fancy, he would have said his heart turned over at the sight of Beth-Ann. Nah, he was the original love-`em-and-leave-`em guy so it couldn't have been that. Just the same, he was glad to see her.

He'd spent the whole morning wrestling with the situation, ever since Seth had made him question his feelings. Something about this woman got to him, bypassed the barriers he'd set about his emotions. He couldn't believe how much he'd missed her. Hell, he'd only known her a few days. This shouldn't have happened.

Now that he knew who Beth-Ann was, did he want to continue with this affair? Until this very moment, he'd convinced himself it wasn't in his best interest to go on seeing her. There were plenty more women out there who just wanted to fool around. He was definitely not into marriage, and despite her protestations and all that bull about no strings, he had a strange feeling she was the type of woman who, once committed, would want the whole box and dice.

Problem was, when she walked in the door, all his careful rationalization flew out the window. The rock-hard boner in his trousers made it perfectly clear where *his* priorities lay. So change of plans. He'd go along for the ride and see where it led.

His old man told him one day he'd find the other half of himself, but he wasn't about to fall for that shit. No, he'd enjoy what life handed him and run like hell if it became apparent the noose was about to tighten around his neck.

He pushed his chair back from the desk and smiled at his visitor. "Beth-Ann, it's lovely to see you. I didn't expect this."

"I thought you might like to share a picnic lunch with me."

She held up the basket, before bending down and placing it on the floor. Then she sidled around in front of him, between his chair and his desk. Riley raised his eyebrows as he watched her. What was she up to?

"Although, if you're really hungry," she said, "I have something else you might be interested in." She braced her arms on the desk and leaned back.

Riley gulped. The pose pushed her breasts up, to the point where they almost tumbled out of the top of her dress. She'd chosen to wear a bright black and red number that hugged her upper body, skimmed her waist and flared out to swirl about her knees. The shoulders of the dress were only an inch or so wide and the neck scooped low to show off her cleavage.

He frowned. "You got a bra on with that?" Stupid question, but all of a sudden, the answer seemed very important.

She pushed herself away from the desk and planted her hands on the arms of his chair. "Check for yourself if you're so interested."

The front of the bodice fell forward and showed off the black bra that almost covered her breasts. In fact, the cups were so small the darker area of her areoles showed above the top of the bra.

"Wanna play?" she said in a breathy voice.

He couldn't help himself. He leaned forward and feathered a kiss across one delicious curve, gratified when he heard her drag in a sharp breath. He pulled her close and buried his face between her breasts, breathing in the warm scent of her skin and the floral perfume concentrated in the valley between.

"Hmm, you smell great and you taste even better." He ran the tip of his tongue across the top edge of her bra. Her nipples hardened and escaped the confines of her undergarment.

"This is a very special dress," she whispered as her fingers tangled in his hair and gave a slight pull. "It has hidden clips on the shoulders. Wanna see?"

She raised her hands and unclipped first one side and then the other. When she released the dress, the fabric slid down and exposed her upper body. Riley dragged in a shaky breath as he stared at the tiny bra. The sight was so erotic, with half her breasts confined and the rest on show, he almost lost it.

His balls tightened and his cock throbbed. He squirmed in the seat, trying to ease the constriction of his jeans. The breath gusted from his mouth in a long, drawn-out groan. Perspiration broke out on his brow. Within minutes, he found himself hyperventilating. Fucking hell, he'd pass out at this rate and miss all the fun.

When she moved her hands around behind her to unclip the bra, he found his voice. "No, leave it on. You have no idea what it does to me to see your nipples playing peek-a-boo like that."

The need to taste raged through him, burning a hole in his gut. He started to push himself upward, his hands braced on the armrests of the seat, but she shook her head and backed away. Sitting on the desk, she parted her legs slightly to balance her weight, her skirt tucked down between her thighs and hands on her knees.

He pushed his chair closer. From this angle, all he had to do was lean forward and savor all that exposed flesh. Before he could convert his thoughts into action, she whispered his name. He jerked his head up and stared at her face instead of her chest. A sexy smile curved her lips and a decidedly sinful gleam glittered in her eyes.

"You want ham on a crusty roll for lunch? Or would you rather have a roll with me?"

She placed the tips of her fingers on her knees and started to walk them up her thighs, and as her hands moved, so, too, did her skirt. Mesmerized, Riley followed the movement with his eyes. When the black and red fabric rumpled up around the top of her legs, she stopped, picked up a fold of fabric and flapped it.

"Oh, it's a bit close in here." She fanned her face with her free hand. "Is it just me, or is it hot?"

Riley gulped, raised his arm and swiped at the perspiration on his forehead. "Darlin'," he gasped, "it's definitely hot, but I think you're responsible. Hell, I'll self-combust at this rate." The throb of his now-painful erection made talking difficult. The roar of his heart racing filled his ears. He hooked his trembling fingers over the armrests of the seat to try to steady himself.

Beth-Ann leaned back, her weight braced on her outstretched arms. For a moment, Riley forgot to breathe as he took in the sight of the half-naked pixie posed before him. His brain seemed to atrophy and all he could do was stare, his mouth open as he struggled to drag in fresh oxygen to feed his tortured lungs.

"Remember those fantasies of mine we spoke about?"

He nodded his head up and down like an idiot, his tongue stuck to the roof of his mouth.

"Hmm, I've been thinking about it and there is one I want to know about."

"Th-th-there is?" He sounded moronic, but he couldn't help himself. His gaze was riveted on Beth-Ann's lower body. She'd moved her skirt slightly, spreading her legs a little wider. He frowned, trying to keep a grasp on the conversation. "Ah, what would that be?"

"I always wondered what it would be like to have a man sweep me off my feet, prop me up on a bench or a table and do the job then and there." She moved the fabric of her skirt another inch. "Spontaneity, ya know?"

Riley was all for seizing the moment. He inched his chair back, but before he could stand up, Beth-Ann leaned close, grasped one of his hands and placed it on her knee.

"Sooo..."

She smiled when he took her offer and started to slide his hand upward. That was enough of an incentive to bring his other hand into play.

"...I thought, seeing as how we don't have a bench, the desk would do just fine."

"Huh?"

He shook his head, his brain unable to process her words. All he could think of was the feel of her thighs under his hands. Satin, but with much more warmth. Smooth and heated. He curled his thumbs further on the inside of her thighs as he reached the apex. Heat of a different kind hit him. He wrenched his head up and stared at the sexy smile on her face, his mouth open in shock.

"Remember your Boy Scout motto, Riley?" She raised her eyebrows. "Be prepared?"

His hands clenched on the top of her thighs as the realization broke over him.

"Holy fuck, you're not wearing any panties."

Chapter Eight

Beth-Ann struggled to keep the "come-hither" smile pinned to her lips. What she really wanted to do was roll around the desk with laughter. The look on Riley's face was priceless. She couldn't believe she'd had the guts to do this, but it sure had some benefits. She reached forward, slid the tip of her finger under his chin and gently closed his mouth.

"Didn't your daddy ever tell you that old one about your face staying that way if the wind changed? You don't want everyone to think you go around in mid-drool all the time, now do you?"

"Um...no." He shook his head and swallowed convulsively.

When Riley flexed his fingers on the top of her thighs, Beth-Ann dragged in a sharp breath and did some fast swallowing of her own. Good gracious, he hadn't done anything yet and her pulse already felt like a freight train on a mad rush to the last station on the line. Her mouth had gone dry, her face felt flushed and hot, and her pussy ached with a persistent throb. Nothing like getting hot and heavy in unusual situations. Talk about an extra dash of spice.

"Am I still in control of this torrid affair?" She raised her eyebrows and waited for his reply.

Riley slid his hands up under her dress and gripped her hips. Her bare hips. His shock appeared to have subsided now and a mischievous grin curved his lips.

"I did tell you that you could call the shots," he reminded her. "You master, me slave. Or rather, you Mistress."

"In that case," she took the time to remove his hands from under the sweep of her skirt, "stand up, slave."

"Your wish is my command, Mistress."

Clumsy in his haste to move, he pushed the chair back hard as he stood. It rolled across the floor and banged into the wall of the office. The crash reverberated throughout the little room. Beth-Ann worked to keep her mouth straight. Heaven knows what anyone passing would think.

"Pick up that picnic basket," she ordered, bursting into chuckles at the disappointed look on his face.

"But I thought we were—"

"The basket," she reminded him as she fought to contain her laughter.

As if determined not to move too far away from her, Riley bent and groped around the side of the desk for the cane basket. When he held it aloft, she indicated he remove the cover. He flipped the tea towel aside and stared at the contents for a moment before he let loose with a crack of laughter.

"How long do you think we're going to be able to stay locked in here," he said when he had himself under control.

"As I said, nothing like being prepared." She grinned as she watched him sift through the contents.

She really had brought ham and crusty rolls for lunch, but that wasn't all. A bottle of red wine nestled in the bottom, the neck resting on the edge of the basket. Wine glasses wrapped in white serviettes hugged the outer curve, a container of strawberries perched on top of them. Beth-Ann reached over and grasped one of the crisp green apples that snuggled beside the filled rolls and held it aloft.

"You've heard about what Eve did to Adam, haven't you?" She bit into the apple, savoring the slightly tart taste on her tongue. "Mind you, I did think you might be more tempted by my final offering."

The apple landed back in the basket and she ran her hand through the mass of tiny, bright-colored foil packets littering the contents like so many pieces of confetti.

"What's your fancy? We have feathersoft, slenderline... Scrap that one, no good. Wrong size." She lifted one eyebrow and stared at the bulge in the front of his jeans.

Oh yeah, Riley was definitely interested. Any worries she might have had to the contrary disappeared in the blink of an eye. She checked out the eclectic selection and snagged one particular, little packet. "We even have a rib-tickler, whatever that may be. Want to give it a try?"

Riley took the red foil square from her hand and tossed it back in among its mates. Then he reached for another before he dumped the basket back on the floor.

"We don't need any sexual enhancers." He leered at her, waggling his eyebrows for effect. "Between the two of us, we'll manage to create enough heat to burn this whole site down."

"Rats. I wanted to see what all the fuss was about."

"Next time."

Those two little words sounded like a promise. They wiped out any worry she might have had about Riley not wanting to continue their affair. In a rush of need, she grabbed the front of his shirt and pulled him into the cradle of her thighs. One by one, she popped the buttons and spread his shirt wide.

"What are you waiting for, slave? Your mistress is hungry."

She leaned forward and ran the tip of her tongue across his chest, teasing the brown discs of his nipples before tracing the fine line of dark hair that arrowed down to disappear beneath the waistband of his jeans. And while she occupied herself with the taste and feel of his heated flesh against her lips, she sent her hands on a quest to discover more.

The snap of his jeans offered no resistance. Beth-Ann eased the zip down and slid her hands around his hips to burrow under the denim fabric and cup his ass. She pulled him in until his bulging hard-on nudged at the ache between her thighs.

"Why, Riley Osborne," she whispered, "how often do you come to work without *your* underwear?" A grin emerged at the fiery blush that stained his cheeks. Fancy that, a man who could blush.

"Ah, I did the late shift with Mel," he said in explanation. "I rushed home afterward for a shower and back here again to open up the site and I was in a hurry—"

"You'll hear no complaints from me," she interrupted. Impatient now, she pushed his jeans down. Her gaze lowered as his cock sprang free. She ran the tip of her finger along the length before curling her fingers around the thickness at the base, grinning when a groan rippled from his throat.

"Although, if you've been hard at it all night, maybe you're too tired for this," she said, tongue-in-cheek, and waited for his response to her choice of words.

Riley gulped at the touch of her hand. It was like a red-hot brand. He tore the edge off the foil packet with his teeth, but his hands shook as he extracted the condom and made a move to sheathe himself in the prophylactic. She took it and rolled it down his cock. Christ, he'd never realized how erotic it was to have the woman take care of the protection issue.

"I take it you don't want me to stop?" She flicked him a cheeky grin. "Sure you don't need to get some sleep?"

"Hell, no," he managed as he pushed her skirt out of the way. "I may never need sleep again."

"A person could die from lack of sleep," she whispered as she took his cock in her hand and rubbed the tip against the inside of her thigh.

Riley jerked in reaction. One hand curved around her hip while the other sought out the heat between her thighs. "Tease me much more and I could expire right here on this spot." *Christ, she was so wet.*

He fell back into the game. "What does my mistress want of me?" He used a suitably subservient tone, his gaze trained on her face as he slid one finger into her warmth.

Arms braced on the desk, she tilted her hips, her head thrown back as she gasped, "Fill me up, slave. Take away the hunger."

"Your wish is my command." Without giving her time to say anything else, he dropped to his knees in front of her.

"Hey, slave, what—"

He lifted her skirt and disappeared under the fabric. Spreading her knees a little more, he buried his head between her thighs. Her scent called to him, an aphrodisiac in itself. He ran the tip of his tongue along her crotch before lapping at her pussy.

"Oh, God, Riley."

Unable to wait any longer, he parted her with his fingers and licked along her cleft, flicking at her clit. He scraped his teeth over the hard little bud until she screamed out his name again. Then he speared her warmth with his tongue, burying his face even closer as he thrust in time with the undulation of her hips.

When he heard her panting breaths, he pulled back and blew softly across the dampness. Her hips tilted and he thought she'd fall off the desk, so great was her reaction. With one final kiss, he stood up, pushing her dress back so he could see the swollen lips of her pussy. Holy fuck, what a turn on.

He grasped her hips, pulled her closer to the edge and drove himself home. For a moment, he held still, his hands anchoring her in place. As she curled her arms about his shoulders, he dropped his head forward to rest on the top of her curls and dragged in a deep breath.

Even though she had instigated this, he felt like a rotten sod for taking her here on the desk. Like a teenager who couldn't wait to find a better place to make out. When he lifted his head and stared at her, she had her eyes wide open, a look of surprise on her face, as if she wondered why he'd stopped.

"I'm sorry," he whispered.

She ran the tip of her tongue along her bottom lip. "What for?"

"You deserve satin sheets and soft music, not this furtive coupling in a temporary demountable building on a busy work site." He gave into temptation, leaned forward and lapped at the moisture on her bottom lip.

She grinned against his mouth. "We had the satin sheets the other night. Let's go for some variety here."

With that, she linked her hands together around his neck and pulled herself forward. Rocking her hips, she drove him deeper still. As he took up the rhythm and thrust hard, her head tilted back and a shuddery gasp escaped. When he withdrew, a little whimper slipped from her lips, only to change to a drawn-out moan when he pounded into her again.

Beth-Ann trembled, not only with the force of his actions, but with the tension that wound tight, deep inside her, barely held in check. Hunger rose, clawed at her throat. Her arms shook, but she hung on, curling her fingers over his shoulders for a moment before dragging them down his chest.

In one part of her mind, she registered the fact that her nails had scored his bronzed skin. "I'm sorry, I'm sorry," she managed to gasp.

The leather covering on the desk struck cold against her back as Riley laid her down and leaned over her, his weight supported on his arms. A shiver traced down her back, mixed with the slight apprehension she felt at her uncontrolled behavior.

"Shhh, it's okay," he whispered. "I need to slow it down a bit."

"No," she begged. "I want you now, hard and fast. I feel like I'll shatter any moment."

"Don't want that to happen." He lowered his head and drew her nipple into his mouth.

Rational thought fled as Beth-Ann lost herself in the carnal pleasure of making love with Riley. She raised her hips and met his thrusts. The breath gusted from her lips as he pushed the tension higher. He ground himself against her and dragged her up to the top of the pinnacle. Harder, faster, until all control unraveled in a firestorm of sensual excess.

As the spasms hit, radiated out from the place where they joined, she cried out. He took the sound from her as he caught her lips in a deep, drugging kiss. His arms wrapped about her and she let go, trusting him to keep her safe.

The utilitarian surroundings of the site office disappeared as the convulsions of her climax swept through her, over her, surrounded her, until there was nothing but Riley and this moment in time. When the conflagration ended, she opened her eyes to find him smiling down at her, that mischievous twinkle evident in his eyes.

"Darlin', you get hotter every time. I thought nothing could be as good as the other night, but you proved me wrong." His voice was husky and his chest heaved as he struggled to drag fresh air into his lungs.

Beth-Ann let her arms collapse onto the desk beside her. Her breathing was just as labored as his. Perspiration dewed her body. Her back stuck to the leather desktop. Riley withdrew and she lay there, totally exposed to him. She flicked her dress down, letting her hand flop again. A wave of heat washed over her, making her aware of her bare breasts and reinforcing her uninhibited actions.

"I'm sorry," she said and averted her eyes.

He reached out with one long finger and turned her face back to him. "Don't you dare apologize. That was the most fantastic thing that's ever happened to me. I wouldn't have changed anything."

She stared at the red scratches on his chest. "I marked you. I've never done that before."

"You can put your brand on me any time you like. I'll wear it with pride. When that one fades, we'll have to do this again, and again...and again."

Beth-Ann felt a moment of disquiet. Riley almost sounded as if he were talking permanence here. Yes, she loved him. More than she thought possible. And yes, she wanted this affair, but she didn't want him to get serious. That way led to a woman's downfall. Before a girl knew where she was, she'd be waiting around for the guy to call. Tailoring her life to suit his. No way was she going to end up like her mother, subject to a man's whims.

It doesn't have to be that way, Beth-Ann.

Cindy's advice echoed inside her head. *Enjoy the moment.* She buried the slither of fear deep inside her and clung to her new theme song. Because she knew one thing for certain, she didn't have it in her to walk away from Riley. But she *was* in charge and she needed to remember that, starting right now.

She lifted her hand and drew the tip of her finger across his bottom lip and down to the scratches on his chest. "I always thought I was a cat in another life."

"Meow." Riley nipped at her finger before standing upright and rearranging his clothing.

He dealt with the condom and zipped his jeans, before doing up the buttons of his shirt, although he didn't bother to tuck it into his pants. Running his hand over his hair, he tried to flatten it back into a restrained style. She grinned, although she still felt a little embarrassed. One look and the rest of the men on site would have a pretty good idea what she and Riley had been up to.

When he held out his hands, Beth-Ann grabbed hold and pulled herself into a sitting position. Somehow, she felt more in control when she was the right way up. She was surprised to say the least when he helped her position her breasts in the half-cup bra before he clipped the shoulders of her dress into place.

"If you ever get tired of the building trade, I can give you a recommendation as a lady's maid." She arched her eyebrows at him and accepted his help to slide off the desk.

A grin tilted her mouth when she turned and saw the mess in the office. The desk was almost empty of the papers and folders Riley had accumulated. In her frenzy, she must have pushed them off the leather top. Pencils lay strewn across the floor, the coffee cup that had contained them smashed into pieces among the paperwork. Good gracious, she couldn't even remember doing that. She hadn't been conscious of anything but Riley and the tumult of emotions inside her.

She reached over and snatched up a crumpled blueprint as it balanced on the edge of the desk. "Hope this wasn't important."

"Who cares? I'll do another one if necessary."

He bent down and grabbed the picnic basket. Grabbing a handful of tiny foil packets, he shoved them into the pocket of his jeans. When he saw her watching, he shrugged, a sheepish grin on his face.

"Can't waste them. I thought we might try out a different one every night." He waggled his eyebrows and twirled an imaginary moustache. "Or maybe two or three, m'dear, if the need arises."

Beth-Ann laughed, ready with a sassy retort, but before she could say anything, there was a loud thump on the door of the office.

"Riley, get your butt out here. Your old man wants to talk to you."

A flush of heat crawled across Beth-Ann's face and she sucked in a sharp breath. Her heart raced. Hands trembled as she patted at her dress and tried to arrange her hair in an orderly manner. "You got a mirror?" she whispered, her voice a shaky croak.

Riley pushed her over to the corner of the office. Fixed to the wall beside a gray filing cabinet was a small speckled mirror. Beth-Ann stared at her image. Her cheeks were bright red with embarrassment, her hair a nest of wild tangles that defied her attempts to straighten them out. The lipstick she'd applied before leaving home was long gone and her eyes had that slumberous I've-just-made-love look about them.

"Shit, I look like I've been pulled through a bush backwards."

"No, you looked like a woman who's been well and truly loved."

"That's the problem." She moved back to the desk and picked up the picnic basket. "I don't suppose there's a back way out of here?"

He shook his head. "We'll just have to brazen it out." He scooped the red hard hat up off the floor and placed it on her head before grabbing his own. "Great image." He grinned as he guided her to the door.

Beth-Ann's heart started to pound. Her palms grew so sweaty she was in danger of dropping the basket. Here it was. The moment she'd dreaded and she didn't know how to avoid it.

Maybe Riley's dad wouldn't recognize her. After all, she wasn't the same fat thirteen-year-old he'd known back in Wattle.

Better he thought she was Riley's bit on the side. She'd have to brazen it out. A groan threatened to break free. Mr. Osborne really *would* think she was brazen, because no one would possibly believe she and Riley had done nothing more than share a bite of lunch.

"Ready?" Riley whispered.

At her sigh and nod of assent, he opened the door to the office. Charlie stood on the bottom step, an older man, one she recognized despite the passage of years, at his side. John Osborne, Riley's father.

He wasn't as tall as Riley, but was just as broad in the shoulders and chest. His hair had a lot more grey than she remembered, his face more wrinkled, but the twinkling kindness was still evident in his steady gaze.

She almost smiled at him as she would with any old friend. She remembered John Osborne with fondness. She'd come into regular contact with him when her father had worked for him. Her mother, with her fixation on food, had developed the habit of sending Beth-Ann down to the site or the office with afternoon tea for her father.

John, well aware of her father's controlling tactics, and the other children's ridicule of the resident fat kid, always treated her as if she were a human being of some worth. He'd listened to her when she rambled on about her woes, encouraged her to share her day with him. In short, he made certain she knew she mattered, and for that, she'd always have a soft spot for him.

Riley took her hand and helped her down the two steps until they were face to face with his father. Charlie, a smirk on his face, had disappeared back into the controlled mayhem that was the building site.

"Hi, Dad. Sorry I wasn't around when you wanted me. We were having lunch."

John Osborne smiled, his eyebrows arched.

"Ah, this is Beth-Ann Harris, a very good friend of mine." Riley pulled her forward.

She lifted her head and stared Riley's father in the eyes, prepared to tough it out. "How do you do, Mr. Osborne? I'm pleased to meet you." *Asinine, Beth-Ann, so polite when you've just been rolling around on the desk with his son.* She extended her hand in greeting.

A large, work-roughened hand enfolded hers. John smiled. "Glad to meet you, Beth-Ann. Used to know a Harris once, back in the old days."

Instead of dropping her hand, he stared at her, his head tilted to one side as he inspected her face. *Oh-oh, here it comes.* Beth-Ann felt her heart skip a beat. Despite her huge loss of weight, she knew she bore a marked resemblance to her father. She exerted a little pressure and tried to pull her hand free, but John was too far in the past.

"Hmm, Harris," he said. "Beth-Ann Harris." All of a sudden, he released her hand and pulled her into a bear hug. "Little Beth-Ann. I thought I recognized you." He held her at arm's length and grinned.

Her heart sank. She didn't dare look at Riley. Just how angry was he going to be because she hadn't come clean? "Um, not so little back then, Mr. Osborne." She managed a weak smile.

He shook his head. "Puppy fat. I knew you'd lose it one day and turn into a raging beauty and I was right, but you've still got that same wide-eyed innocent look in your eyes. The eyes gave you away. I'd have known you anywhere." He lifted the edge of the hard hat. "Still got that great red hair, I see. Glad you didn't go the way of most women these days and tamper with the color."

Beth-Ann thought back to the *lunch* in the site office and almost cringed. Some innocent she was. And the bottle of semi-permanent hair dye in her bathroom made her feel guilty as sin for some reason.

John turned his gaze on his son. "How come you didn't tell me you were seeing Beth-Ann?" Without giving time to answer, he tucked his arm through Beth-Ann's and turned her away from the office. "I haven't kept in contact with anyone from Wattle. You're old enough now to understand why I chose that option, but I have to say, I missed our little talks when I moved to the city. So how are your mom and dad?"

She let him guide her across the site and over to the security booth. She could feel Riley's presence behind her, and she still hadn't looked at him to gauge his reaction. "Dad died when I was still at school and Mom when I was eighteen."

"Ah, sorry to hear that, love. I warned your father he needed to change his life style. All that alcohol and excess weight had to take its toll. I'm glad to see you did something about it. Guess you found that control you always used to go on about."

"I guess I did."

He dropped a quick salute on her cheek. "You and I will have to catch up soon and talk about the old days. Get Riley to bring you over to the house." He lowered his voice, his mouth near her ear. "Guess you also made that son of mine eat his words, too, hmm?" His eyes twinkled as he smiled at her.

Beth-Ann dared a look at Riley. His face was devoid of expression as he watched the by-play between her and his father. She wanted to cry. *Please don't let him break it off,* she silently begged.

"I'll leave you two to say your good-byes." John turned on his heels and started to walk away. Then he paused and looked back over his shoulder. "When you're done, Riley, I'll meet you in the office. I'd like to know what the police had to say."

With John gone, Beth-Ann turned to Riley and crossed her arms over her chest, the picnic basket held in front of her like a shield. "Are you angry with me?"

Riley slid around behind her, took her by the shoulders and moved her to the side of the security booth, away from the curious eyes of the men on the site. "I always knew," he whispered.

Shock dragged Beth-Ann to a halt. She spun around and stared at him. "You knew?"

"Yep."

"When? How?" He'd known the whole time? She squeezed her eyes shut as she remembered their first encounter. Oh my, what must he think of her?

"Oh, not right at the beginning, but certainly after that first night at your house."

"How?" She shook her head as she tried to make sense of it all. She'd been so careful not to let slip any incriminating comments about her earlier life and she'd put all the photos away. Anything that could identify her.

He took the basket from her and dumped it on the ground before he pulled her into his arms, fitting her body to his. "There's a small photo in a silver frame on top of your fridge. You and your parents, taken, I'd make a guess, just before your dad died."

Darn, she'd forgotten that one. She pulled away from him and planted her hands on her hips. "So you knew I was that fat kid who followed you around like a bad smell. What was it? A pity party, take the fat girl out for an airing? Or is this a sop to your conscience because of what you said to me when I was thirteen?"

Riley grasped her by the shoulders and gave her a slight shake. "Beth-Ann, you are not fat. Look at yourself. You're a vibrant, sexy woman. Any guy would give his right arm to spend time with you."

He paused to take a deep breath. "Size, or lack of it, had nothing to do with it. And before you ask, yes, I do remember what I said to you that day down by the football field. I think it was the first time in my life I'd ever been really nasty to anyone, male or female. I've regretted it ever since, which is why the memory remains so clear in my mind."

"You remembered me?" She searched his eyes, trying to find the lie.

"Sure did." He grinned. "Every time I turned around you were there. This sassy-mouthed kid who used humor to deflect the barbs of all the other kids in school. I always admired that in you. Okay, so you were fat, and I'm glad you lost the weight if only for your own health, but that's not who you are."

"But you were so mean. You told me no man would ever be turned on by me." The memory, once so sharp and painful, seemed to have lost some of its sting. She shook her head. Fancy that.

"So you proved me wrong, didn't you? Darlin', you push every button I can think of. You make me hotter than any woman I've ever been with, but it's not just the sexual thing. It's you, the person. You have a way of befriending everyone you meet. Your mind is razor-sharp, your ready wit makes me laugh, and I find myself wanting to spend every spare minute with you. In short, Beth-Ann Harris, I like you. I mean, I *like* you, if you can grasp the distinction I'm trying to make."

His words of praise stroked her ego, until her intense fear of commitment kicked in. She pushed it aside, trying to ignore the implications of his final words. She'd deal with that later.

A rush of guilt rose to the forefront of her mind. She bit her lip and glanced at him before she dropped her gaze again. How was he going to feel when he realized—and he would, he was a pretty astute man—that she'd had her own ulterior motives for going out with him.

"So, what made you decide to commit to this red-hot affair with me?"

She winced at his choice of the word *commit.*

"Was it my raving good looks? Or maybe it was the fact I picked up on your pun on holes. I've got to say that was the most fun I've ever had when I've introduced myself to a client. Normally I deal with boring old businessmen. What tempted you to take a chance on me, hmm?"

Beth-Ann couldn't for the life of her come up with a witty answer. She raised her head and stared at him, to find him frowning down at her. She wanted to close her eyes. *Here it comes. This is when he gets angry with me.*

All of a sudden, he let out a crack of laughter. "That's it, isn't it? Revenge. You wanted to get back at me for those nasty comments when I was a kid. I'm right, aren't I?"

"Maybe in the beginning it started out as revenge," she admitted with a grimace. "But I responded to you before I even realized who you were. The penny didn't drop until you called me *ma'am.* It reminded me of your father and the way he used to address my mother."

Riley laughed. "Dear old Dad will be happy his lessons on manners stuck." He pulled her into his arms again and dropped a quick kiss on her up-turned mouth. "I was full of rage and pain when I made those cracks. I'm sure you're aware of all the gossip about my mom that floated around town, and let me tell you, it was fact, not rumor. She'd just walked out on me and my dad and no woman would have gotten a fair hearing right about then, not even a thirteen-year-old full of hero worship."

"I knew about your mother, heard my parents talk about it," Beth-Ann said. "I felt so sorry for you. All I really wanted to do that day was to offer you my sympathy." She gave a slight grin. "Oh, and check out your naked chest when you stripped off your football jersey"

"Somewhere inside of me is a sixteen-year-old heart going pit-a-pat for that compliment." He chuckled. Then he sobered, the smile wiped from his face. "I cut you off at the knees that day and I'm so sorry for that. Do you forgive me?" He ran the tip of his finger across her bottom lip.

Beth-Ann shivered. All he had to do was touch her. "I'll forgive you if you forgive me for not telling you the truth and for being so petty as to want a little revenge. Anyway, your comments were the impetus for me being so determined to lose all those pounds when I finally had control of my own life."

She reached up, snagged a lock of his hair and pulled him down to her. He took quick advantage and cut off any further words with a heated kiss, knocking her hard hat off in the process. She groaned at the thrust of his tongue and reciprocated in kind. When he broke away, her chest was tight with the need to gulp in fresh air.

And maybe something else?

The big "C" word—as in commitment. Not something she wanted to deal with right now or she may well run screaming from the building site.

"Very soon you're going to tell me why your excess weight as a child matters so much," he said.

She jerked in reaction as his words bit deep, but chose to keep her own council.

He frowned. "It wouldn't have anything to do with this need to be in control all the time, would it? I remember quite clearly the issues your father had with control. Your mother was a living, walking advertisement to the effects of blatant male chauvinism and dominance. Just because I was only sixteen doesn't mean I didn't notice what was going on around me."

"That's a rather long jump to make, isn't it?" She raised her eyebrows in haughty disbelief.

With a grin, he dropped another quick kiss on her lips. "Discovery is part of the fun, darlin'." He turned her around and walked her to the front entrance of the site. "Now, out of here, woman. I've got work to do and dear old Dad is waiting."

"Will I see you tonight?" She hated herself for asking, but she needed to know she hadn't screwed this up with her admission that she'd wanted her taste of revenge.

"I'm on guard duty with Mel tonight, but not until eleven. Want to go out for a bite to eat beforehand?"

Beth-Ann bit her lip. "I can't. I've got the two guys from the block of apartments across from my house coming over for dinner." She grinned. "Well, a cooking lesson and they get to eat their creations. You could still pop in if you want."

"Hmm, I don't know. I'd kind of like to have you to myself, but we'll see. I'll ring you."

When he tilted her head up and claimed her lips in another scorching kiss, she lost herself in the taste of him. Once again, her heart raced and her blood heated. Oh, boy, Riley Osborne was dynamite. One touch and she burst into flames.

A barrage of wolf whistles dragged her back to the present. A group of men had ceased work and stood watching them. The lascivious grins on their faces said it all. Her cheeks were hot as she pulled away. "I'd better go."

"Hey, before you do, I'll take one of those crusty rolls. For some reason, I have an insatiable appetite." He reached into the basket and snagged the plastic-wrapped package. His treasure held aloft, he turned to walk away.

"Thought you'd had your lunch, Riley," Charlie called out as Riley made for the office.

Beth-Ann grinned.

Charlie didn't know how close to the truth he was.

Chapter Nine

Riley hovered outside the front door of Beth-Ann's house. The damn dog that had announced his arrival the other night ran up and down the fence-line, the sound of its frenzied bark a disturbance in the quiet suburban neighborhood.

Great way to get a watchdog. Just move in next door to the mangy critter. He grimaced and shook his head. He'd better get himself on the other side of the door before someone called the cops and reported a burglar or a peeping tom. Did peeping toms hang around at—he flicked a glance at his watch—seven-thirty in the evening?

He felt like an idiot even being here, but he couldn't stay away. Beth-Ann drew him like a moth to a flame, and like that luckless moth, he'd probably keep beating himself against the fire until she grew sick of him and tossed him out.

A frown caught him unawares. Now why the hell did that thought hurt so much? He was supposed to be the big macho male, not the least concerned about emotions and the like, but somehow, he'd lost his perspective with Beth-Ann. The mad rush over here to break up her cozy cooking sessions with two unknown men was a perfect example.

Shit, he was pissed off that they were a part of Beth-Ann's life, for Pete's sake, and he hadn't even met the men in question.

Keep it cool, Riley, keep it cool.

The phrase hammered at him as he raised his hand and rapped on the door, wincing when he applied more force than he should have. His brow pulled down in a frown as he waited for a response.

Muffled words came to him through the thickness of timber. He leaned to one side and pushed his ear up against the door in the hope he could hear Beth-Ann's voice.

All of a sudden, the barrier disappeared and Riley, his balance shot to pieces, found himself on a fast trip to the floor. He flung out a hand and clutched at the doorframe before he hit the deck. The next thing he knew, someone grabbed hold of the front of his shirt and lifted him clear off the floor. His feet peddled as he tried to gain some type of purchase on the slippery tiles in the entranceway.

"What are you, mate? Some damn pervert who gets his jollies hanging around single women's places?"

A sharp shake accompanied the low, gravelly voice. His mangled shirt slipped from the waistband of his jeans, pushing the big beefy fist up under his chin. He gagged as the stranglehold impeded the passage of air into his lungs.

Riley opened his eyes wide and stared at the gorilla that held him. He was pure muscle. His shoulders damn near filled the whole doorway. The arm holding him up bulged and rippled as it applied more pressure to his windpipe. Riley's eyes widened a bit more as he tried to grab some air.

Speaking was a physical impossibility. All he could do was stare at the roadmap of a face with its deep grooves, beady squinted eyes and the squashed nose that had seen the fast end of its own share of fists.

The gasping sound of his breathing beat at his ears. A black haze began to collect in front of his eyes. In a moment of total clarity among the torture of trying to breathe, he noted the way the overhead lights glinted on the shaved dome of the thug's head and highlighted the big love heart tattooed there, a name blazoned in red across the black outline.

"Answer me, slime bag, before I punch yer lights out."

Now that the shock of the attack had worn off slightly, Riley decided it was time to extricate himself, *before* he lost consciousness from lack of oxygen. He grabbed at the clenched fist and shoved, trying to dislodge the grip on his ruined shirt. It was akin to trying to shove a locomotive out of the way. *Totally fucking useless.*

"Beffff-Aggg..." He was right, speech was useless. He kicked out with one booted foot. Maybe steel-capped work boots would do the job. And all the while he twisted and squirmed in the ape's grip.

"Maxwell, put him down. He's a friend," Beth-Ann screamed out.

The brute let him go. Riley's feet touched down, sliding out from underneath him and before he knew where he was, his ass hit the cold tiles. The force of it jarred up his spine and slammed his mouth shut. He grunted as he bit down on his lip, the sting evidence that he'd split the skin.

Beth-Ann raced across the living room and dropped to her knees beside him.

"You big bully, Maxwell. Look what you've done." She pulled Riley's head to her chest, her fingers tangled in his hair. "Oh, poor baby," she crooned.

Riley dragged in a hoarse breath and buried his head between her breasts, one nipple a provocative point that nudged at his cheek. Who said good things couldn't come out of minor inconveniences? He couldn't have asked for better if he'd staged this fiasco himself. It kind of made up for the embarrassment of being shown to be less than adequate in front of his current lady.

Beth-Ann squirmed and pulled on his hair when he nuzzled at her breasts. "Are you all right?" As the tip of his tongue teased the pebble-hard point, she gasped and pushed him away.

"Riley Osborne, you're incorrigible. Half choked and you can still find the right place to land." She grinned at him and smoothed her thumb across his mouth to blot up the small bead of blood that shone bright crimson where he'd bitten his lip.

"That's why you love me, isn't it?" he joked in a croaky voice.

"That's *one* of the reasons I love you," she responded, caught by the glitter of his brown eyes.

Her heartbeat faltered as she realized she'd admitted her love for him, and in front of witnesses. She just prayed he'd think it was one of those throwaway lines everyone used on occasion. Because if he didn't, she'd just handed him the means by which he could control her.

By sheer force of will, she kept the smile on her face. "Are you really okay?" She stood and tugged at his arm, helped him to stand, then brushed off his rear end. Riley cleared his throat and rearranged his shirt, minus a few buttons, so he looked reasonably tidy again.

"I am now, but who's your muscle?" He nodded toward the bouncer who still stood at the open front door.

"That's Maxwell, from across the road." She planted her hands on her hips and faced Maxwell. Her lips twitched at the scowl on his face. "Make nice, Maxwell. Now come and meet Riley. He's the man I told you about, the one who came to see about filling my hole for me."

She spun around in surprise when Riley snorted, and back again when Maxwell coughed as if he'd choked on something. The two men slapped each other on the back and burst into laughter. She heard the slightly higher pitch of her other visitor as he, too, started to chuckle. *Men.*

After a moment, it registered how she'd phrased it. She grinned. She was at it again. "Okay, enough already with the play on words, guys. And Graham," she raised her voice over the continued hilarity, "you'd better not let that sauce burn."

Maxwell slammed the front door shut and extended his hand to Riley. "Sorry about that, mate. I didn't know Beth-Ann's fella was comin' over."

"No harm done, but I'm going to yell before I hit the driveway next time. What the hell do you bench press?"

"Oh, I'd say at least one-ninety with one hand."

Beth-Ann held up her hands. "Uh-uh, don't get him started on his muscles or we'll never get dinner ready." She squealed as Maxwell picked her up in a bear hug, carried her into the kitchen and deposited her on the bench. He remained by her side, his head pressed to her chest and one beefy arm about her waist. She glanced at Riley over her shoulder, frowning as she noted the discontented look on his face.

"I thought you'd ring," she said as he moved to stand on her other side.

Riley glared at Maxwell as he hugged Beth-Ann. An avalanche of jealousy rolled over him. How dare the big lout put his head on her chest? That was *his* resting place. God help him, he felt like that sixteen-year-old school kid again with a fit of the greens because another jock dared to look at his girl.

"I swapped with Arthur so I could stay and...er, visit. He can do tonight and I'll fill in for him on his next shift." He cast a confused look at the second guy as he sidled up and hung himself on Maxwell's other arm.

Couldn't have been much more than twenty or so. A trifle on the short side and no muscle to talk about. At least this one didn't have all the telltale trademarks of a boxer like Maxwell. No danger there.

"Oh, goody, a sleepover. Are we invited?"

Ooo-kay. Problem solved. He didn't need to be too brilliant to work out that Maxwell and this guy were an item. He suddenly realized what the word tattooed across the love heart on Maxwell's head was. *Graham.* It was time to put the little green-eyed devil on his shoulder to rest. Riley almost grinned in relief as Maxwell dragged his arm from around Beth-Ann, slung it about the smaller man's shoulder and hugged him.

Beth-Ann giggled and elbowed Maxwell in the ribs.

"Get real, Graham," Maxwell said. "We're not invited. This is a party for two. Get the picture?" He grinned as his partner pouted. "Go shake hands with Riley and be good."

Graham flounced away from Maxwell and made his way around to Riley. "Hi, I'm Graham and I'm seriously offended," he said as he offered his hand. "No party. What a kill-joy." He balanced his other hand on his hip.

Riley took the limp hand and shook it, almost bursting out laughing when Maxwell giggled at Graham's antics. It was so incongruous to hear that girlish sound out of such a bear of a man.

"Oh, you bad boy," Maxwell said to Graham, a wide grin on his face as he waved a limp wrist in the air.

Beth-Ann jumped down from the bench and faced the men. "Enough with the teasing, or we'll never get this dinner cooked." She grinned at Riley. "Don't mind the guys. They're hamming it up to get a rise out of you. A lot of hetero males feel their masculinity is threatened in the company of gay men."

Maxwell leaned over and slapped Riley on the back so hard if he hadn't grabbed for the edge of the bench, he would have ended up on the floor again.

"Don't mind us, mate," he said. "We've come to the conclusion most straight men seem to expect that type of performance so we lay it on thick. Anyway, welcome to the dinner party. You staying and having something to eat?"

"No one will be eating anything if we don't get this meal into the oven," Beth-Ann said. "Maxwell, you put the mince into the dish. I want a layer of meat, the next one pasta sheets, then Graham can put some of the white sauce over that. Keep going until the dish is full, but remember to save some of the sauce to go on top."

Riley smiled as his little powerhouse of a pixie bustled about, flinging orders left, right and center. She did like to be in control. He crossed his arms over his chest and leaned back on the kitchen bench to watch, only to have her grab him by the shirt and drag him over to the refrigerator.

"You can make a salad to go with the lasagna. No work, no feed," she said with a frown.

He tipped her a salute. "Yes, ma'am," he said, to be rewarded with a smile that curled his insides and kicked his libido into top gear.

⚒ ⚒ ⚒

Beth-Ann cuddled up to Riley, her feet tucked beneath her on the couch. It had been a good night. Maxwell and Graham were hilarious as usual, which made the dinner conversation hop. Riley was just as bad once he got going. Tonight she'd caught sight of the fun-loving teenager he used to be before his mother shattered his trust in human nature.

"I'm glad you stayed." She wriggled around until she found a more comfortable position on his chest for her head. Sighing, she relaxed again.

"Yeah, I'm glad, too," he said. "Maxwell and Graham are a riot. It's nice to meet your friends. It's another way to get to know more about you."

As he ran the tip of his finger up and down her arm, she shivered in reaction. Warmth streaked under the skin, invading her blood and sweeping throughout her body, pinpricks of heat that threatened to burst into flames. One touch and he had her panting to experience his special brand of magic. Hormones went on the rampage, sexual tension gripped her belly, and she knew it wouldn't take much to fan the flames into a raging conflagration.

"You know all about me," she protested as she tried to damp down the fire inside. Much as she'd love to jump his bones, quiet times like this were much more meaningful. "You knew me when I was a child."

He chuckled. "All I knew was I had this shadow that never left me. I'd turn around and there you were."

Beth-Ann grimaced. "I was pretty pathetic, wasn't I? I had this major crush on you when I hit thirteen, but even before then, when I was a little kid, I liked to be around you at your dad's building yard. Somehow, you made me feel safe."

Riley removed his arm from around her shoulders and sat forward to work his boots off. He surprised a squeal out of her as he picked her up and repositioned her. When he was finally still again, she found herself stretched out on the couch with Riley cuddled in beside her. She grinned. Couldn't have done it better herself.

She slid her hands around his waist and hugged him to her. The fire inside flared a little higher, the tension escalated just a tad. And it wasn't necessary to ask how he felt. The fabric of his jeans was no barrier to the insistent prod of his hard cock as it nudged at her belly.

Images of the two of them doing it right here on the couch immediately crowded her mind, but not yet. She wanted to enjoy the closeness of this interlude before they got to the sex part. It was quite a discovery to realize it was as satisfying as the afterglow that came with a good romp in the sack.

"How do you feel now?" he said.

It took a moment for her to get her mind back on the previous conversation. "What are we talking about here? Safety or sex?"

"Both. You were a feisty little brat back in those days. Shy at school, but a sassy little thing when you were at the yard. You and Dad used to spend hours together."

"He listened to me. Not many people did that back then. With your dad, I could be myself and not have to worry about the fat exterior. He saw me as a normal kid, not the over-inflated tub of lard I was."

"I remember *your* father quite clearly. Even as a kid, I could see your old man had some issues he needed to address. He used to mouth off down at the yard about a woman's place being in the kitchen. *'Keep 'em barefoot and pregnant, and if you can't do that, keep 'em in the kitchen where they can do some good.'*"

At Riley's words, Beth-Ann's head filled with images of her childhood. Memories surfaced, but this time, instead of anger, her normal reaction to her father, a sense of sadness for him filled her. Because there was one thing he'd never learned. You didn't need to manipulate or browbeat someone to get them to love you and to stay with you.

"Yeah, that was my dad, all right," she murmured. "The original control freak. Don't get me wrong, I loved him, but he used to make me so angry because of the way he treated my mother. Her answer to his tantrums was to spend all her time in the kitchen so she didn't annoy him."

She propped her elbow on Riley's chest and rested her chin in her cupped hand. Although she kept her gaze fixed on his face, her thoughts were back in the little town of Wattle.

"Eating at our house was like sitting down at a fancy restaurant. If there weren't four courses for each meal, my father wanted to know what she'd done with her day. If the house wasn't polished to within an inch of its life, there'd be hell to pay. In his eyes, that was the only use females had. That, and warming his bed whenever he wanted to scratch the itch, regardless of how she felt."

"I'd heard my dad talk about it, but I didn't know it was that bad," Riley said.

"The problem was my mother equated all that food with love. If I didn't eat what she put in front of me, I didn't love her. It was only after you made that crack at me that I started to see where I was headed."

Riley lifted her, scooted over on the couch and brought her down to rest atop him. Beth-Ann wiggled until she was comfortable. Her chest rested on his and her legs parted and framed his thighs. Her pussy started to ache as she felt him beneath her, her panties already wet with wanting him.

She grinned at him. "Pretty hard pillow you make, my friend, but I'm not one to complain." She ground her hips down, chuckling as his cock hardened even more beneath her.

He gripped her hips and held her still. "Enough of that, wench. I have something important to say."

Eyebrows raised, she waited.

"Beth-Ann, I really am sorry if I hurt you back then. I can make all the excuses I want about my mother et cetera, but the fact of the matter is it was just plain nasty. I was a total ass and I hope you didn't take it to heart."

"Hey, don't sweat it. You were instrumental in me taking control of my life. I started in small ways, like feeding my pockets with half my dinner every night." She started to chuckle. "My mother couldn't understand why I wanted pockets sewed on to all my clothes. Or why I always had so many dirty clothes in the wash."

Riley stared at her. "You're kidding, right?"

She shook her head. "Uh-uh, I didn't want to hurt my mother so I started to take the food from the table and feed it to the dog through my bedroom window. Dad never did figure out how a work dog could get so fat. After a while, I got smart and kept a plastic bag in my pocket to shove the food in. That dog followed me around like a bad smell for the rest of its days."

He grinned. "I can understand why." The smile disappeared and his face grew serious. "So is this where your issue with control came from?"

"Nah, I don't have a problem with control." *Liar, Beth-Ann.* "I just like to order my own life."

Beth-Ann didn't want to talk about this any longer. He'd cut a little too close to the bone. No way did she want to tell him the extent of her problem, that because of him and his juvenile comment, she had no, or very little, self-confidence where men were concerned.

Which was why she always chose losers. Inside, where it counted, she still felt like that fat kid. No way, no how, was she ever getting married and ending up like her mother.

Had she forgiven Riley for his nasty crack? Yeah, she had. She even understood why he'd said what he had at that time in his life. He was hurting and he'd lashed out. But just because she'd tossed out her plan for a little revenge didn't mean she'd be stupid enough to give her life into the keeping of any one man. She might love him to pieces and she could commit to a red-hot affair with him, but as far as a permanent relationship went, forget it.

She almost burst into laughter. Why on earth was she in such a stew? Riley was a self-confessed, love-`em-and-leave-`em womanizer, even if he did go for exclusivity while he was with a woman. He wasn't into taking over a woman's life. All she had to do was keep control of her emotions and remind herself she didn't want a life-long commitment either.

"Enough of the deep and meaningful," she said. "Wanna fool around?" She used her arms to brace herself on his shoulders and sat upright. Scooting down a fraction, she balanced right over his rigid erection.

He hissed and arched his hips, driving his hardness against the hot ache between her thighs. She bit her lip to contain the groan that threatened to break free.

"We haven't finished talking," he said in a ragged voice.

"No more talking," she whispered as she leaned forward, her weight balanced on her arms, and took his mouth in a hungry kiss. He opened his mouth and she brought her tongue into play, darted and withdrew, until he met her halfway. Then the duel was on and she reveled in the taste and the feel of him.

His eyes had a glazed look when she retreated and stared at him. Her breathing matched the rapid rate of his. Eye contact maintained, she undid the buttons of his shirt one at a time and ran her fingers over his perfectly delineated muscles. When that wasn't enough, she dropped her head and followed the same path with the tip of her tongue.

"Lady, I'm going to expire on your couch," he groaned as he slid his hands under her skirt and grasped her hips.

"What a way to go," she crowed before she left a trail of butterfly-soft kisses across his chest, closing her mouth over one nipple.

"What the—"

All of a sudden, Riley jackknifed into a sitting position. Beth-Ann grabbed for his shoulders and hung on so she wouldn't tumble off onto the floor.

"Holy smokes, woman, you've got no panties on again." His voice was a mixture of horror and excitement.

"Remember the motto?" She grinned at the look on his face. "Be prepared?"

Riley gripped her hips and pulled her in close so she snuggled into his lap. "Are you telling me you've been running around all night with nothing on? What about Maxwell and Graham?"

He couldn't believe she'd been half-naked all night. Yeah, okay, it was a sexual turn-on that she'd been ready and waiting for him, but the idea that she might have flashed the other men filled his head and just about drove him crazy.

His mind spun back to the moment when Maxwell had picked her up and deposited her on the kitchen bench. Her denim skirt barely reached mid-thigh and when the gorilla had hauled her around, it had slid up to expose even more of her legs. The idea that another man might have opportunities he felt were his alone annoyed the hell out of him. He knew he was being unreasonable, but he couldn't help it.

"Maxwell and Graham...you could have..." He stopped and tried to gather his thoughts. "What if Maxwell and Graham—"

A gurgle of laughter bubbled out of her. "Riley, get real. The guys are gay. They're not interested in me beyond friendship."

"Doesn't matter." He shook his head. He sounded like a spoilt kid and it didn't take much brainpower to work out where the anger had come from. Jealousy. Plain and simple. "In the future I want you to keep your panties on unless I tell you different."

Wrong move, idiot. He'd done it now. Beth-Ann's eyes narrowed and she pulled back from him, although she couldn't go far because his hands held her anchored in his lap.

"Riley, you might share my bed at the moment, but if you think that gives you the right to control my actions, you can get your ass out of here right now."

He winced at the ice in her tone, at the pursed mouth and the flash of anger in her eyes. He'd blotted his copybook big time. It was time to retrieve some of his lost Boy Scout points, even if he had to grovel.

"Darlin', I'm sorry. I didn't mean for it to come out like that. I don't want to take over your life, but... Well, the simple fact of the matter is I'm jealous at the thought that you might have flashed those men."

She stared at him for a moment, her gaze narrowed. Then it was like someone had thrown a switch inside her and the glower disappeared and the sun came out again. Her eyes lit up and her sensual mouth softened into a cheeky grin. His little pixie was back again.

"I only took them off five minutes before they left," she said with a lift of her eyebrows. "And, anyway, you're to blame. You started this no-panties lark at the nightclub." She stuck her tongue out at him.

"You little rat." He started to chuckle. "You let me make of fool of myself, let me think you'd been like that all night, and all the time—" He broke off and pulled her to him, dropping kisses all over her face. "Ms. Harris, you're a tease."

She used her weight to try to push him backward. He let her have her way and flopped onto the couch, her body still pressed to his. He was ecstatic to be back on good terms with her. It hurt to have her angry with him.

"About being prepared," she said, pausing for effect.

"Hmm?" He pushed his hands under the back of her skirt and cupped the cheeks of her ass, bringing her closer to his throbbing cock.

"If you look under the fruit in the bowl on the table in front of the couch, you'll find I thought of everything."

With a little effort, he reached for the coffee table placed parallel to the couch. Hooking his finger over the edge of the yellow fruit bowl, he dragged it closer, nudging the phone out of the way as he did so. His arm wrapped around Beth-Ann, he raised his shoulders so he could see into the dish.

A frown creased his forehead. What was she talking about? Oranges and bananas wrestled for position among the glossy red apples. He lifted the first few pieces of fruit out of the way and stared. A grin surfaced as he rolled the oranges aside, snagged the half dozen little packages hidden underneath and waved them aloft.

"I take it we're going to christen the couch tonight." He shook his head. "Women. Who can read them? A great bed up the hallway and she wants to get down and dirty on the couch."

"This is a great couch, but it's never seen any action. You're supposed to initiate me into some of the finer points of having an affair. Adventure, remember? So, I thought..." She didn't finish the sentence. Instead, she lowered her head and ran the tip of her tongue along his bottom lip.

No further invitation needed, he opened his mouth and drew her in, took control of the kiss and dragged them both into a sensual web. She took the power back from him, broke off the kiss and nibbled at his bottom lip. Then she laved it with her tongue, flicked at the corner of his mouth and plunged deep.

It was obvious she wanted to set the pace and he was more than happy to let her run with it. He was an equal opportunity guy and had no problems with the woman being on top, so to speak.

Her lips a warm brand against his skin, she slid down his throat, nipping at the pulse that beat a mad tattoo and signified his growing excitement. She pushed the shirt away from his chest, lowered her head and ran her wet mouth across his skin. All the while he kneaded her bare ass and prayed she wouldn't stop.

"Touch me," she whispered as she unsnapped his jeans. "I want to feel you."

She lifted her hips slightly and moved back a fraction. A tortured growl rumbled from his throat at the loss of her weight. He trailed his hands over her bottom, angled forward until he could run the tip of his finger along the swollen folds of sensitive flesh between her thighs. Perched over him, her knees on either side of his hips, she was open to him. Hot and wet with wanting him.

Tension coiled in his gut, drove the blood down to swell his already rock-hard cock even more. He groaned as she opened his zip and released him from the confinement of his jeans. And as she wrapped her hot little hand about him, he inserted a finger into her waiting warmth.

She clenched her muscles at his invasion, releasing them and tightening again. Without any instruction from him, she eased up and down, riding his hand, taking his fingers as deep as she could. He watched her face, saw the glaze that filmed her eyes as she pleasured herself. Her mouth was slightly open. The tip of her tongue bathed her lower lip in moisture. He wanted to grab her and devour her.

And all the while her hand worked on his cock, gliding from the base right up to the tip, curling around and sliding low again, to start the process all over. Molten fire flashed through him. His heart thumped so hard, it was a wonder he didn't pass out. When she reached further to cup his balls, his chest tightened and his hips arched in involuntary action.

"I can smell your desire," he whispered, his words prompting her to increase her pace. "I want to taste you, take your heat into myself, drive you crazy."

She shuddered and opened her eyes wide to stare at him. "My turn tonight." Her breath came in sharp little pants, her voice husky. "You get to lie there and enjoy it. Where's that condom?"

Riley withdrew his hand and dug down the side of the couch where the condoms had fallen. He managed to capture one between two fingers, holding it aloft and squinting at it.

"Hey," he chuckled, "this is one of those with the little finger thingies on the sides of it. Supposed to titillate the G Spot or something." Then he gasped as she applied a little pressure and exerted an added friction on his cock.

"Lady, for someone who's been accused of not being adventurous," he groaned, "you sure know how to stir up the waters in this paddling pool." He started to sweat as the tension rose to an almost unsustainable level inside him.

With a grin, she grabbed the condom from him and tore at the foil with her teeth. "You ain't seen nothing yet, Riley Osborne," she mumbled.

She moved back a little further on his thighs and fitted the bright red rubber over the head of his cock. Fucking hell, he didn't think it was possible, but he felt himself swell even more. He couldn't believe how much a turn on it was to have a woman do the job for him. The females he normally played around with left all thought of health safety and birth control up to him. He kind of liked the turn-around.

Her little tongue clamped between her teeth, she started to roll it down.

All of a sudden, a sound cut through his ragged breathing and dragged him from the sensual haze he'd fallen into. He groped for rational thought, struggled with a surge of disappointment as Beth-Ann stared at him, a film of shock dragging the color from her face. He lifted his head and glared at the offending object emitting the persistent noise that had shattered the moment. Talk about a passion killer.

He had to clear his throat before he could speak. He glanced at the coffee table, then up at Beth-Ann. "Phone's ringing."

Chapter Ten

Beth-Ann shook her head and tried to adjust mentally to the strident ringing. She shivered, as if someone had dashed cold water in her face. Forget the face. Her whole body felt like she'd emerged from an ice-cold shower. She looked down to see her hands still wrapped about Riley's penis. Her fingers uncurled of their own accord. Closing her eyes a moment, she breathed deep and tried to find a way out from the sexual tension that still held her in thrall.

With a silent curse at the unwanted intrusion into her little fantasy world, she leaned forward and pressed the button to put the phone onto speaker. She wanted to ignore it, but she couldn't. Not only had Riley given Mel this number in case there was a problem at the site, but she was Cindy's emergency contact should something happen to either of the children.

"Hello?" Darn, she sounded like a weak-kneed female. She coughed and cleared her throat and tried again. "Yes, who is it?"

"*I know he's there.*"

The caller had somehow muffled his voice. It sounded as if it echoed through a long pipe padded with cotton wool. An obvious attempt at disguising his identity. Beth-Ann looked at Riley, her brows raised in enquiry. She held her finger to her pursed lips to warn him to keep quiet for the moment.

"Who is this? What are you talking about?"

155

"You don't need to know who I am. He knows and he's going to pay."

His tone was full of menace, the words slurred as if the speaker had imbibed too heavily. She opened her mouth to speak, but Riley shook his head. He lifted her weight and swung his legs down off the couch, before placing her back on the plump cushions.

His movements brisk, he stood and righted his clothes. For a moment, Beth-Ann almost burst into giggles as he held up the unused red condom as if he didn't know what to do with it. He shoved it into his pocket and sat down beside her.

"Who the hell is this?" he said, his head cocked to one side as he waited for the answer.

"You know me, Riley Osborne. Examine your conscience for all the people you've hurt."

Riley frowned and ran his hands through his ruffled hair. "Look, mate, I don't have a clue what you're talking about. If you explained it to me I might be able to help you."

The sound of harsh, guttural sobs filtered down the line and filled the room. Beth-Ann held her breath as an unaccountable surge of misplaced sympathy swept through her. The man sounded broken, as if he'd lost his best mate.

"You can't help me. I've lost it all," he whimpered.

"Tell me about it, friend. What's got you so upset?" Riley said.

"Don't you call me friend. You're no one's friend."

Beth-Ann shivered. The man on the phone had screamed the words out in a vitriolic stream of hate. If he'd been standing in the living room, she had a feeling he'd have thrown himself at Riley and pounded him into a pulp. Or gone down trying.

"It's because of you she left me and took the kids with her. Now I gotta sell the house, too. And if I have to lose it all, so do you."

"How did you know where I was?"

"I'm watching you. I always know where you are and I've seen the little lady. Does Ms. Harris know what a bastard you are?"

The tone started out reasonable, but by the end had descended into a venomous caricature of the human male. Beth-Ann gasped as she realized she'd been dragged into the spotlight by his words.

"I'm going to make you pay. I'll hit you in your pockets. That's all people like you understand."

He laughed, a maniacal sound that to Beth-Ann was like a fingernail scratching on a blackboard. She shuddered and grasped Riley's hand, reassured by the warm touch of his skin.

"You stay away from this house, you understand me?" Riley's voice was sharp and cloaked in a heavy threat. "You come near this woman, you touch her, and I'll hunt you down and make you sorry."

"I don't want to hurt the little girl, I only want you. You don't even know how I'm getting in, do you? Not as smart as you thought. You like fire, Mr. Osborne, sir?"

The man severed the connection and the only sound that remained in the room was the hollow echo of the empty line. Beth-Ann switched off the phone before turning her gaze on Riley.

"I take it that's the guy creating the havoc at the building site. You haven't been playing around with his wife, have you?" She was pleased with the even tone of her voice.

"What the hell do you think I am? I don't muck with married women."

Beth-Ann breathed a silent sigh of relief. Now that small matter was out of the way, fear for Riley crowded in. "Do you recognize the voice?"

Riley stood and paced across to the other side of the room, a deep frown on his face. He curled his hands into fists at his side and beat against his thighs with a repetitious thud that sounded louder than it should have. With each mark, Beth-Ann could almost see his mind turn over as he tried to reason it out.

"There...I don't know. There's something familiar about it, but I can't put my finger on it."

"He sounded like he had his mouth covered. A hanky maybe." She paused, not certain she should mention what was on her mind. "Ah, Riley, it couldn't possibly be Charlie, could it?"

He stared at her, astonishment on his face. "Charlie? Are you kidding? No way would it be anyone who has been with us from the beginning. Charlie, Jason, a couple of the others— we're like family."

Beth-Ann shrugged. "I just thought I'd ask. Charlie seemed to think you needed to be taught a lesson."

"I'll bet it had something to do with women and settling down. He's always at me to get married." Suddenly, the look on his face changed. "Turn the lights off," he barked.

She responded to the ominous tone without thinking, jumping up to flick off the overhead lights. Now only the soft glow of the table lamp drove back the darkness. Riley strode over to the large window at the front of the house and eased back the curtain, his body hidden behind the thick folds of fabric. Beth-Ann joined him.

A spasm of fear lodged in her heart, making the fine hairs stand up on her arms. The breath caught in her throat as she tried to peer outside. Everything was silent, even the dog next door. "I don't think he's out there. Pixie would have started to bark by now if he was."

Riley dropped the curtain and turned to face her. Despite the dimness of the room, she could see the perplexed look on his face.

"What?" She frowned at him.

"Who is Pixie?"

His mouth quirked as he asked the question, as if he were trying to contain his laughter, despite the seriousness of the situation in which they found themselves.

She slid her arm about his waist and guided him over to the couch. "Pixie is the dog next door. Stupid name for a dog that comes up to my waist." She grinned in an effort to lighten the atmosphere.

"I don't believe it." He shook his head. "I think of you as my little pixie. You're so small I could pick you up and carry you around in my pocket." He dragged Beth-Ann down beside him, keeping her hand tucked in his as he reached for the telephone with his other hand.

"I've got to ring a cop friend of mine. He's looking into the sabotage at the site for me."

She disengaged her hand and stood up. "You make your call and I'll freshen up the coffee. I have a feeling you're going to need it before the night is done."

She could well be right, Riley mused as he watched her leave the room. His jaw clenched at the idea of this idiot threatening Beth-Ann. Whoever this guy was, he'd kill the sod if he came near his pixie. Okay, so he was blowing air out of his ass; he wasn't about to kill anyone. But if he got to him before the cops did, he'd thrash him to within an inch of his life for even knowing where she lived.

Life without Beth-Ann all of a sudden seemed untenable. He'd gone in so deep with her she colored every area of his existence, and when he wasn't with her, thoughts of her crowded out everything else. It should have scared him witless, but for some unaccountable reason, it didn't. This was going to require more examination.

He heard the clatter of crockery from the kitchen and it helped to drag his thoughts away from his love life and back onto the seriousness of the nocturnal phone call. Without any more delay, he punched in Seth's home number. He knew Seth was on day shift so it was no point ringing the station. He drummed the tip of one finger on the table as he waited.

"That you, Seth?" he snapped out when the call was answered.

"Who the hell else would it be, Riley? What are you doing ringing me at..." There was a slight pause and then Seth started to speak again. "Shit, it's nearly midnight. I've only been asleep for an hour or so." His voice sharpened, his tone official and brisk. "You got a problem on the site?"

"Remember the woman I told you about, the one who pushes all my buttons? I'm at her place in Ashfield. Twenty-one Lucy Street to be precise."

Seth chuckled. "So what do you want me to do about it? You're a big boy, you can look after yourself."

Riley grinned at his friend's teasing before he wiped the smile from his face and concentrated to recall all he could of the vitriolic telephone conversation. "Our boy called here tonight. He—"

"Your cell phone or her land line?" Seth interrupted.

"Her home phone, so he followed me, knew where I was. *And* he managed to find out her name and phone number."

He slid across the couch as Beth-Ann entered the room with two mugs of steaming coffee in her hands. She placed the beakers on the low table in front of the couch and curled up beside him, her hand on his upper thigh. He ignored the flash of heat that entered his blood and focused on his call.

"You still there, Riley?" Seth said.

"Yeah, just thinking," he responded. "Look, it's evident it's someone who has either worked for me or I've had dealings with. He claims I took everything away from him and he's going to do the same. He's able to get onto the building site without the security guards being aware and now he's mentioned fire."

"Have you contacted Mel and…"

Sounds of movement filtered down the line and Seth's voice faded for a moment. Riley pressed the receiver closer to his ear. "Can't hear you, Seth."

"Sorry, just getting dressed. Okay, you get onto Mel and tell him I'll send a car around. The guys can help him check over the site. Can you leave your ladybird or did you get disturbed at an inconvenient moment?"

Riley shook his head. Seth would never change. Any chance to have a shot at him, just like in the old college days. "I'll meet you at the site, but I'm worried about Beth-Ann in case he's still out there."

He hooked his arm about her shoulders and pulled her to his side. All his protective instincts rose to the fore as he gathered her close.

"I'll have a car do a patrol through her street," Seth said. "I don't think we have to worry about her, but it doesn't pay to be too lax in these matters. I think he's more likely to follow you back to the site if he's still there. It's you he wants to harm."

"All right, Seth, I'll see you there in a short while."

Riley ended the call and contacted the building site and spoke to Mel, warning him of the possibility of an arson attack. When he finally placed the receiver back on the cradle, he hugged Beth-Ann to him with one hand while he took a hasty swallow of coffee.

He dropped a quick kiss on her parted mouth before bending to retrieve his footwear. When fully dressed again, he pulled her to her feet and walked to the front door.

Beth-Ann turned into his arms for one last hug before he opened the door. Within the last half hour, something had changed. She knew she loved Riley, but now she realized how much. The thought of him being hurt pounded at her brain. A cold shard of icy fear speared through her veins and lodged in her heart. Life would never be the same again if she lost Riley. She clutched at his shirt and blinked her eyes as tears threatened to well up.

Darn, she was made of sterner stuff than this. "You be careful, you hear?"

"Yes, ma'am," he joked.

"I mean it, Riley. I want you to ring me later and let me know you're okay. And tell Mel to be careful, too. He's a nice man."

When Riley tipped her chin up, she raised herself up on tiptoes to meet him. His lips glided across hers in a gentle caress, somehow more heart-wrenching than the full, open-mouthed erotic kisses that had wrapped her in a sensual cocoon earlier. Her heart threatened to jump right out of her chest when he pulled away.

"You lock the doors after me and don't open them for anyone unless they're in uniform and flash you a badge. Seth will have a patrol car do a drive-past. I don't want anything to happen to you."

His jaw clenched and a grim look spread across his face. Beth-Ann wanted to offer him comfort, but there was nothing she could do. It was up to Riley and Seth to catch this bozo. She tried to lighten the situation with a little humor, at least send him on his way without worry for her clouding his judgment.

She pulled back and struck a pose, hands planted on hips, breasts pushed forward. "Shoot, and here I was, all set to indulge in another of my fantasies."

Riley grinned. "And what was this one and how come you didn't let me in on it?"

"I always wanted to be on top. You know, be the dominant one. Maybe I should pursue a career as a dominatrix." She shook her head. "Nah, can't do that. Don't own a whip or a pair of black boots. I guess I'll just have to be content with making you lie back and let me do the riding." She made a comic face at him, glad when he started to chuckle and the shuttered look on his face eased.

"Hold that thought, pixie," he responded. With one last hard brush of his lips, he opened the door and stepped outside, slamming it after him.

✗ ✗ ✗

Riley hooked the leg of the chair with his boot and pulled it up to the desk. He flopped down, stretched his long legs out and sighed. "What the hell is this guy trying to do?" he asked of no one in particular.

"He's yanking your chain, buddy," Seth said from the other side of the desk.

"And doing a damn good job of it." His father eased into the office and dragged up his own seat. "If you'd caught him tonight, you would have put him through a brick wall, you were so angry."

Riley leaned down and dragged out the bottle of whisky from the bottom drawer, along with three small, heavy-based tumblers. When he held the bottle up and both men nodded, he poured a measure into each glass and slid them across the table.

He took a mouthful and swallowed, glad of the artificial heat that streaked through his system. His father was right. If he'd got his hands on that guy tonight, he would have... Suffice it to say, he wouldn't have been responsible for his actions. How dare this jerk involve Beth-Ann? That was what really made him see red.

His thoughts skidded back to Seth's comment. "How do you mean, he's jerking my chain?"

"Buddy, he's making you sweat," Seth replied. "I don't even think he had any intention of showing up here tonight. He just wanted to stir the pot a bit. What do you reckon, John?" He turned to Riley's father.

"We've gone over this place with a fine-tooth comb. No sign anyone else has been on site. No indication of fire or any attempt at arson, so maybe it was all a load of bunkum just to get your motor revving. Give you something else to worry about." He yawned as he uttered the last words. "Sorry, I've missed my beauty sleep."

Riley stared at his dad. His face was pale, dark circles under his eyes making the pallor more pronounced. Every time he breathed in, Riley could hear the wheeze that made his father cough until he gagged, one of the debilitating effects of the protracted cold he'd caught. Damn it, his father should be home in bed. Riley wouldn't have rung him, but he was part-owner of the business and had a right to know.

"There's one thing I can't understand though," John said.

"What's that?" Seth reached over for the whisky bottle and poured himself a shot before doing the same for Riley and John.

"I don't know, it's just a feeling I have. This fellow seems to know the site, so how can it be a past employee? None of them have been here. Also—" He paused to take a sip of his drink.

A surge of impatience hit Riley before he squashed it. His dad would get all the facts out in his own good time. No point in rushing things.

"Okay, I'm thinking out loud here so bear with me," John said. "This guy knows the trade. The equipment he's targeted for sabotage is essential to keep the project on line. Okay, they're all things easily replaced or fixed, but it slows the progress while we sort it out."

"He's in the trade," Riley said. "We already worked that out."

John raised his hand to cut Riley off. "No, hear me out. All the stuff in the beginning was nuisance value. The most dangerous thing was when he sawed through those support beams."

"Good thing I found that saw on the floor beside the beams or I wouldn't have given it a thought. I'd hate to finish the job and find out later the whole structure was unstable. Lives could have been put at risk." Riley shuddered when he thought about what could have happened. He'd seen buildings come down before, admittedly after something like an earthquake, but it wasn't pretty.

Seth sat forward. His glass hit the desk with a clunk. "That's it."

"What is?" Riley frowned and tried to make sense of Seth's comment.

"He wanted you to know about the beams."

"That's the point I wanted to make," John interrupted.

"Think about it," Seth said. "The guy knows this site, that building out there." He gestured toward the door of the temporary office. "If he's in the trade as we think he is, he left that saw on the floor so you *would* find it. It was another way to slow you down. He knew you'd check it out before you continued with the project."

"Another way to slow me down," Riley repeated in a thoughtful voice. "Hmm, so this is all to prevent me bringing the contract in on time."

"What's the worst that could happen if you don't," Seth enquired.

Riley stood up, tossed off the last of his whisky before he recapped the bottle and stowed it back in the bottom drawer.

"This is the biggest job we've taken on to date," he said. "Bring it in on time and the client has promised us the contract to build the new resort up on the northern beaches. So, yeah, a lot rides on it. It will make the reputation of the company and we stand a good chance of picking up all the government jobs. Plus we'll incur huge monetary penalties if we miss deadline."

Seth stood and stretched, his hand moving up to cover a yawn. "And who knows that?"

"I've offered all the workmen a bonus if this makes deadline, so everyone on site is aware how important it is to finish on time." Riley grimaced as he realized how difficult it'd be to pin this on one of his present employees. It would be like looking for the proverbial needle in a haystack.

"Here's what I want you to do," Seth said. "Go over all employee files, see if you have any malcontents among them. Anyone you've demoted maybe. Someone with an axe to grind. Hell, *anyone* you've pissed off."

He walked toward the door of the office, then paused. "I'll keep regular patrols in the area and you get back to me as soon as you go through your personnel files. We'll take it from there." He opened the door and sketched a salute to the other two men. "I'm outta here. Not only do I have to get some sleep before my shift in the morning, but I have a lovely lady keeping my bed warm for me. I'll speak to you tomorrow."

"Before you go," Riley called out, "what about Beth-Ann?"

"Sorry, I forgot to tell you." Seth turned back toward the room. "I sent a car out to check on her. She's locked up tight in her little house, probably asleep by now. We've put Lucy Street on the regular route so they'll do a drive-by every half hour. Just tell her to keep her door locked at night. I don't believe she's a target. I think our saboteur just wanted you to know how close he's watching you."

Riley sighed and dropped down into the chair behind the desk as Seth closed the door behind him. He ran his hands through his hair, before propping his elbows on the desk and lowering his head into his cupped palms. He should drag out the employee files, but he was just too damn tired.

"I can't believe any of the guys would be responsible for this," his father said. "Most of them have been with us for years."

"Yeah, I agree with you, but we have to start somewhere." He glanced at his watch. "You should get yourself home and into bed, Dad. It's late and I still have to ring Beth-Ann to reassure her I'm all right."

"I'm not a geriatric yet," John retorted. He grinned. "So maybe I am, as far as age goes, but I don't feel it. But you're right, it's time to go."

He winced as he stood up and stretched his back. "Maybe I am getting old. I feel every muscle tonight." He paused and stared at his son. "You serious about Beth-Ann?"

Riley shook his head. His dear old dad had never questioned him about his relationships before. "Why do you ask? It's never mattered in the past."

"I don't want to see that little girl hurt. We used to have some very in-depth chats when she hung around the yard. She suffered enough when she was a kid. I'd hate to see her go through any more. Her father was a good man, but he sure had some problems with the whole control issue. Treated his wife and kid like they were subordinates in the army."

"His daughter has her own problems with control. She likes to be on top at all times." Riley smiled slightly.

He suddenly realized what he'd said. His father was pretty broad-minded, but this was Beth-Ann. He grimaced. "I don't mean that in a sexual way. She sees her excess weight as a kid as a lack of control over her own life, so now she likes to be the one in charge. And that applies to every aspect of her life."

Yep, that was his pixie. He grinned as he thought back to earlier in the evening. She'd been hellbent on being on top then in the most intimate way possible, but he wasn't about to tell his father that.

"So are you?" John asked again. "Serious I mean. I know you usually walk away when a woman gets too close and I've worried that my lousy relationship with your mother, and your experience with Denise, might have soured you for all time. But I get the feeling Beth-Ann might be different. You have this goofy look on your face whenever you mention her name."

Riley wiped his hand over his face. Shit, his father could read him like a book, because tonight, when that call had come in from whoever was causing problems on the site, he'd realized something. Beth-Ann *was* different. Oh, he wasn't about to sprout the big "C" word. Commitment wasn't his game, but he had a feeling he wasn't going to be able to walk away from her in a hurry.

"Okay, so she *is* special," he said, "but don't go and hang out the church bells. That's not my scene."

His father frowned and then the dark look disappeared from his face as if he'd come to a decision. Riley waited.

"There's something I've never told you," John said, "but I think it's time." He rested his hip against the side of the desk and stared off into space.

"Despite my experience with your mother, you know I believe intrinsically in the concept that there is one special person out there for each of us. A soul mate, if you will."

He held up his hand as Riley gave a snort and opened his mouth to speak.

"No, let me finish. Your mother was second best and I believe she knew it. Oh, I loved her, just not as much as I should have. There was a woman when I was young, someone I believed was the other half of myself. We were all set to get engaged when she died. I never got over it and I think your mother was aware of that, although I never told her about Melanie."

"Dad, you don't need to tell me this." Riley couldn't stand the sadness on his father's face.

"Yep, I do. I don't want you to end up old and lonely. I want you to promise me when you find that one woman you can't live without, you'll think about settling down. Don't let my experience sour you." He grinned. "And, yeah, I know men don't normally spill their guts like this, but I wanted you to understand. Don't want you to end up a crusty old bachelor like me."

Riley walked around to the opposite side of the desk and dropped a hand on his father's shoulder. "Thanks, Dad. I appreciate the confidence. If Mom felt you didn't love her, I guess it helps to explain why she was the way she was. Not that it excuses her." He wasn't ready yet to go that far.

He walked John over to the door of the office. "I promise, if I suddenly find myself in a position where I can't live without that one special woman, I'll stop my fooling around." He raised three fingers to his forehead. "Scout's honor. Now get out of here so I can ring my girl and put her mind at ease."

His father's words filled his mind as he closed the door and moved back into the office. He hadn't known there'd been another woman in his dad's life. John had never spoken much about his earlier years, but it helped to understand some of what Riley had witnessed as a kid. Not that his father had been a bad husband, at least it didn't look that way from the outside.

It had always been his mother he'd blamed for the break-up of the marriage. Maybe it was time to rethink his stance on commitment and marriage. He propped his chin on his closed fist and stared into space for a moment.

Nah, still couldn't see himself as the marrying type, but he could see himself committed to one woman and that woman was his little pixie. He reached out and slid the telephone closer, a grin on his face as he acknowledged how much he was looking forward to hearing her voice. She made him laugh, made him feel special. And the sex? There was only one word for it.

Wow.

A certain part of his anatomy sprang to life as his body responded to the raunchy thoughts cluttering his brain. He was already in way too deep, and for the life of him, he couldn't walk away from Beth-Ann right now even if he'd wanted to.

Which he didn't.

Hell, his father was more on the ball than he'd realized, because one thought hit him smack between the eyes.

Beth-Ann Harris was important to his future happiness.

Chapter Eleven

Beth-Ann rolled over on the large, empty bed and grabbed for the phone as the shrill ring broke the silence. She hadn't really been asleep, just dozing as she waited for Riley to call. It'd been hours since he'd left to go to the building site. In fact, she'd assumed he'd forgotten his promise to call or had become so caught up with the security issue that contacting her was low on the list of priorities.

"Riley, is that you?"

Her question came out on a gasp as it suddenly hit her that it could have been the twisted individual who'd rung earlier. She held her breath as she waited for a response. A cold wave of fear swept over her, pebbling the skin on her arms. Her heart pounded in her chest and the blood rushed through her veins. Her clammy hand tightened around the receiver, ready to slam it down if it wasn't Riley.

"Hi, pixie. Were you waiting up for me?"

A fractured sigh feathered across her lips. The tension seeped from her body and she sagged back onto the mound of pillows behind her. Her hand trembled when she lifted it to push the hair back from her face.

"Are you okay?" For the moment, it was all she could think of to say, so great was her relief.

"I'm fine. Whoever it was didn't turn up at the site, although we searched the place from top to bottom. Seth thinks he's just out to stir me up, at least tonight anyway. But it does mean we have to be more vigilant about security from now on."

Beth-Ann moved the phone over onto the bed and curled up on her side, her bent arm tucked under her head. The overhead fan stirred the humid air, but didn't give any comfort from the heat, despite the hour. Summer in Sydney could be the pits.

She gave a slight grin. Some of the heat could well be the internal variety, generated by the sound of Riley's voice. She only had to think about him and her body reacted. Now if she had him here in her bed, instead of on the other end of a telephone line... With an effort, she dragged her mind back to the matter at hand, to the idiot who'd decided to target Riley. "Are you sure you don't remember the voice? Something about that call—" She broke off, trying to organize her thoughts into some semblance of order.

"It's funny you should say that, I keep thinking I know this person. I sort of half recognized the voice, but I can't pin it down. Just when I think I've got it, it eludes me."

Anger that Riley should be put through this flashed throughout Beth-Ann's body, followed by a surge of protectiveness. She gasped with astonishment. Now *that* she'd never felt before. Not for any of the men she'd gone out with in the past. Her friends, yes, but a boyfriend? It was a good indication of how important Riley had become to her.

"I hope they catch the guy," she said, "because I'm going to give him a mouthful for doing this to you."

Riley laughed. "Aw, that's sweet, but you'll have to get in line. I get first shot. I'm damn angry he had the gall to involve you, even if it was only through a phone call."

He paused. Then he changed the drift of the conversation. "I forgot to ask how the roof repairs were going. I can't believe I spent the evening at your place and didn't even take note. I don't think I looked at the ceiling once. Some substitute insurance rep I am."

Beth-Ann laughed. "Riley, we sat right in the living room, no more than a couple of meters away. How could you not notice?"

"Um, dare I it say it? I was so eaten up with jealousy because of your cooking companions, I didn't even think about it."

Her eyes opened wide as she took in his words. He really *had* been jealous. If she wanted revenge, here was her chance. She could drop a bomb on him and tell him she didn't want to see him anymore, not now she had him lusting after her. That had been part of the original plan. To get Riley to the point where he admitted she turned him on.

She'd had evidence and more of that fact, but revenge was the last thing on her mind. It had ceased to matter. Now it was all about how *she* felt, the love she'd buried deep in her heart, because to admit it was to give another person control over her. Just the same, the thought that Riley was jealous warmed her all over.

There was silence on the other end of the phone. The only way she could see to handle this was with humor, her normal fallback tactic. "I can't believe you were jealous of a gay couple. Graham acts so blatantly homosexual most of the time, more for effect than anything else. Bet he'd get a kick if he knew he inspired good old-fashioned jealousy." She chuckled.

"Yeah, well, I didn't know they were gay, did I? Come on, Maxwell doesn't exactly look the type." He burst into laughter. "All right, I know there's no type, and I'm talking through my hat, but I can't help how I feel."

Beth-Ann pulled herself upright and punched the pillows behind her into a more accommodating shape. "To get back to the subject."

"Which is?"

"My hole." She grinned and went on before he could interject again. "In my ceiling. Your men have patched the area and plastered over it. Jason rang me to say he'll be over tomorrow to put the final coat of plaster on—the skim coat, I think he called it—and then he'll come back the next day and paint the whole area."

"Hmm, that's strange."

Riley's voice had taken on a thoughtful tone. Beth-Ann frowned as she tried to work out where he was going with that comment. "What is?"

"It's normal for the painters to leave the builders to prepare the area and just come in and do the painting. Still, I know Jason is a stickler for detail so maybe he wants to assure himself the final coat of plaster is perfect. He'll do a good job for you. He's a great tradesman, but he can be a bit of an old woman at times."

"You leave poor old Jason alone," she joked. "He's a nice man."

"Don't get me wrong. I like Jason. He's a solid family man and does great work. He's had a few problems, but seems to have overcome them now."

"So can I wear my wet tee shirt?" she teased him, just to get his reaction.

"Like hell. That pleasure is mine."

She started to chuckle. "Riley, I'm not serious. The fact that you saw it was pure accident. And if you're so hung up on my mode of dress, when are you coming to see me again?"

"Much as I'd like to come and crawl in beside you—you are in bed, aren't you?—it's pretty late. I need to go get some sleep and so do you. I'll be on duty with Mel and Arthur for the next few nights. Not that I think anything is going to happen, but it doesn't hurt to stay vigilant."

Beth-Ann felt a stab of disappointment. Part of her had hoped he'd return after he'd finished at the site. She mentally castigated herself for her selfishness. The poor guy had been put through the wringer tonight. He needed to be on deck tomorrow and she was keeping him from his rest.

"Give me a ring when you can, `kay? Otherwise I'll worry about you."

"How do you feel about dinner with me over the next few nights?"

She shook her head. She must have missed something here. Didn't he just say he was working? She pulled the receiver away and stared at it before she clamped it back to her ear. "I thought you said—"

"I don't go on duty until eleven. Think you can stand it if I come over straight after work? We can order in some takeaway and have dinner together before I have to get back to the site."

As a warm surge of excitement flowed through her, her lips tilted into a pleased smile. Yeah, she was going to see Riley. "I could cook," she suggested.

"I don't want you to go to any trouble."

"It's no problem as long as you're not too fussy. Plain, wholesome food is what you'll get. Now hang up and go get some rest and I'll see you after work tomorrow. I'll look forward to it." Already her mind was busy with what she'd cook for dinner. *Wonder what he'll do if I serve myself up with nothing but strawberries and whipped cream?*

She swallowed a giggle as he said goodbye. The phone back on the bedside table, she snuggled down and flipped the thin cotton sheet over her nakedness. Good thing she hadn't told him she slept in the raw when the temperatures were high. He'd never have gotten off the phone.

And speaking of temperatures...

The mere thought of seeing Riley tomorrow had her in a lather. She kicked the sheet away and ran her hands over her breasts. Her nipples were hard and throbbing. The breath caught in her throat and her heart thumped with a loud insistent beat.

God help her, she was too involved now to even contemplate a life without Riley.

⚒ ⚒ ⚒

Cindy ticked the days off on her fingers. “Tuesday. Wednesday. Thursday. And again tonight. Girl, this will become a habit.”

Beth-Ann opened her mouth to issue a sassy comeback, then hesitated. Her thoughts slid back over the last three days. Riley had managed to ring her from the building site whenever he had a spare moment, and every afternoon at five o’clock he left work and came straight home to her.

“It’s scary,” she whispered in response to Cindy’s teasing comments.

“What is?” Cindy snagged hold of Peter’s collar as he raced through the living room. She dragged her son to a halt in front of her and waited until he raised his head. “Peter Phillips, you will quit it with this rampaging through Beth-Ann’s house. Because if you don’t, I’ll change my mind and make you come with me to the Parent-Teacher interviews. Is that understood?”

As she watched the butter-wouldn’t-melt look on Peter’s face, a smile twitched at Beth-Ann’s mouth, chasing the black mood away.

“Yes, Mom, I understand. Sorry, Beth-Ann. I promise I won’t do it again. Pleaseee don’t make me go with you. Kids shouldn’t have to put up with school at night as well as daytime. That’s not human.”

"I think the word you're looking for is *inhumane*," Cindy managed with a straight face. "Now go find your sister." She watched, a grin on her face, as he started out the back door. "And make nice with Julianna, thank you," she called after him. Eyebrows raised, she turned back toward the living room.

Beth-Ann started to chuckle, then burst into outright laughter. "Is that kid of yours ten or a hundred and ten? He is totally aware of how to get around you. He's no one's dummy."

"Don't I know it!" Cindy perched on the arm of the couch, her legs crossed. One pink-tipped foot, clad in a strappy black sandal, swung in time to the music that played in the background. "That kid is way smarter than I am."

Cindy crossed her arms over her chest and stared at her. Beth-Ann knew what was coming and part of her was sorry she'd mentioned it. At the same time, she really needed to talk about it, if only to get another woman's take on the situation.

"So what's got you scared?"

Yep, right on the mark. "This whole situation with Riley," she said with a sigh.

"Have you enjoyed yourself?"

"Yes, but I like him coming over."

With a loud guffaw, Cindy slid off the arm of the couch and plopped down beside Beth-Ann. "Girl, you're supposed to like it. Why spend time with him if you aren't having fun? He's one of the sexiest men I've seen in a long time. Bed-time must be fantastic."

"Cindy, get your mind out of the gutter. But you're right, he is sexy and that's the funny part."

"What is?" Cindy frowned. "The fact that he turns you on? Or the fact that you have sex on tap at the moment?"

"That's just it." Beth-Ann stood and paced across the room as she tried to sort out the jumbled thoughts whizzing through her brain. "I thought it was all about having an affair. Hot spicy sex and a lot of fun. But these last few days, we haven't done it at all. Do you think he no longer wants me?"

"He still comes over, doesn't he?" Cindy raised her eyebrows. "Did he say anything?"

"Riley isn't into wham-bam-thank-you-ma'am. He said if he hasn't got time to make it special for a woman, he won't get into the 'quickie' thing."

"So what on earth do you do? Is that boy dead below the waist?"

The comment made Beth-Ann grin. No way was Riley dead. "He comes home straight after work, has a shower and helps me get dinner. After we eat, we just cuddle up on the couch and talk. Oh, and neck a lot. The man has no problems down below, let me assure you."

"So he likes being with you. Where's the problem? A relationship should be more than just sex."

"That *is* the problem." She had worried this subject to death over the last few days. She loved the fact Riley came over every day and that was the crux of the matter. She loved it too much and had begun to depend on his companionship, even if it was spiced with growing sexual tension.

"We have dinner and watch television like an old married couple. That's what scares me. It's like we jumped a stage in the middle and went right to the happy family stage. I don't want this to become a habit."

Cindy flicked a glance at her watch, stood up and straightened her top over her taupe trousers. "Girlfriend, you worry too much. I know you love the guy, but has he said anything to you?"

She shook her head.

"So don't twist yourself into knots analyzing it. Go with the flow and see where it leads. It's not like you have to commit to marriage or anything. I've known relationships like this to go on for years, each a part of the whole, but each partner remaining independent. That way you retain control of the situation."

She walked to the back door and called her children before turning back to Beth-Ann. "Don't worry so much. Enjoy his company and see where it goes. Hey, he could decide he's had enough in another week or two."

A shard of ice slithered through Beth-Ann's veins at the idea of Riley calling it quits. The thought of not seeing him again hit her right in the chest. A burst of pain filled her entire body. Oh, boy, she was in deep trouble.

Before she could say anything else, the children raced in the back door, all noise and enthusiasm.

"Beth-Ann, are we gonna bake cookies tonight?" Julianna asked with a slight lisp.

"No," replied Cindy, "you are both going to be good children and mind what Beth-Ann tells you. Understand, Peter?" She turned to her friend. "You sure Riley won't mind this?"

"What won't Riley mind?" a deep voice said.

Riley poked his head around the back door and scared the life out of Beth-Ann. She hadn't expected him for at least another hour. Her heart rate accelerated and a grin lit her face. Thank God he hadn't come a few minutes earlier. It was one thing to discuss him with Cindy, but she didn't want him to know how hung up she was on this whole relationship.

"Sorry I'm early, but I'm going to have to get to the site by nine tonight. Mel's baby-sitting so his daughter can go to Parent-Teacher interviews."

He stepped through the back door and, moving to Beth-Ann's side, leaned down to drop a quick kiss on her mouth. Curving an arm about her shoulders, he smiled at the other woman. "Hi, Cindy, how's it going?"

Beth-Ann took one look at Cindy and started to laugh. She snuggled close to Riley's chest and buried her head to stifle her chuckles.

"Okay," Riley said. "Do I walk out and come in again? Because I think I missed something."

"Guess what we're doing tonight?"

As he waggled his eyebrows and a lascivious grin spread across his face, she raised her head and pursed her lips to contain the laughter.

"Nuh-uh, not that," she crowed, although a spurt of disappointment swept through her. Getting down and dirty with Riley was top on her list of to-do things. She'd missed the intimacy of making love over the last few days.

"We're baby-sitting Peter and Julianna tonight so Cindy can go to Parent-Teacher interviews. And that means an early dinner to fit in with the kids."

Riley frowned. "What is it with these schools? Do they all have their interviews at the same time?"

"Are you sure you don't mind, Riley?" Cindy said. "I could take them with me."

"Nah, I'm just joking around. I don't mind at all. In fact, that Peter of yours could teach me a thing or two if his comments from the other day are anything to go by."

Cindy gasped. "Oh, no, what'd he say? I know he's picking some shocking things up from school." She grimaced. "I think part of it comes from not having a dad in the house."

"It's not a problem," Beth-Ann interrupted. "I dealt with it and Peter knows not to break his word to me, don't you, young man?" She cast a flinty gaze at the ten year old who was about to give a surreptitious tug on his sister's ponytail.

Riley reached around her, snagged a lock of Peter's hair and gave it a slight jerk. He didn't say anything. He didn't need to. Peter released his hold on his sister and stared up at the male authority figure in front of him.

Beth-Ann covered her mouth with her hand so Peter wouldn't see her smile. She couldn't believe how easy that had been for Riley. He'd sized up the situation at a glance and promptly dealt with it. *And* without a fight.

He would make a good father. Startling images of tiny versions of Riley sprang into her mind. For a moment, she felt an unaccountable ache deep inside her womb, as if something were missing. Like a baby of her own. Hers and Riley's.

She banished the thought, along with the pictures, and tried to rid her imagination of the image of Riley's child cuddled in her arms. She was so not going there. Kids meant permanency, and Riley wasn't the happy-ever-after type. Neither was she. Darn it, why was it so hard to remember that?

"I'll just go and refresh my lipstick. Then I better get a move on," Cindy said and disappeared up the hallway to the bathroom.

Beth-Ann was glad of the diversion. She gathered the children up and settled them in front of the television with a cartoon video. Riley joined her in the kitchen where she was halfway through dinner preparations.

"Hope you like spaghetti bolognaise. It's the kids' favorite." All of a sudden she felt nervous, as if her earlier thoughts regarding having Riley's child were painted on her face. "Um, you want to stir the sauce while I put the water on to boil?"

"Okay, I'm ready to go. I shouldn't be longer than a couple of hours tops." Cindy leaned over the kitchen bench. "Wanna walk me out, Beth-Ann?"

Hmm, now why does Cindy need an escort off the premises? Beth-Ann shrugged. It was obvious Cindy had something to say and didn't want Riley to hear. She dried off her hands on a paper towel and tossed it onto the bench. "Be right back," she said as she followed Cindy out the back door.

She waited until they were on the driveway beside Cindy's car. "What's the problem?"

"Ah, not certain if I should say this." Cindy hesitated, chewing on her bottom lip for a moment.

"May as well spit it out now you've started. I mean, how bad can it be?"

Cindy propped her arms on the top of the open car door. "You were scared about the whole business of Riley coming over for dinner et cetera and feeling like an old married couple, right?"

She nodded, not certain where Cindy was going with this.

"I couldn't help but notice Riley's shaving gear in the bathroom and the pile of washed and ironed clothes on the linen basket."

"So?" Beth-Ann shrugged. "He comes over straight after a hard day on the building site. Just because he's the boss doesn't mean to say he doesn't get his hands dirty. He brought fresh clothes the first night so he could shower before he went back for his security patrol with Mel. I wash the dirty ones so there's a fresh change for the next day. I don't see it as a problem."

"All I wanted to say is that you're both acting like an old married couple already. He comes *home* from work, gives you a kiss and starts on the dinner. He's moved some of his clothes over. And don't think I didn't see that stack of blueprints for some building or other on the coffee table. So now he's bringing his work home?"

Cindy slid into the front seat of the car and slammed the door. "You're worried about the whole independence thingy? Well, from where I'm standing, you're halfway to being committed already."

"No way." Beth-Ann shook her head so hard the curls bounced across her forehead. She struggled to breathe. She suddenly felt as if her lungs had deflated. She shoved a hard fist between her breasts and dragged in a harsh scoop of fresh oxygen as a panic attack threatened.

"Careful, girlfriend," Cindy warned, her voice raised as she turned the key in the ignition and the engine roared to life. "You know what the next step is, don't you?"

"What?" Beth-Ann's voice was a thin thread of sound as she mentally reviewed her relationship with Riley over the last few days.

"He'll want to move in. After all, he's already started, made himself comfortable. Bet he even props his feet up on the coffee table. That's a sure sign. First comes commitment and then comes control, if you're not careful, that is. Forewarned is forearmed."

Beth-Ann watched Cindy maneuver the vehicle out of the driveway. Her heart belted out a loud tattoo in her chest. She opened her mouth and gasped like a stranded fish. Visions of her father's treatment of her mother rose in her mind.

His utter lack of tender feelings toward her mom. The control freak at work. His demands that he be first in his daughter's life, as well as his wife's. And after her mother had spent the day with polishing cloth in hand, a frenzied dervish who scrubbed all the timber in sight, including the coffee table, her father would come home, plop down in front of the television, beer bottle in hand, and his dirty work boots propped on the polished surface of the coffee table.

It hit her, hard and fast, dragged an agonized moan from her open mouth and drove the breath from her lungs again.

Riley propped his feet—okay, minus the work boots—up on the coffee table as if he had a perfect right to do so. *And* he had her running about like a perfect idiot as she made him coffee, cooked his meals and washed his clothes. All right, let's be honest here. He didn't ask her to do it. She waited on him because she enjoyed it. It made her feel needed. As if... As if...

Heaven help her, she couldn't even finish the thought.

She stumbled slightly as she turned toward the house. She had a decision to make and she needed to do it as soon as possible. But one thing worried her.

Was she already in too deep to extricate herself? Because there was one thing she was honest enough to admit, if only to herself, and it scared her witless.

She needed Riley Osborne.

Chapter Twelve

"This is not going to work, darn it."

Beth-Ann folded her arms across her chest and paced about the living room. It had only been forty-eight hours since they'd looked after the children for Cindy. She cringed when she thought of that night. After Cindy's revelation about how at home Riley had made himself, she'd freaked. She'd been withdrawn for the rest of the night, not that Riley had said anything, although she'd caught the occasional puzzled look on his face.

What made it worse was that he was perfect with the kids. He knew exactly how to reach them. Peter, in particular, benefited from having a man take an interest in his life. He saw his dad every second Sunday, but from all accounts, it wasn't enough.

"I thought if I tried to distance myself from Riley, I could get things into better perspective, but he fills my thoughts every moment of the day," she whispered.

She'd called him on his cell phone yesterday and told him she had things to do and he couldn't come over after work. The disappointed timbre in his voice had almost been her undoing. Another few minutes on the phone and she'd have begged him to come see her.

"Aaagh, why do I do this to myself?" Beth-Ann cast another glance at the wall-mounted clock in the living room. Riley would have been at the site for three hours now. She wondered how it was going. Had there been more sabotage?

The thought of Riley in danger did strange things to her equilibrium. If something happened to him, it would shatter her. She might never see him again.

A cold lump developed in the pit of her stomach. Tears filled her eyes and she had to blink to clear her vision. She swallowed down the nausea that filled her throat. Twenty-four hours away from Riley and she was a basket case.

What if some sick creep was stalking him right at this moment? She had a mental picture of the villain lying in wait for Riley, ready to bash him over the head as he walked by. Her mind went into overdrive and provided her with a whole range of equally traumatic scenarios.

Riley, beaten to a pulp. Covered in blood as his life ebbed away. Arson, with rapacious flames licking at his skin with unimaginable pain.

"Stop it, Beth-Ann. You're being stupid," she warned herself.

She reined in her imagination, but the sense of fear remained. If something happened to Riley, she would be devastated. She'd have lost the most important person in her life and she hadn't even told him she loved him.

With a shake of her head, she tried to think rationally. She flicked a glance around the pristine neatness of the living room in an effort to distract herself. She'd polished the house to within an inch of its life. What didn't move had been brushed, washed, scrubbed and sorted. It had been the only way to keep her thoughts off Riley. Now there was nothing left to do. The heavens preserve her, she'd turned into a replica of her mom.

Her thoughts turned back to her childhood. Mom always said she liked doing things for her husband, that is was part of the loving. Given how much she'd enjoyed cooking for Riley the last few days, maybe there was something to it.

Do you love Riley, truly love him?

"Oh, yeah."

Miss him when he's not around?

"More than I thought possible." She glanced over to the back door. "I miss his work boots parked by the door. Heck, I even miss his washing. I like seeing his jocks and jeans on the clothesline with my panties and tee shirts. I am one sick puppy."

The internal voice clamored for attention. She let it have its way.

What are you going to do about it, because if you walk away from this, it could be the worst mistake of your life?

The ball was in her court. After the cold reception she'd given Riley when he'd called today, he might never contact her again. It was up to her to mend the fences. He was smart enough to know she'd tried to distance herself from their relationship. Hell, he may well have had enough of her and be ready to move on to the next woman.

She could sit here and drive herself crazy with wanting him. Or she could get off her butt and go find out if he still wanted her. As far as commitment went, she didn't have a problem with being exclusive just as long as Riley didn't mention the marriage word. Just because she loved him didn't mean he had to move in and take over.

Cindy was right. He'd made himself at home here, but she liked it, liked that he felt comfortable enough to do so. It didn't have to go any further. He had his place of residence and she'd retain hers. A simple solution and one she wasn't about to forgo. Because, like it or not, she loved Riley Osborne and couldn't imagine life without him.

Go do something about it.

Darn, that persistent little voice inside her head was at it again, but this time she listened and took its advice. Because it suddenly seemed important that she tell Riley she loved him. Right now. Tonight!

Within minutes, she'd showered and towel-dried her hair until it curled about her face. It didn't take long to slip into panties and a brief cotton shift dress. Flat sandals and she was ready.

She phoned for a cab and used a few precious seconds to make up a picnic basket, remembering an earlier promise she'd made to Mel. When she heard the toot of the cab's horn at the front of her house, she grabbed her purse and the basket, and made for the front door. On an afterthought, she backtracked and snagged one of the little foil packets out of the fruit bowl on the coffee table.

Her heart raced and she had to struggle to catch her breath when she slammed the back door of the vehicle and gave the driver the address for the site. Doubts filled her. Was she doing the right thing? Riley was working. She should have waited until tomorrow and called him to come over to discuss this. But if she did that, the fear of commitment would overwhelm her again and she'd back down. Then where would she be? Without Riley, that's where.

With eyes closed tight, she leaned back on the plastic-covered seat of the cab and breathed deep, trying to center herself. In less time than she thought possible, she felt the vehicle slow.

"We're here, luv. This do you?"

She blinked. The driver slowly drew the vehicle to a halt in front of the security booth at the construction site. Mel emerged from the building and stood like a sentinel, a frown on his face as he watched her open the back door. She slid some money through the front window to the driver and without waiting for her change, clutched the picnic basket and her purse to her chest and made her way over to the guard.

"Hello, little lady, what are you doing here at this time of evening? It's almost midnight." Mel, his portly belly restrained by a thick leather belt from which hung a pistol holster, approached her, his brow furrowed in concern. "You shouldn't be out on the streets at night on your own. Too dangerous, that's what I tell my girls."

"Hi, Mel." Beth-Ann glanced at the sidearm. "Is there any need for that?" She pointed to his belt. "Riley's not in danger, is he?" Fear for Riley's safety rose up again to cloud her mind. Her stomach churned and the taste of bile filled her mouth.

Mel patted the gun at his side. "Nah, but the police licensed us to carry firearms just in case. It's been as quiet as a cemetery here the last few nights. Hard for a man to stay awake when there's nothing to do."

He guided her into the security booth. "You still haven't explained what you're doing here. Is Riley expecting you?"

Now that she was here, Beth-Anne wondered at her sanity. An attack of nerves hit her and she tightened her trembling hand around the handle of the picnic basket. Her purse slipped from her grip and hit the floor with a thud. The clasp broke open and the contents sprayed out. Before she could do anything, Mel bent with a grunt and gathered up the bits and pieces all women found it necessary to carry around with them.

"T-t-thanks, Mel," she stuttered as he passed it to her. As he bent and retrieved the final object and handed it to her with a grin, a wave of heat washed over her and she didn't need a mirror to know her face was bright red.

A tiny, silver-foil packet.

The type you don't share with anyone but your partner.

How mortifying. Beth-Ann tried to retrieve the situation. She held out the cane basket. "Um, I didn't forget my promise, although I made it up in a rush. Hope you like strawberries."

Mel took the offering. His eyes twinkled as he grinned at her. "My wife loves strawberries. Maybe I'll take some home after my shift."

He placed the basket on the bench behind him. "I assume you want to see Riley. He's been like a bear with a sore head for the last day or so. I guess you're responsible, hmm?"

She grimaced. "Yeah, I think so. Which is why I need to see him. I know I shouldn't be here, but I really need to talk to him. Is that possible?"

Breath held, she waited for his reply. She couldn't, she simply couldn't, go home now, not after having come this far.

Mel stared at her for a moment. "You know I'm not supposed to let anyone in, don't you?"

Not game to trust her voice in case she begged, she nodded.

"Let me contact Riley and we'll see."

He grabbed a radio off the bench and thumbed the button on the top. As a mixture of static and high-pitched squawks filled the little office, Beth-Ann winced. Mel adjusted the knob and lifted it to his mouth.

"You there, Riley?"

As she waited to hear Riley's voice, butterflies raced through her stomach. She dragged in a deep breath and held it. Gracious, at this rate she'd die of asphyxiation before the night was over. With a conscious effort, she exhaled.

"Riley here, Mel. You got a problem down there at the gate?"

Tension made his voice sound terse. It grated on her ears and once again, she doubted the wisdom of her actions.

"No, no problems, but you could have one," Mel said with a sly wink at Beth-Ann. "I've got a visitor for you."

There was another bout of static before Riley's voice came over loud and clear.

"At this time of night? You been drinking, old man?"

His tone was more relaxed now. Beth-Ann breathed a sigh of relief and the panic subsided. Riley was okay. First hurdle over. Now for the rest.

"A little slip of a thing, red curls, sassy attitude. Recognize her?" Mel's mouth spread in a grin as he teased his boss.

"Beth-Ann? Beth-Ann's here?"

Mel turned to her, the smile still in evidence. "You happen to be Beth-Ann?" He extended the radio to her, gave her the thumbs-up sign and sauntered out the door of the security booth.

She was glad of the privacy. If Riley rejected her advances, she'd prefer to suffer the embarrassment on her own, not with the fatherly Mel an ever-watchful eye to her downfall.

"Riley, it's me."

"Darlin', what on earth are you doing down here at this time of night?"

The radio enhanced the sexy tone of his voice and started the blood pounding through her veins. A shiver trickled down her spine at his endearment. "I need to talk to you. Can I come on the site?"

"It can't wait until tomorrow?"

She shook her head before she remembered he couldn't see her. "I'd rather do it tonight."

Her heart took a downward tumble when there was utter silence from the radio. With another squawk, Riley's voice floated over her again.

"All right, there hasn't been any problems for quite a few days now so I guess it's okay. Have Mel sign you in and I'll meet you at the front entrance to the building."

He clicked off the radio and silence filled the room. Beth-Ann depressed the switch on the top and placed the walkie-talkie on the bench. Despite it being summer, a cool breeze had sprung up by the time she stepped from the security booth. She shivered and her nipples tightened into hard little points. She crossed her arms over her chest as Mel approached her.

"How'd you go?"

"He said to go to the main entrance and he'll meet me there." She couldn't help herself. A smile surfaced and the heat of another blush swept over her face.

Mel reached into the office, grabbed a book from the bench and flipped the pages over. He handed it to her along with a pen. "Put your name down there and I'll switch on the spotlights so that you don't fall and hurt yourself on all the building materials the workers leave around. I should make you wear a hard hat, but I'll let you go this time, seeing as how the site's closed down for the night."

Beth-Ann scrawled her signature and handed back the logbook. As Mel walked her to the gate, her stomach churned. She had a sudden feeling this would prove to be the most important night of her life.

Mel gave her a brief hug before he ushered her through the entrance. "Whatever it is, if you both love each other, you'll find a way to make it happen." He nodded to where Riley stood outlined by the floodlights against the front of the partially completed building.

"Thanks, Mel." She went on tiptoes and dropped a quick kiss on his weathered cheek. "You're my hero."

"Aw, get on with you, girlie. That's what my daughters say when they want something." He grinned. "Now go ease the bad mood of that hero over there."

⚒ ⚒ ⚒

Riley watched her walk across the cluttered building yard. His mouth quirked. He could see clear through her dress where the powerful floodlights backlit the fabric. The blood rushed south and his cock swelled as he focused on the outline of her muscled thighs. She might be tiny, but what she had she kept in shape. He did like a woman with muscles in all the right places.

It crossed his mind that she was here to break up with him, to sever the intimate relationship they'd developed. He grimaced. Not that it had been very intimate the last time he'd seen her. Two kids running around kind of throws a spanner in the works. Bit hard to get it on with a ten year old on the back of the couch.

Not that he minded the kids being there. He'd never spent much time with children, never thought about them, truth be told, but it surprised him how much he'd enjoyed himself. Wouldn't mind a rug rat or two, but not yet. Maybe sometime in the future. And for some reason, there was only one possible person he could see as the mother of his munchkins, and at the moment, she was striding across the site as if she were going to war.

Again, he wondered why she was here, and whether it had anything to do with the reason she hadn't been available last night. *And* the coolness he'd felt from her on the night they'd looked after Peter and Julianna. Like someone had coated her with ice. In the end, having two kids there didn't matter a damn. She hadn't sent out the right signals anyway.

He couldn't believe how much he'd missed her. He'd turned into a grouch. Boy, he had it bad. Not as bad as his dad had predicted, but close enough. The big "L" word, the one he'd avoided since that last big showdown with his ex-fiancée. Now the question was whether or not to admit it to her.

"Riley."

She drew to a halt and looked up at him and he felt like he was ten feet tall, because if he didn't miss his guess, what was reflected in her eyes was the same emotion he suffered from.

Love.

The stuff that was supposed to make the world go round. He almost groaned at the clichéd load of bullshit that swept through his mind. Who the hell cared what it did for the rest of the world? Right now it sure made the blood pump through *his* veins.

With his hand extended, he stepped forward a pace. She ignored the gesture and moved right into his arms. He closed his eyes and gathered her close. *Thank God*, he thought in silent prayer. If she'd come to break up, this sure wasn't the way to do it.

His hand trembled as he grabbed the radio from his belt and depressed the on-off button. When he heard Mel's voice among the static, he said, "You can turn the lights off now. I'll radio through if we need them again."

Without giving Mel time to answer, he cut the connection, and radio still in hand, moved Beth-Ann back so he could see her face. "You okay?"

"I am now. I missed you. I just didn't realize how much until I saw you tonight."

Her lips trembled and she blinked as if she was struggling against tears. Riley could have sworn his heart shredded as he watched her. A flash of fear painted her features just moments before the lights went out and it was a no-brainer to work out why. Her problems with commitment, if he didn't miss his guess.

"Here, you take this," he said and handed her the radio. He took her hand, moved over to the entrance and bent down to grab the flashlight he'd left there when he'd come out to wait for Beth-Ann.

"Riley, I want—"

"Let's go inside and we can talk, okay?"

He led her through the bottom floor of the building until he came to the last apartment. This one was almost finished except for the painting. He intended to furnish it and set it up as a showroom so the client could make a start on the sale of the rest of the apartments.

Heaped in one corner of what would be the main living area was a mound of painters' canvas drop-cloths. He guided Beth-Ann over and indicated to her to sit. She lowered herself down and curled her legs up under her. His mouth tilted in a smile. It seemed to be her favorite position. He placed the flashlight to one side so the beam of light illuminated the pile of canvas.

"Comfortable?" he asked as he squatted on his haunches in front of her.

Beth-Ann nodded and tried to find her voice. Her heart beat so loud she was sure he could hear it. She dragged in a deep breath and opened her mouth to speak, but he held his hand up so she waited. "*Coward,*" screamed the little voice inside her head. Anything to delay the moment when she must tell him how she felt.

"You didn't come to tell me to get my sorry ass out of your life, did you?" he said with a lift of his eyebrows.

She shook her head with a vigorous movement, the verbal denial trapped inside.

"And you weren't busy last night. You were scared, right?"

A nod of the head. It was all she was capable of. She loved him all the more for making this easy for her.

"You don't hate me?"

Anything but. Beth-Ann shook her head again and bit her lip.

"Cindy said something that caused you to freak out. Made those old fears of commitment and lack of control raise their ugly heads, true?"

Once again, she nodded.

"Beth-Ann, you keep up all that nodding and shaking and I'll start to think you're one of those little dogs the teenagers stick on the back dash of their cars. You know, the ones that nod their heads whenever the vehicle moves." He gave a soft chuckle at the wide-eyed look on her face. "Say something already."

"I was so afraid something would happen to you and I hadn't told you that I loved you." As soon as the words left her mouth, she gasped. She hadn't meant to burst out with it like that. She closed her eyes, only to snap them open again when he leaned forward and dropped a light kiss on her lips.

"Well, I'm sure glad we got that out of the way because I love you, too."

Now the tears did come. They welled up and overflowed to trickle down her face. Then she started to laugh at herself. Here she was, the happiest she could remember being and all she could do was cry.

"You're not going to get hysterical on me, are you?"

Riley lifted his hand and wiped the dampness from her face with his thumb. His gentleness almost caused another outpouring. She started to shake her head again, then grabbed him by the shoulders and pulled. Perched on the balls of his feet as he was, the slightest tug and he overbalanced.

He thrust his hands down to take his weight, but Beth-Ann was ready for him. She wrapped her arms about his waist and hugged him to her, spreading her legs to make a cradle for him between her thighs. A heartfelt sigh slipped from her lips as he lowered his body until his rigid muscles brushed her breasts.

That wasn't the only thing that was rigid. Thank God for testosterone.

"Hi, Riley. I'm Beth-Ann and I love you," she whispered. Now she'd said it once, she couldn't believe how easy it was.

"Hi yourself." He grinned. "I love you, too. And that's what all this fuss was about, wasn't it?"

Beth-Ann inserted her hands between them and started to slip the buttons of his shirt undone. She felt starved for the feel of his hot body against her own. All the while she kept her gaze fixed on his.

"I freaked. All those old fears rushed in and took over. It's this whole issue with always having to be in control of my own life."

He wiggled his hips a bit closer, grinding his hard erection against the sensitive flesh between her thighs. When she moaned, he leaned down and captured the sound with his mouth. She opened her mouth, felt the sweep of his tongue and reciprocated in kind. Damn but he tasted good.

When he pulled back, she tugged his shirt from the waistband of his jeans and slid her hands across the contours of his back, her palms flattened to capture his heat.

"How do you feel now?"

It required an effort to concentrate on his question. All she could think of was the feel of his hot flesh. She shivered as he pressed his hips closer. His rigid cock nestled against her pussy. Her clit throbbed in anticipation of things to come.

"Loving you meant I had to step outside my comfort zone," she whispered as she struggled to keep her hips still. "But now I'm hooked and you're just going to have to deal with it. Think you can handle it?"

"You bet your boots I can. We'll deal with the control issue as it pops up. I'll try not to crowd you. This is a new thing for me, too. We'll just continue as we've been doing and see where it goes. Okay?"

She started to nod, then caught herself at his grin.

"Any other problems you want I should address?" he said with a lift of one eyebrow.

"Just one question." She reached down beside her and felt for her purse. Clicking it open, she rummaged around inside until she heard the crinkle of foil paper.

"Hmm?" he murmured as he lowered his head and nibbled along her jaw.

"When do we get to fool around?" She waved the silver-wrapped prophylactic in his face, a grin from ear to ear.

He snagged it in his teeth and dropped it on her chest.

"A lady after my own heart."

"You'd better believe it," she said and placed her palm over the aforementioned part of his anatomy.

Chapter Thirteen

Beth-Ann lifted her head, ran the tip of her tongue along the seam of his lips and dropped a light kiss on the corner of his mouth. She felt the shiver that raced through him, and under the palm of her hand, the thump of his heart. His face was all seriousness, his gaze fixed on hers. Without conscious thought, she tilted her hips. When he groaned, she couldn't help but grin.

"Do I get to be on top this time?"

Riley stared at her for a moment, then started to chuckle. He lowered his head to rest in the curve of her shoulder. His body shook with laughter. "Darlin', you can have anything you like."

"Promises, promises," she retorted and angled her head back when he nibbled at the column of her neck. Fire burst to life inside her. When he swirled his tongue around the furled edge of her ear, a delicious sensation feathered through her.

With one simple movement of his mouth, he had reduced her to a mindless mass of emotion. All she could do was feel. As he moved down and brushed at the hardened peak of her breast, her back arched and she whimpered.

"Riley," she whispered in entreaty.

"I'm right here," he said as he rubbed his mouth back and forth.

Heat seeped through the thin cotton and her nipples hardened even more. A moan slipped from her lips when he took the crest, dress and all, into the warmth of his mouth and suckled. Beth-Ann lifted her shoulders off the pile of drop-cloths, clasped his head to her and tried to catch her breath.

It was useless. All she could do was hang on for the ride until the gathering tension in her body burst free and she was her own person again. She groaned in disappointment when he pulled away, only to sigh with renewed satisfaction when he moved across and lavished the same attention on her other breast.

"Hey, Riley," she murmured.

He lifted his head a fraction, his eyes glazed as he stared at the wet patch on her dress. "Don't interrupt a guy when he's feeding," he quipped.

Beth-Ann wanted to laugh. Riley had a way of lightening the tension before he'd allow it to build again until she couldn't stand it. Making love with this man wasn't just a bout of physical gymnastics designed to satisfy a biological urge. It was funny, and sweet, and an all-consuming fire that swept her along until she had no choice but to give in and experience the ultimate. In the end, he may well make her cry, but he also made her laugh and his humor was part of what she loved about him.

She pushed at his shoulders before he could lower his head again. "Don't be so greedy. No one else is going to swipe your...food before you get to it."

"No one will get a chance," he growled in a deep voice.

"Stand up a moment." She pushed on his shoulders again, trying to scoot out from beneath him.

"Huh?"

A chuckle escaped at the bemused look on his face. "Those jeans of yours look like they're painted on. I love to check out the shape of your ass, but right now I'd rather see you out of them."

"Your wish is my command."

He moved back until he was on his haunches. Pushing himself to his feet, his hand went immediately to his belt buckle. Beth-Ann almost laughed at the eagerness he showed, but his fingers were all thumbs as he fumbled with the stiff leather about his hips.

"Why don't you let me do it?" She grinned at him. "Another first for me. Undressing a man instead of the other way around."

Riley wasn't about to look a gift horse in the mouth. There was something erotic about being undressed by a woman. As Beth-Ann balanced herself on her knees in front of him, he dropped his hands and let her at it.

He sucked in a ragged breath as she lifted her hands as far as she could and slid her palms down his chest. When she came to his recalcitrant belt, brand new and still stiff, she ran the tip of her finger across his belly. The muscles contracted in response, the small involuntary action enough to make her smile. Then she leaned forward and pressed a hot kiss right above the buckle.

"Hurry up, I'm dying here," he groaned.

"Not before I've had my way with you," she retorted as she deftly undid the belt and slid it an inch at a time out of the belt loops.

The light played across her face, highlighting the delicate planes of her cheekbones and glinting off the fiery red curls. She was so damn beautiful she made his heart ache. He hadn't planned on getting this serious about any woman, but with Beth-Ann, it was all new. He fell a little in love with all the women he courted, or at least the idea of love. But not once since Denise had he wanted it to be anything more than time spent in the pursuit of mutual pleasure.

Ah, but Beth-Ann. She was different.

His hips jerked as she undid the snap of his jeans and lowered the zip. Not many women he'd trust to unzip him when he had a raging boner. It was too easy to damage the equipment, so to speak.

He stopped her as she started to slide his jeans down. "Hey, let me get my boots off first. Somehow it seems tacky to make love with your footwear on." Bending over, he grabbed the first boot and wrestled it off, almost ending up on his ass on the floor. With a few more undignified hops to stay upright, he managed to remove the second one.

The moment he was free of them, Beth-Ann pulled him back to stand in front of her. He wasn't about to voice any objections. When she slipped her hands inside the back of his jeans and inserted them under his jocks to cover his butt, he started to shake. He expected her to slide them down, but she lowered her head to press her cheek against his throbbing cock.

Unable to help himself, he arched his hips forward in reaction.

She grinned up at him. "Down, boy, we have all night."

Then she surprised the hell out of him when she suddenly whipped both jeans and jocks down his body. Eager now, he lifted his feet at her urging and she pulled the denim from him. At the same time, he shrugged the shirt from his shoulders, rolled it into a bundle and tossed it across the room.

"Your turn now," he whispered past the lump in his throat.

Beth-Ann couldn't keep her eyes off the nest of curls at the base of his belly and the thick cock that jutted out from his body. She sucked on her finger, then trailed the wet tip down his length. Riley's hands clutched at her hair, pulling her closer.

"Not fair, Beth-Ann," he groaned.

"What isn't?" She repeated the action, this time swirling the dampness over the head, wiping up the tiny drop of fluid on the top. Then she sucked her finger again, closing her eyes briefly at the taste of him.

"I'm standing here with not a stitch on and you're fully dressed. What's wrong with this picture?" Riley said, his voice a husky drawl.

With a grin, Beth-Ann kicked her sandals off and whipped the shift dress over her head. Without standing, she lifted her bottom and slid her red silk panties to her knees. With a definite twinkle in his eyes, Riley bent down and dragged them the rest of the way, flinging them aside. She started to giggle as she reached for him and pulled him down.

"What?" He shook his head in bemusement.

"Heaven help us if anyone comes in here. Our clothes are spread from one side of the room to the other." She frowned as he lifted her arm and twisted to look at her side.

"No one will come. And I've heard about being prepared, but this is ridiculous."

She opened her eyes wide. "You've lost me. What are you going on about?"

A shiver caught her unawares as he ran his hand along the outer curve of her breast. Using two fingers, he pulled something away from her body. She caught a flash of silver as he held it up.

"You had the condom packet stuck to the side of your boob."

She laughed. "That's because you make my temperature rise so much my body is covered in perspiration." Oh, it was good to joke with Riley, even in the midst of the most intimate act a man and woman could share.

"Hot stuff, eh?"

He didn't wait for an answer. He took her mouth in a soul-shattering kiss, driving the blood through her veins with a flash of fire. She met the thrust of his tongue with a deliberate parry and withdrawal, tempting him into play, the dance a weak imitation of the supreme surrender. And this was one surrender she didn't mind making.

While he skimmed his hands down her body and back up again to cup her breasts, Beth-Ann was on her own voyage of discovery. She trailed her fingers across his buttocks, before clasping him tight and pulling him in until she could feel the heat of his cock brush the aching place between her thighs. She arched her hips, desperate to take him deep. The breath gusted from her lips. A soft sob erupted from her throat as he pressed closer still.

She pushed up and tried to roll them onto their side, frustration growing when she found him too heavy. "Riley," she whispered against his lips.

He reared back a moment, his weight supported on one outstretched arm. Beth-Ann took the opportunity offered to her and tipped him over onto his back. She knew darn well he'd allowed her to do it. One look at the grin on his face said it all.

"Thought you'd forgotten you wanted to be on top," he said on a whisper.

With an agile twist, she lifted over him, one knee braced on either side of his hips. "Not likely. I want to experience what it's like to call the shots. You get to lay there and do nothing, okay?"

She frowned and looked around. "Where's the condom."

Riley started to chuckle. "Stuck to your chest again. I've heard of man magnets, but condom—"

"Enough already," Beth-Ann interrupted with a smile. She peeled the little package from between her breasts and tore it open. Then she slid back down Riley's thighs and took him in her hand. She marveled anew at his tensile strength, overlaid with a slick softness that made her fingertips tingle.

Her hand wrapped around the heat of him, she grinned down at him. "Ever wondered if it would break if a woman got too violent?"

He burst out laughing as if she'd said the funniest thing in the world. His eyes crinkled and his mouth curved as he tried to catch his breath. Oh, she did like a man who could enjoy a bit of silliness.

"There's no bone in there so how could it break," he managed between chuckles.

"So why is it called a boner?" While he went off into another paroxysm of hilarity, she positioned the condom and rolled it down over his thick hardness. Lifting up, she settled over him, taking him into her yielding flesh.

The laughter disappeared from his face. "Hey, wait, it's—"

"Too late," she whispered as she took him as deep as she could. Her body stretched to accommodate him and a gasp slid from her mouth as she felt the full length of him. "Oh, my," she whispered as she stared at him, caught in the almost feral glitter of his dark eyes.

She couldn't believe how much deeper he was this way. She liked being able to see his face as she lifted herself up slightly before sliding down again, one careful inch at a time, her bottom lip caught between her teeth as he filled her.

His hands came up and grasped her by the top of her thighs, his thumbs angled in to tangle in her pubic curls. His hips rose and fell in time with her jerky movements. She leaned forward and rested her hands on his chest, her weight braced, and the rhythm became easier. Smooth enough to twist a spiral of heat deep in her womb.

"You feel like fire," he whispered. "So hot." He parted her, searched for and found the hard little nub of her clit.

Sensation hit her. She cried out, unable to stop her frenzied movements as his hips angled to drive his rigid cock even deeper. She bit her lip on a sob and struggled to catch her breath. Tension coiled deep inside, spreading down to coalesce into a conflagration at the point where they joined.

A series of little spasms hit her. The explosion of her climax was imminent, ready to crash through her, when suddenly Riley curled shaky hands about her shoulders and rolled to his side. He withdrew with a rapid heave of his hips. Left her stranded with eyes wide and her breath frozen in her lungs.

In a daze, she curled onto her side, her legs pulled up to her chest. Riley stumbled away from the erotic nest among the paint drop-cloths, grabbed for his jeans and hopped about as he pulled them on. He zipped them up, but left the clip at the top undone.

Beth-Ann swallowed, tried to find her voice. What had gone wrong? One minute she was on the edge of another Riley-brand, cataclysmic orgasm. The next she was... Shit, she didn't know what she was. It was all she could do to acknowledge the gnawing tension that still clawed at her insides, the intense wave of disappointment that brought tears to her eyes.

Damn Riley Osborne. He had some serious questions to answer. If this was how he got his kicks... And, bloody hell, it was the second time!

She dragged a loose fold of paint-stained canvas up to cover her nakedness. Anger flashed through her. She pushed herself into a sitting position and opened her mouth to give him a good piece of her mind. There were nasty names for women who did this type of thing. Wonder what they called men?

Before she could speak, Riley squatted in front of her, grabbed her by the upper arms and dragged her close enough to press his lips to hers. When he drew back, he placed his mouth near her ear.

"There's someone else in the building. I heard a crash a moment ago," he whispered.

His voice was so quiet Beth-Ann had to struggle to make out his words. "I didn't hear anything." She took her cue from him and kept her voice lowered.

"Darlin', you were moaning so loud you wouldn't have heard a bomb go off." He placed one long finger over her lips before she could say anything else.

"You stay here and I'll go see who it is. Neither Mel nor Arthur would come over to this part of the building when they know I'm here with you. And you can bet your bottom dollar Mel told Arthur about your visit."

She reached up and lifted his hand away from her mouth, entwined her fingers with his. "You be careful, you hear? This could be that weirdo who was on the phone the other night."

"Probably just kids." He blew her a kiss before he stood up. "You keep the flashlight with you. I know the building well enough to negotiate it in the dark." Then he disappeared out the door of the apartment.

✼ ✼ ✼

Beth-Ann tried to track Riley's movements. After a few moments, she gave up. For such a big man he sure moved quietly, *and* in the dark.

Her body still hummed with unrelieved sexual tension. Her pussy was still wet. She rubbed her legs together and tried to banish the insistent throb between her thighs. Whoever it was on site had lousy timing. Talk about being left high and dry. Well, maybe not dry.

"Gross, Beth-Ann. Get your mind off your body. Riley could be in danger out there."

She dragged herself upright and pulled at the paint cloths until she found one that wasn't too large. Twisting it about her body like a sarong, she tucked the loose flap down between her breasts. It was scratchy against her skin, but it was better than being spread-eagled like a naked sacrifice. At least it gave her some measure of dignity.

For a moment, she thought about getting dressed. She shrugged and discarded the idea. Riley was probably right and it was nothing but kids. That being the case, he'd soon be back and they could take up where they'd left off.

Kicking the surplus canvas behind her so it trailed like a wedding dress, she shuffled across to the doorway and stared out. Once away from the pool of light cast by the flashlight, darkness pressed in on her. Suddenly, worry for Riley's safety filled her.

Fear gathered hold again. She wanted to go after him, but knew she couldn't. If it wasn't kids and the saboteur was on site, she would be more a hindrance than help. She pressed a hand to her middle as nausea churned in her gut. *Please let Riley be safe.*

When she turned to go back to the makeshift bed on the other side of the room, she heard a slight noise behind her. Nothing more than a shuffle, but ominous. She tried to spin around, but the bulky canvas twisted about her feet. Bending from the waist, she worked to free her legs and in that moment, a shadow detached itself from the darkness of the hallway and erupted into the room.

A clenched fist hit her in the back and she went over. Her knees cracked on the hard surface of the bare concrete. Tears filled her eyes, but she blinked them away. Her breathing accelerated along with her heartbeat. Her mouth dried and she struggled to swallow.

On hands and knees, the bulk of the canvas flipped over her arm and clutched to her side, she scrambled away from the menacing figure behind her. When she reached the edge of the pool of light, she stopped and took a deep breath, focused, and let it rip.

"*Riley!*"

One name. The one person she knew she could rely upon to rescue her from the disastrous end to her night of passion.

"Shut up, missy. I don't want to hurt you."

The voice was gruff, that of an older man, and one she recognized. She shuffled back even further and pushed herself upright, wavering on shaky legs until she found her balance. Her knees stung like a bitch. The canvas loosened about her body and she dropped the excess and tightened it around her breasts.

"Jason?" she said in disbelief, her voice a raspy croak. She cleared her throat and tried again. "Jason, is that you?"

The figure edged forward until it stood on the edge of the circle of illumination. Beth-Ann backed away, as far from him as she could get and still remain within the light.

The painter looked like a derelict off the streets. His shirt was creased and dirty, buttoned in only two places. The shirttails hung over jeans that had seen better days, the knees torn and muddy. His hair flopped forward over his forehead and made the wild look in his eyes even more of a threat.

He was the total opposite of the man who'd painted her ceiling just a few days ago. That man had been the perfect gentleman, helpful and kind, thoughtful. More the fatherly type. The sort of person a girl could go to if she had a problem.

Now he was twitchy, his body in constant movement as he swayed from side to side. His eyes were blood-shot, his face creased in a look of hate. And she was sure she could smell alcohol.

Then she saw what he had in his hands and remembered the comments the caller had made that night at her place. In one hand, he clutched a bundle of dirty rags. It was what else he carried that made the blood run cold in her veins.

A beaten and twisted can with a distinctive brand name on the side. Small and square with a handle on top. The type that normally came filled with gas. Fuel. Petrol. Whatever you liked to call it, it would start a hell of a fire if ignited.

"Jason, what are you doing here?" She crept around the circle of light as he moved closer.

"He took it all," he screamed, his face twisted. Spittle sprayed from his mouth, dribbling down his chin. "He has to pay."

"What do you intend to do with that?" Beth-Ann indicated the can of gas.

As her heart skipped a beat, she pressed her hand to her chest. Perspiration broke out on her forehead and she raised her arm to wipe it away. Fear left a sour taste in her mouth, like day-old garlic. She swallowed convulsively and tried to squash the flutter of nerves that caught at her stomach in a fresh wave of nausea.

"He made her leave. And the kids, too." Jason burst into noisy sobs, lifting the back of his hand, dirty rags crushed in a tangled lump, to swipe at his nose. He dropped his gaze and stared at the contents of his hand as if he hadn't seen them before.

Beth-Ann took the opportunity to gather up the surplus canvas about her feet and try to move around the circle toward the door. If she could just get a little further, she could run hell for leather out into the hallway. Surely Riley had heard her scream and would be on his way back by now?

"Stay where you are," he screeched and dropped the bundle of rags.

The spit dried in Beth-Ann's mouth as he moved in front of her, his arm extended. She halted, breath held as she waited for his next move.

Horror clawed at her mind as he unscrewed the cap from the gas can, poured some of the contents over the bunch of rags on the floor and upended the rest down his front. It soaked his shirt, the excess gathering in a pool at his boots. One thin finger of fuel crept across the floor toward her feet like a living entity. Beth-Ann wanted to take flight, but fear kept her frozen in place, her gaze trained with morbid fascination on the streak of fuel.

Jason grunted and the noise drew her head up. He slipped his hand into his pocket and retrieved a cigarette lighter, held it in front of him, his finger ready to flick it into life.

Dear God, he was actually going to do it.

It was bad enough he was willing to die, but if he went any further with this lunacy, in all likelihood he would take her with him.

Think, Beth-Ann, think. Find something to distract him.

"You don't want to do this, Jason." She made her voice as soothing as she could. "What about your wife? She won't have you there to take her shopping any longer. She'll miss you."

"That's what this is all about," he screamed. "He took my wife."

Oh-oh, wrong thing to say.

He waved his hand about in front of him and Beth-Ann was afraid he'd carry through with his threat. She tried to reason with him.

"Are you talking about Riley?" She shook her head. "He isn't with your wife. He's with me and I'll bet your last dollar he's not the type to play around with married women."

"That's not what I mean. My wife would never play around with any other man."

She stepped up closer to him, not through any sense of false bravery, but because she figured she was doomed anyway if he ignited that fuel. First, she wanted to see if she could reach him. He'd seemed so sane, so nice, when he'd painted her ceiling.

A wash of alcoholic fumes hit her in the face as she moved up beside him and placed her hand on the arm that held the lighter. She coughed, then dragged in a shaky breath and tried to think of something to say.

"Why don't you tell me about it?"

One tottering step at a time, she guided him over to the mound of drop-cloths, away from the puddle of gas on the floor. She pressed him to sit, surprised when he obeyed. Anyone with a smidgeon of sense would turn and run right about now, but Beth-Ann felt sorry for the guy. Perhaps if she could get him to talk she could defuse the danger to Riley.

"I used to be foreman for Riley once. You didn't know that, did you?"

He didn't give her time to answer or even shake her head.

"I'm not just a painter. I'm a good builder, too. He said I was drinking on the job, that my work had become slipshod, so he demoted me."

She crouched on her knees in front of him, wincing as pain shafted through her. "What happened then?"

"There was less money coming in and things got hard at home. The wife and I fought about it when she wanted to buy things for the kids. And then she left me because there wasn't enough money." He started to cry. Big, fat drops that overflowed the red-rimmed eyes and rolled down the creases in his face.

Tears of sympathy filled Beth-Ann's eyes and she had to blink to clear them. "Did you tell Riley you had problems making ends meet at home? I'm sure he didn't even know your wife had left you. You talked about taking her shopping only last weekend at my place."

"He wouldn't care," he spat out amid the guttural sobs that now tumbled from his slack mouth.

"Don't get mad with me, Jason, but you do seem to have a bit of a problem with alcohol. Has it always been this way? If you're really honest with yourself, do you think maybe Riley had a good reason to demote you?"

She held her breath and waited for him to explode with vitriolic abuse against Riley. He said nothing for the moment, the silence punctuated by the occasional shuddery sob.

"If I were the boss, I'd have sacked me on the spot," he admitted.

A sigh of relief escaped her at the change of tone. He'd gone from crazed to reasonable as if he'd turned things over in his mind. She edged closer, her knees cushioned on the pile of canvas, and placed her arm about his bony shoulders.

"What about at home? Did you go on with the drinking when the money got tight? It's a normal reaction to stress with some people. Maybe it was the alcohol your wife couldn't handle and not the lack of funds. Women will put up with anything for the man they love. Happiness isn't judged by the amount of money and what you can or cannot buy. Most of us would live in a tent if it's with the right man."

He leaned into her and slid his hand about her waist. "You're a nice girl. I hope my daughter turns out like you."

He was so quiet for a moment she thought he'd fallen into a drunken stupor. Suddenly, he snorted and sat up straight, although he kept his arm around her, whether for comfort or to keep her from getting away she didn't know.

"She told me if I stopped with the drink she'd come back. *And* she'd bring the kids. I miss them. I try to pretend everything is the same, but it isn't. But I've been drinking in secret for so long I'm not certain I can stop."

"There are a lot of places you can go for assistance. If you talk to Riley, I'm sure he'd help you find one."

He wiped his face with the sleeve of his shirt. "I knew it wasn't Riley's fault, but I had to blame someone. Because I couldn't face the fact that I was responsible for my own problems." He pulled his arm away and turned to face her. "You think he'll help me, even after all this?"

Before Beth-Ann could answer, there was a noise at the open door to the apartment. Jason reacted with lightning-quick reflexes, despite his state of intoxication. He grasped her by the throat and started to scramble to his feet, forcing Beth-Ann to go with him. Either that or be strangled.

All of a sudden, she remembered her naked state as her foot tangled in a swatch of canvas and loosened the makeshift drapery she'd twisted around her body. It had slipped her mind while she'd been concentrating on Jason's problems. As the painter dragged her with him so she faced the doorway, his bulk huddled behind her, she tried to clutch at the binding across her breasts.

Jason held the lighter up, his finger poised. His accelerated breathing was like an assault to her ears as he pressed his cheek to hers and tightened his arm about her neck.

"Stay back," he yelled, "or she'll go up with me. I've got nothing to lose."

Her knight in shining armor—or rather, denim jeans with the top clasp undone—stepped into the doorway. His hair was disheveled, his upper body naked, as if he'd just risen from bed. Her bed, in fact, given the state of her undress. Everyone would know exactly what they'd been up to.

Beth-Ann tried to shake her head, troubled at her thoughts. How absurd to even think about that, let alone worry about it, in this situation. Her life was a risk and that's all she could come up with?

Jason was crazy with grief and alcohol. She was just plain crazy.

"Are you all right, Beth-Ann?" Riley's voice was soft, filled with concern and rigid self-control.

"I'm okay," she managed and wanted to burst into hysterical laughter at the incongruity of the statement.

Bile rose in her throat at the stench of her own fear and the mixture of alcohol and gas fumes. She swallowed hard and stared at Riley.

"Actually, I do believe I need help," she croaked.

Chapter Fourteen

Mel by his side, Riley froze, heart pounding in his chest. The sweat broke out on his forehead. Mouth dry, he had to force himself to swallow.

His vision narrowed until all he could see was Beth-Ann, held in the arms of a man he'd trusted. Riley tried to clip his radio onto his belt, but he fumbled and it fell to the floor at his side. He couldn't have cared less. All he could do was stare at his little pixie.

When he'd heard her scream his name, he'd been down the far end of the first floor. He'd used the radio to call for Mel before belting back here. Under normal circumstances, he knew the building better than the back of his hand. Tonight he found every obstacle possible and promptly ran into it and delayed his progress. Thoughts of Beth-Ann at the mercy of some maniac had filled his mind and almost turned him into a blithering idiot.

"Go call the cops," he whispered to Mel, coughing as the acrid smell of fuel caught at the back of his throat. If that bastard hurt his pixie, he'd kill him.

"Already done," Mel said out of the side of his mouth. "Had Arthur contact Seth when I called him to take over at the front gate."

Riley nodded, but didn't take his eyes off the tableau on the far side of the living area of the apartment. The glow of the artificial light turned Jason's face into a macabre caricature. In contrast, Beth-Ann had a sickly white pallor that tugged at his heartstrings.

He dragged in a shaky breath and tried to gather his scattered wits. He wanted to go in there and knock Jason's block off, but he had to restrain himself for Beth-Ann's sake. "What's this all about?"

"If you hadn't taken the foreman's job away from me, she would still be here." Jason waved the lighter about. "You took it all away. It's your fault."

Hands raised in front of him, Riley took a step forward.

"Stop," Jason screamed. "Come any closer and she goes up with me."

"Come on, buddy, it can't be that bad. Put the lighter down and let Beth-Ann go and we'll sort this out." As much as he wanted to charge into the room and tackle Jason to the floor, for the moment, he couldn't do a fucking thing. Jason's hand trembled on the lighter. One flick and it would all be over. God help him, he couldn't lose Beth-Ann.

"You took it all from me," Jason said again. "It's always been your work. The most important thing in your life. So I'm going to hit you where it hurts most."

He looked down at the woman he held against his chest. "I'm sorry you have to go with me, but there's no other way. I liked you. You treated an old man with respect. I'm sorry."

With Jason's attention focused on Beth-Ann, Riley inched forward another step. He heard a slight noise behind him and cast a quick glance over his shoulder. Two policemen, in their distinctive blue uniforms, filled the entrance to the room, crowding Mel out of the way. Seth pushed forward and stood shoulder to shoulder with him. Riley gestured for him to remain silent for the moment.

"Jason, you'll have to level with me. I still don't understand what you're talking about," Riley said.

Beth-Ann tugged at the arm about her neck, her eyes full of entreaty. When Jason loosened his hold a fraction, she sucked in fresh air, the sound harsh and wheezy.

"Don't be angry, Riley. Jason needs help. Your help. He thinks you're responsible for his wife leaving him and taking the kids with her," she managed to whisper.

"I'll give him help all right," Riley muttered.

Beth-Ann ignored the stark horror on Riley's face, concentrating on reaching Jason. She tried to tilt her head to look back at him, but this close, it was impossible. The hand holding the lighter wavered from side to side in front of her face. Taking a chance, she reached out and grasped his forearm and pulled it close, surprised when he let her. She hugged it to her chest, intent on establishing the same type of rapport she'd had with him earlier.

"No, Beth-Ann," Riley yelled.

She pinned Riley with her gaze as she tried to gather her thoughts. Vaguely, she noticed Seth and the policemen, but she didn't have time, or the energy, to focus on them at the moment. She had to reach Jason.

"Jason, you know Riley wasn't responsible for how things turned out, don't you? Your wife didn't leave because he demoted you. We talked about this before."

His chokehold on her throat loosened even more. She dragged in another deep breath. "I'd like to turn around so I can see your face. It's so rude to talk to someone without looking at them. Is that all right?"

Experimentally, she started to twist, a little at a time. He dropped his arm so it settled about her waist, the lighter still clutched in one shaky hand. When she faced him, she reached up, wrapped her arms about his neck and gave him a hug.

"Ah, poor Jason. It's been so hard for you, hasn't it? Trying to keep up appearances, not letting anyone know your wife has gone."

"I've been so lonely. I miss her and the kids."

He chuckled, the sound bizarre given the situation. A shiver traced its way down Beth-Ann's back. Her eyes stung from the petrol fumes, but she ignored it. There were more important issues at stake. Namely, her life.

"Never thought I'd miss the way the girls hogged the bathroom," Jason said. "Strange what you don't appreciate until it's not there."

Beth-Ann cupped her hand over his cheek, sure something as simple as a little human touch could only help the situation. "Remember what we spoke about earlier?"

He nodded.

"Riley isn't responsible for your problems. You said yourself that you would have sacked him had you been the boss. He gave you a chance to clean up your act and I'll bet he's still willing to help you do that. All you have to do is ask."

"He'll toss my ass in jail," Jason whined. "I'll never get my family back."

"No, I'm sure your wife will stand by you. She said she'd come back if you stopped the drinking, didn't she?"

When he nodded, she continued, "Well there you go. She loves you and wants to be a family again, but you have to get help by dealing with the alcohol addiction. Don't you see?"

Riley shook his head in disbelief as he listened to Beth-Ann. Her life was on the line and all she wanted to do was help the man who threatened her.

Seth sidled a step closer to Riley. "Fucking hell, she's going to talk him to death," he said in a lowered voice. "She could have grabbed for the lighter by now. I'm going to give it a go. On the count of three, we'll rush him."

Hand on his arm, Riley restrained him. "No, give her a chance," he whispered. "I think she'll talk him around." He turned his attention back to Beth-Ann.

"You know the police are involved," she said. "There's nothing we can do about that, but it doesn't have to go any further. If you give me the lighter, we can both walk out of here and Riley can get you some help. I'll even go and talk to your wife for you."

Jason stared at her. "You will?"

"Sure will."

She pulled back from his hold and he let her go. When she lifted her hand, he placed the lighter in her upturned palm. Taking his hand, she guided him like a child toward the door.

Riley couldn't believe she'd done it. His pixie was an amazing lady. She seemed to gather people to her, misfits included, and make them her friends. Right now, Jason stared at her as if she were his only lifeline.

He wanted to grab the painter and thrash the crap out of him. He could have lost Beth-Ann. God help him, he couldn't live with that. Despite the seriousness of the situation, his mouth curved into a smile as she clutched at the top of the sheet of canvas she'd used to hide her nakedness.

Seth and the two uniforms converged on Jason and took him into custody. Beth-Ann stood silent, a dazed expression on her face. He stepped forward and gathered her into his arms. His eyes prickled with tears of relief. Crap, now he wanted to cry. Big macho men didn't cry.

They did, if they'd almost lost the one thing that gave their life meaning. The thought hit him right between the eyes. Well, how about that? Dear old Dad was correct. When it was the right woman...

"Okay, you two take him in. I'll be there after we secure the scene," Seth said.

Riley shuffled about so that he and Beth-Ann faced Seth. As awkward as it was, he wasn't about to let go of her for anything. "Jason, I'll find you a good lawyer, and when Seth gives me permission, we'll talk, okay?"

Jason nodded and faced forward, his hands cuffed behind his back. With one cop on either side, he left the room. Seth ushered everyone else back into the hallway. For the first time, Riley realized his father was there as well.

"Dad, I didn't... How...?"

"Arthur called me. I *am* part-owner of this business after all." He concentrated on Seth. "Jason's been with us for ages. I'd like to go down to the station with him. Is that all right?"

"Yeah, don't see that as a problem. He might open up more with an old friend there. Riley seems to be the one he has it in for. Go in the patrol car and I'll run you home later."

As John turned to go, he cast a quick look at Riley. "Remember that promise you made me, son?"

Riley nodded, a grin on his face.

"I get the feeling I'm about to collect on it and I heartily approve." John smiled before hurrying down the hallway to catch up with the officers.

Beth-Ann held herself rigid in Riley's arms. She was afraid if she let go she would shatter into a million little pieces. Tremors racked her body, starting deep inside her and radiating outward. Her skin felt icy cold and for some reason, she couldn't concentrate on the conversation going on around her. Her entire focus was on the makeshift sarong she wore and the way it scratched at her skin, as if she'd become hypersensitive.

All she could think of was the fact that she was naked under this sheet of canvas. She dragged herself out of Riley's embrace and started back into the room only to have Seth bar her way.

"I need to get my clothes," she said, surprised at how her voice wobbled.

"Sorry, Beth-Ann, it's a crime scene now. No one is allowed in there for the moment."

Tears filled her eyes and she blinked to keep them at bay. "But I need my dress. I can't stay in this." She plucked at the canvas over her breasts. Why was it so important? She was decently covered.

Riley stepped up and placed an arm about her shoulders. "Come on, man, don't do this to her. You can see how distressed she is. *You* get them for her."

"Don't ever say I don't do anything for you, buddy." Seth disappeared into the room to return moments later with Beth-Ann's cotton shift crushed in his hand.

When he passed it to her, she slipped it over her head and smoothed it down her body. Dragging the canvas sheet out from underneath, she let it fall to the concrete floor.

"What about my...um, underwear?" she murmured as a wave of heat rushed up over her face.

"Think you'll have to go without," Seth said with a grin at his mate. "I wouldn't recommend you put these on."

He held up his hand and a pair of red satin panties dangled from his forefinger. Beth-Ann reached for them, then pulled back. Her nose wrinkled in disgust. Her underwear was soaked, the smell of petrol pungent.

"One guess where they were," Seth said.

Rats, another night without panties. She glanced at Riley, a half grin on her face. It was ridiculous to find herself in this situation. In one part of her mind, she knew it was a release from all the tension of the last half hour or so, but all of a sudden, she wanted to burst into laughter.

"Shit, I'm going to have to staple your panties to you in the future to keep them on you," Riley said. "Never known a girl who could lose her underwear so often."

There was an instant of silence before Riley opened his eyes wide as if he'd only just realized how that sounded. Seth gulped audibly, coughed to clear his throat and then gave up and dissolved into a raucous bout of laughter. Beth-Ann started to chuckle and Riley joined in, the laughter cleansing after the tense scene with Jason.

When he finally had himself under control, Riley hugged Beth-Ann to him. "Let's go over to the office. I can't stand the smell of gas any longer." He reached across and tried to grab the soaked panties from Seth. "I'll take those, thanks. Don't think I like the idea of my best mate having a pair of my girl's panties. Not kosher, old boy."

Seth held them away from him. "Sorry, old chum. Evidence, don't you know?"

He chuckled as he walked up the hallway. When Riley prompted her, Beth-Ann, with a silent command to her feet to move, shuffled along beside him like an old woman.

She blinked as she stepped outside. The floodlights were on and it was like emerging into daylight. She couldn't even hazard a guess as to what the time was. All she knew was that she felt unbearably tired. Not surprising, really, given what had gone on.

�✖✖

Riley sat in the large executive chair, Beth-Ann wrapped in a blanket and cuddled on his lap. He propped his booted feet on the edge of the desk, settled back and gathered her close.

Now that all the hoopla had finished, and Seth and the boys in blue had gone, he had time to think. Earlier thoughts crystallized in his mind.

I could have lost her.

The image of Beth-Ann with Jason's arm wrapped around her neck wouldn't leave him. One false slip, one slight movement of Jason's hand and boom—a blazing inferno and no Beth-Ann. He may as well have thrown himself into the mix because without her, his life would be meaningless.

Yeah, all right, very melodramatic, Riley.

He shook his head. Too bad. It was the way he felt.

After a fierce hug for the little sprite on his lap, he moved her back and tilted her so he could look into her face. She'd regained her color and the tremors had stopped. Now she looked tired out, with bruised shadows under her eyes. She gave a big yawn and freed her hand from a fold of blanket to cover her mouth.

"Sorry. It's been a long night."

"Darlin', that is an understatement. This has been the worst—and the best—night of my life."

Beth-Ann frowned. Okay, she could understand the worst, but the rest was just plain confusing. She stared at Riley, trying to read his mind.

He'd treated her like a porcelain doll since they'd entered the office. Hot coffee, a warm blanket and lots of hugs. He'd run interference when Seth had questioned her. In fact, he'd looked after her every need, but she was over the shock now. A little tired, but that was all. It was time to take control of her life again.

She sat up straight, balanced on his thighs. "Explain the best part. Somewhere along the line I missed it." With a wiggle, she managed to get her bare feet on the floor and push herself upright, ignoring the disappointed look on Riley's face.

"The best thing that came out of tonight is that I realized how important you are to me." His boots hit the floor as he sat up. "And I now know my father is right. There's one special person out there for each of us. We just have to find them."

He rested his hands on her hips and moved her so she stood between his spread thighs. Then he grinned up at her as if he'd found the mother lode of the biggest gold mine in known history.

A sensation of warmth rolled over her. She cradled his cheek in her palm. "I love you," she whispered past the lump that formed in her throat.

"I love you, too, and that makes it easy. So when are we going to do it?" He wrapped his arms about her waist and laid his head on her chest.

Beth-Ann frowned. This night had gone on too long. Once again, she'd lost the thread of the conversation.

"Easy? Do it? Sorry, you'll have to explain. I think I'm too tired to take it in." She caught herself in another deep yawn.

"When do you want to get married? We'll have to time it in with your work so we can have a honeymoon. I can get away at any time. Dad will fill in for me."

"Whoa." Beth-Ann grabbed his arms from around her back and pulled. He stared at her, his face puckered in a frown as she stepped away from him.

The air caught in her throat, making breathing difficult as the old fears rose up and swamped her. She struggled to clear her mind against the mental fog that threatened to take over.

"Just when did you decide we needed to get married?" Ice coated each word as she dropped it into the conversation pool. An accompanying shiver raced through her body and raised the fine hairs on her arms.

Riley stood and approached her, but she held him off with a raised hand.

"Beth-Ann, I love you."

"I know, but give me one good reason why that should plunge us into matrimony." Beth-Ann felt her tenuous grip on her emotions slip a notch.

"I've never been so scared in my life. You could have died tonight. I want to spend the rest of my life making certain you're safe. If I know what you're doing, whom you're with at all times, I'll be able to anticipate any trouble."

Shades of her mother. She started to shake as she saw her mother's life in vivid color mentally flash past her eyes. He was scared? Hell, he'd just about scared the living daylights out of her right then.

"There's no need for us to get married. We can care for each other without that. Why can't we just go on as before?"

She held her breath while she waited for his answer. Her gut cramped when she focused on all that marriage meant, at least to her. Arms wrapped about her belly, she bent forward and tried to slow her rapid breathing.

"Hey, you know the old saying, don't you?" he said.

He grinned, inviting her to laugh with him, to share the joke she just knew was coming. All she could do was shake her head.

"We've had this raging hot affair, now you have to make an honest man of me."

The joke fell flat. Beth-Ann couldn't have raised a smile to save herself.

"Riley, what you're proposing doesn't have anything to do with love. It's all about control. *You* have to know what I'm doing? *You* have to know where I am? That's the same type of control my father exercised over my mother. I won't do it."

"Damn it, Beth-Ann, that's not what I mean. I know you have issues with remaining in control, and we can work on that, but after we're married."

She shook her head like a little robot. Right now, it seemed the only movement she was capable of. "I won't marry you, no matter how much I love you. However, I'm quite happy to go on having an affair with you. You can visit whenever you have spare time."

Riley couldn't believe how the conversation was going. How dare she belittle their love like this? Couldn't she see how important this was, for both of them? He didn't want to control her. He just wanted to love her.

A flash of anger swept through him. "I won't have a hole-in-the-corner affair with you, Beth-Ann. If you won't make an honest man of me... Well, the way I see it, it's marriage or nothing. Can you live with that?"

The words spewed out of his mouth, shocking the hell out of him. He hadn't meant to say that, but it was too late to take it back.

He knew the exact moment the anger hit her. It made her tired eyes glint and raised flags of bright red high on her cheekbones. She stepped up so close, her breasts brushed at his chest.

"You, Riley Osborne," she ground out through clenched teeth, "are a moralistic hypocrite. What happened to your no-strings-attached policy? It was fine to fool around with me before, but all of a sudden, because you want to take over my life, it's marriage or nothing."

He reached out his hand to run it over her cheek, letting his arm drop to his side when she winced and pulled away. "I made a promise to my father that when I found the one woman I couldn't live without, I'd marry and settle down. And whether you like it or not, you *are* that woman."

She ran the tip of her fingers across his chest. "Come on, Riley. We had fun together. It doesn't have to stop," she cajoled him, a sexy smile on her face, her lips parted in invitation.

A shudder rocketed through him at her touch. His cock tightened right on cue. He dragged in a sharp breath and, with a strong admonition, silently told his body to stand down. Now was not the time. Sex was easy. It was the relationship that needed work.

He shook his head. Somehow, he knew if they were to get past Beth-Ann's hang-ups about commitment, he had to stand firm.

"Please, at least think about it," he begged. "We don't have to get married straight away. We can just live together until you get used to the idea and see I'm not trying to control you."

Beth-Ann shook her head.

"I love you too much to continue with furtive couplings on the office desk or in partially completed buildings. I want to marry you and be there for you every day. Go to bed and get up in the morning with you beside me. Corny, I know, but I can't live with a part-time affair feeling as I do. It has to be all or nothing."

"You're serious, aren't you? So what are you saying? No marriage, no sex?" She backed away from him, toward the door of the office.

He remained still, bit his lip against the pain that ripped through his gut. "All or nothing," he reiterated, his voice hoarse with longing.

"Then I guess it's over, because I can't give you what you want. I'm not strong enough."

Her voice broke on the final word. She dragged the door open and fled into what remained of the night, or rather, the early hours before dawn.

Riley stared at the open doorway, more shattered than he'd ever been before, even when his mother had left him.

"I'll wait," he whispered. "For however long it takes, I'll wait."

⚒ ⚒ ⚒

"You're a big grouch. You're no fun any more."

The petulant voice slapped Beth-Ann right in the face and forced her to focus on the pint-sized munchkin who stood in front of her, hands planted on tiny hips. Julianna threw her a look filled with disgust, turned on her heel and stomped out the back door.

Beth-Ann stretched out her legs and sat up, her hands curled into fists in her lap. She released her breath on a sigh and shook her head. Out of the mouths of babes.

"My daughter is correct. You've turned into a first-class grump." Cindy walked in the back door and sauntered across the living room. She dropped a brown paper package, the name of the local hardware store blazoned across the outside, into Beth-Ann's lap, then plopped down onto the couch beside her.

"Seriously, sweetie, I'm really getting worried about you. You've done nothing but wallow for a whole week now. You refuse to answer his calls or even say his name. For the entire time, I don't think I've seen you get out of that tatty old robe of yours."

She paused and stared, her eyebrows raised. "However, it seems you took a shower and washed your hair while I was gone. The tee shirt has seen better days, but it's a definite improvement."

Beth-Ann tried for a weak grin. "Pathetic, wasn't I? You should have kicked my butt."

"Nah, everyone has to grieve, but now it's got to stop. So what are you going to do? And why on earth did you have me rush down to the hardware store and buy a builder's tool belt?"

With a grin, Beth-Ann stood, grabbed Cindy's arm and pulled her to her feet. She turned her around and pointed her toward the back door.

"I wasn't really being a grouch this morning although the term certainly applies to the rest of the time. No, I've been churning your words over and over in my mind and now I've come up with a plan."

Cindy planted her heels at the door and refused to respond to any further prompting. "Hah, good to see you finally realized marriage doesn't mean control. It will only happen if you turn yourself into a doormat and you're not the type."

She let Beth-Ann edge her over the doorstep. "So what *are* you going to do? And you still haven't explained that." She pointed to the couch where the brown paper package sat.

Beth-Ann grinned. "None of your business, girlfriend. The only thing I will say is that you helped me to see things clearly. You and Barry, your ex."

Cindy grinned. "Not ex for much longer. Damn, I'm going to have to give up all those ex-husband jokes now we're getting married again."

"You totally floored me with this news. From what you told me, the early years of your marriage were rotten, but you're still willing to give Barry another chance." Beth-Ann shook her head in astonishment.

"I love him." Cindy shrugged. "It's as simple as that. Neither of us is the same person we were when we got married. Maybe now, after having had this time apart, we'll make a better job of it the second time around. If I don't give it another shot, I may regret it for the rest of my life. Loving someone means you have to open yourself up to the possibility of being hurt emotionally, because if you don't, you could miss out on the greatest happiness you'll ever know."

A grin tilted her lips and she winked. "Okay, lecture over, but I hope you've taken it to heart."

"I have, but I still can't believe that all those times I baby-sat for you, you were off seeing Barry. You sure had me fooled."

Beth-Ann shook her head. "Now vamoose, my friend. I have to go out."

"I'm going, I'm going. I know when I'm not wanted." Cindy chuckled, then her smile disappeared and a veil of seriousness settled over her face. "Hey, good luck, okay?"

Within minutes of Cindy's leave-taking, Beth-Ann had changed clothes, locked the house, and was on her way to the building site with the help of the local cab company. She made use of the time to try to still the rapid beat of her heart, but to no avail. When she stepped from the vehicle in front of the security booth, her pulse rate was even higher.

"Hello, little lady." Mel stepped forward to greet her.

"Hi, Mel. Is it okay if I go see Riley?" Her voice quivered slightly as she uttered his name.

"Sure, he's in the office but he—"

Beth-Ann didn't wait to hear the rest of his answer. She scooted into the security booth, grabbed a hard hat and jammed it on her head. Straightening her back, she marched as fast as she could on her strappy high-heels across the site to the office. A few wolf whistles came her way, but she ignored them and she didn't make eye contact with anyone.

When she reached the bottom step to the office, she jolted against a man on his way down. She raised her head and stared. John, Riley's father.

"Beth-Ann. Are you all right? I nearly knock you over."

"I need to speak to Riley. Right away, if I could?"

She exhaled noisily, trying to steady her breathing. Leaning closer, she whispered in John's ear.

He reared back and looked at her, a twitch to his lips as he tried not to laugh. "I love it," he pronounced. He nodded toward the closed door. "Come on."

Her heart raced as she followed him up the steps. He opened the door and poked his head through, using his body to hide Beth-Ann for the moment.

"Riley, visitor for you. I have a lady out here who says she has a hole that needs filling and only you can do the job." He ushered Beth-Ann into the office and slammed the door behind her.

She hovered there a moment as a shiver of shock slid down her spine. Dear heavens, she hadn't planned on there being anyone else here. Riley stood on the far side of the room, his back pressed against the filing cabinet. Seated behind the desk, flicking through the files spread out on the surface in front of him, was Seth. A uniformed officer stood behind him. She cursed her luck, but it was too late to back out now, because if she did, she might never have the nerve to attempt this again.

Riley opened his eyes wide and stared at the vision over by the door. For the last week he'd dreamed about her. He'd picked the phone up numerous times to ring her, then slammed it down again. When he did get up the gumption to make the call, all he got was her sassy voice on the answering machine, or her friend Cindy. He'd been tempted to beg Cindy for her help, but he knew he couldn't. Beth-Ann had to conquer her fears and come to him. Anything else would lead to unhappiness. And now, here she was.

His father's comment when he'd announced Beth-Ann just now had floored him, and one bet it had come from her. No one else knew about the play on the word "hole" or what it actually meant.

She ignored the other men in the room and tottered toward him on thin spiky heels so damn high it was a wonder she could walk at all. He frowned. What on earth was she doing wearing a knee-length fur coat in the middle of summer? Although he had to admit the white fur, the collar pulled up to create a frame for her petite face, was a knockout with her red hair. Sexy as all get out, even if the red hard hat did mar the picture somewhat.

"I saw your advertisement for a handyman in the local paper," she said.

Riley waved frantically over her shoulder to tell Seth and his sidekick to get the fuck out of the office. With a cheeky grin, Seth complied. Riley dragged his attention back to Beth-Ann. He didn't know where she was going with this, but he was more than happy to play along. Hell, he was happy just seeing her.

"You were saying..." He held his breath and waited.

"I heard you needed a handyman. Will a handywoman do instead? I'm a specialist with my hands and I know exactly what to do with a handyman's best tool. Come to that, I have a full set of tools of my own."

For a moment, she remained still, although she clutched the sides of the coat together with hands that trembled. Dragging in a deep breath, she suddenly pulled the fur wide.

Riley stared, his mouth open in shock. He snapped it shut and tried to think of something intelligent to say.

"*Fucking hell.*" He took a deep breath. "I don't just have to staple your panties onto you. I'll have to do something about the rest of your clothes as well."

He couldn't take his eyes off her. Under the white fur, she was naked. Nude. Bare-bottomed, totally exposed. All she had on were the black high-heels and set low about her hips, the hammer angled down in front, was a brown leather, builders' tool belt, complete with a set of tools.

His mouth twitched and he wanted desperately to laugh, but he controlled himself. He wasn't out of the woods yet.

"You realize this is a permanent position we're talking about?"

Beth-Ann breathed a sigh of relief that he'd taken this stunt in stride. He had a perfect right to toss her out on her naked ass for her pig-headedness. Thank God he hadn't.

"I'm looking for a job that will carry me through the rest of my life, until death do us part."

He opened his mouth to speak, but she cut him off.

"I haven't learnt all the tricks of the trade yet, but with a little help, I will." Pulling the hard hat off and dropping it to the floor, she tilted her head on one side and smiled. After a moment's hesitation, she let the coat slide off her shoulders and down her body. "How are you on instruction?"

"I've heard of pixies in the bottom of the garden, but I'd rather have one by my side for the rest of my life." He stepped forward and opened his arms. "As well as in my bed," he said and waggled his eyebrows. "And we'll learn together. No control, just lots of love. How do those working conditions sound?"

Beth-Ann stepped into his arms and lowered her head to his chest as his arms tightened about her. Tears sprang to her eyes, but this time they were tears of happiness. What an idiot she'd been. A hell of a way to learn that love doesn't mean giving up control of your life.

"I hope I'm going to have a chance to christen my shiny new tool belt. Can't have it going to waste."

"Darlin', I'm sure we'll find a use for it. There must be occasions when you need a hole filled up."

Beth-Ann grinned and wiggled closer. Her bare breasts brushed at his chest. "As long as I get to play with your tools as well."

Alexis Fleming

Thirty-seven moves in thirty years have taught *Alexis Fleming* to make friends where she can and what better way than through the voices in her mind. Alexis' world is peopled with interesting characters and exciting possibilities that come to life in each and every book she writes. Her first love has always been romance, whether on this world or the next. Hot, sizzling relationships with a dash of comedy and a few trials and tribulations thrown in to test her characters.

When she isn't tied to her computer creating sizzling stories, Alexis, along with her husband and a demon cat called Chloe, runs a motel situated on the edge of a National Marine Park in Jervis Bay, New South Wales, Australia.

Alexis believes you can never have too many friends and loves to hear from her readers.

You can visit with Alexis at www.alexisfleming.net or email her at alexisfleming@hotmail.com, or join her newsletter group: http://groups.yahoo.com/group/AlexisFlemingNewsletter

Looking for more by Alexis?

Enjoy this excerpt from

A Muse Me

© 2006 S. L. Carpenter

A contemporary erotica full of humor as only S.L. Carpenter can do.

Eugene watched as the letters disappeared from the computer screen one by one. The words vanished, leaving the pages empty, just like the void of creativity in his imagination. For over three months he hadn't been able to write a single scene, page or paragraph that read or felt right. Everything was meaningless. His passion was gone and everything he wrote was dull and lifeless.

For a writer, this was a slow death. Writer's block was more painful than constipation after eating spicy Mexican food.

His small, lonely, microcosmic world had shrunk around him and now he needed to get out and have an experience to inspire and awaken the inner being and set loose his alter egos. The walls needed to be knocked down so he could spread his wings. Basically a good fucking and a drunken binge might do the trick. Not necessarily in that order.

He had written thirty books filled with romance and sex. Two were made into low budget movies for cable, with terrible acting and fake breasts. He had a nice apartment and a kick ass computer set up for writing. California was a hotbed but his bed had run cold.

Lately, though, he had lost his urge to write. If the muse for his inspiration were a place, it was the Sahara desert. He needed a change of mind, a change of scenery. In the most basic of terms he needed to run away and find his muse.

He wrote under the name Dorris Daye. People told him there was a stigma problem with men writing romance and erotica. He was asked to think up something different than Eugene S. Finkter. His middle name was Scott. He liked his name but knew his parents had cursed him to a life of constant teasing.

Something had to be done. A drastic transformation in his hum-drum life to make him think differently. To get out of the rut he was entrenched in.

So he pondered his possibilities. A vacation to someplace different. Las Vegas? Naw, just gambling and hookers there. Hmmm. Florida? Hmmm, naw, it's set up for retirement and other than spring break I'd end up in bed with a grandma with no teeth. That actually has advantages though. He needed exotic, he needed the Caribbean.

Eugene needed Aruba.

Enjoy this excerpt from

Let's Pretend

© 2006 Raine Weaver

A tantalizing contemporary treat available now at Samhain Publishing.

Ronnie swung the door open with a crippling yawn, then gave her visitor a venomous stare. "Coleman? What are you doing here? What time is it?"

That irresistible smile blazed forth. "You look like Linus of the Charlie Brown series standing there with your blankee."

She pulled the fleece coverlet around herself. For the first time she was grateful that her taste in sleepwear didn't lean toward sheer and frilly, or anything like the slinky negligees Kayla always wore. She felt awkward and exposed enough in her brushed-cotton gown. "I'll bet you say that to all the big-headed kids. What do you want?"

He entered unbidden, walking straight past her into her kitchen and starting her coffeemaker. "I wanted to catch you before you left for work. Be sure we're on the same page, so to speak."

She sighed heavily, trying her best to be angry with him. It was difficult. He'd brought the fresh air and newness of the morning into her tiny kitchen, just by walking in the door. "Brant. I haven't showered. Haven't changed. Haven't had any caffeine, haven't even faced a mirror yet. I may look like Linus, but I feel like Pigpen. Give me a break."

He looked surprised, as if it had never occurred to him to notice how she looked. "Oh. Sorry. I was just so enthusiastic about our little game...go ahead and get ready for your day. I know how you are about your 'routine'. I'll entertain myself. Where's Kayla?"

Ronnie's eyes shot to every alternate corner of the room. Uh-oh. This could be sticky. She had no idea how close the two of them were.

She opted for honesty. "She...she stayed out all night. I don't know where she is. I hope that's not a problem."

"Why should it be? I can catch her later," he responded simply. "Here, buddy."

She reached for the small paper bag he held out to her. "What's this? I can't accept..."

"Oh, don't get your undies in a wedge about it. Do you wear undies under that thing?" He grabbed the hem of her gown and began to ease it up.

"Stop that." She slapped his hand, fighting off a nervous giggle as her body temperature soared dangerously high. "It's none of your business."

"Oh, but it is *now*, Ronnie-rum." He snared her fingers and pulled her to his side. "It might be important, if we can get Pang to take the bait."

She pulled her hand back, retreating. "You keep your nose out of my underwear, Coleman. What's in the bag?"

"Open it."

She obeyed and, frowning, immediately handed it back to him. "I don't use this stuff."

"What's the big deal? It's only lipstick and perfume."

No, it wasn't. It was proof that he didn't think she was attractive enough as she was. "I don't use much of this stuff, unless there's some special occasion. When I go to the office, I'm going to do a job, not to—" Her objection died on her lips. It wasn't true anymore, was it? She *did* have an ulterior motive—trying to attract Paul Lang.

"The perfume's generic. As for the lipstick—the dark red one's for drama. And the gloss is just a dusky-rose sort of tint. Sort of like your lips," he added casually, apparently not noticing the color come to her cheeks. "After all, the original purpose of lipstick was to attract the attention of the male by subtly mimicking the female's swollen, flushed labia during sexual stimulation."

She buried her face in her blanket. "Thanks, 'buddy'. That really makes me want to run into the bathroom and smear it right on."

"Why are you embarrassed? What's wrong with letting a man know you're sexually interested and available?"

Why was he always asking her questions she couldn't answer? "You seem to have made an intense study of human nature."

He shrugged, handing her half a cup of coffee. "When you know what motivates people, you know why they behave the way they do. And you know what pleases them. Helps in the escort business."

She fidgeted indecisively with the bag. It wouldn't hurt, she supposed, to add a little color and scent to her business attire. Especially if it ended this awkward conversation. "All right. I'll try it. But just a *little*. Wouldn't want to attract *too* much attention to my labia."

He spread his arms wide. "That's all I ask. Now get ready. I'll drive you."

"No." The man was taking over her *life*. "I prefer to drive myself."

"Okay. Then I'll bring a little something later, and we can have lunch together. Now, now, don't say no. How about a simple donut in a plain paper bag? What could be wrong with that?"

✯ ✯ ✯

She should have known better.

She should have known she couldn't trust him.

Brant strolled into her office promptly at twelve thirty, captivating the ladies with his smile. All work stopped at the sight of the navy-blue knit shirt stretched across the broad band of chest, and the showy red-and-gold bag he carried before him, the one he set triumphantly upon her desk for all to see.

It was the trademark bag of "The G-Spot", the boutique well-known in certain circles for selling intriguing little objects and clothing to enhance the sex life of eager couples. The name of the store was emblazoned across the bag; and the fact that the bag was so small made it seem even more intriguing.

She slowly massaged her forehead as he leaned across her desk, his voice deep with amusement. "Whassup, Ronnie-rum. Did you miss me?"

"Please tell me," she mumbled, her mouth hidden behind her hand, "that you have an *edible* donut in that bag."

"Two, in fact." He smirked. "Edible? Of course. What other kind would they be?"

"I was afraid they might be...you know, maybe the little round rubber rings you put around a...that men use for..."

"Yessss?" The smirk became a pudding smile.

Samhain Publishing, Ltd.

It's all about the story...

Action/Adventure
Fantasy
Historical
Horror
Mainstream
Mystery/Suspense
Non-Fiction
Paranormal
Red Hots!
Romance
Science Fiction
Western
Young Adult

http://www.samhainpublishing.com

Printed in the United States
127056LV00001B/102/A